The Write Choice

Allie Samberts

Editing by Megan Carver

Cover Design by Jillian Liota, Blue Moon Creative Studio

alliesambertswrites@gmail.com

www.alliesamberts.com

To Jillian, Jill, Julia, Elizabeth, and Sandy.

Marriage and motherhood are hard AF.
Having friends to share the funny stories with takes some of the load off.

Thanks for traveling these roads with me. Your humor, grace, and righteous anger give me life.

Author's Note

THE LEADE PARK CREW will always hold a special place in my heart. While this book marks my departure from the town that started it all for me, I'm so proud to have created such unforgettable characters who have resonated with so many of you.

Of course, I love the swoony men of Leade Park, but the ladies are special to me in a different way. Mac and Jenny both held parts of me. Katie is no different. The way she struggles with the mundanity of motherhood, and how she tries to find her passion for art again once her kids are a little older, is something I feel deeply connected to.

But Katie can be prickly. She's a born-and-raised New Yorker, but more than that, she experiences anxiety. It's something that can set anyone on edge. I should know—I've been dealing with it most of my adult life. While she doesn't experience any of the more extreme manifestations of anxiety, there are descriptions of her her personal anxiety in this novel.

Katie also has coping mechanisms that are less than healthy—namely, she has overused alcohol in her past. While there are no descriptions of her drinking on the page here, she does frequently talk about her past alcohol use and her current struggles staying away from it. While I do not have lived experience with substance use disorder, I made sure to have several sensitivity readers who do. I'm indebted to them for their insight, and for their help in describing Katie's situation thoughtfully and realistically.

You should know, too, that these characters use profanity. They got accidentally pregnant in their past, too, which they discuss on page. There are also two on-page explicit scenes for you to look forward to (or avoid) in chapters 18 and 21.

That said, if any of these are things that might trigger you in any way, you may want to come back to this one when you feel ready.

And if you or someone you love is experiencing difficulty with substance use, you can call the SAMHSA National Helpline at 1-800-662-4357 or find more information at samhsa.gov.

To all my readers, thank you from the bottom of my heart for coming to Leade Park and staying a while. I hope you have found something in these characters that has made you feel seen. More importantly, I hope your stay here has left you happier than when you arrived.

Prologue
Katie

No one really talks about the routine you fall into when you have a baby. Maybe no one falls into a routine with a baby. I can certainly see how that could be the case, but I don't have many mom-friends to compare notes with. I don't have many friends left at all, actually, but that's something everyone *does* tell you. Anyone who has ever delivered, adopted, or interacted with a baby will tell you that your friendships are about to change. And by "change," they mean disappear. That's been the case for me, at least. I haven't seen my work friends since my maternity leave from the art gallery started. I haven't seen my out-of-work friends since I got pregnant and stopped drinking.

When I think about it, I know that should probably bother me. I'm almost thirty years old, and the only friends I had were ones I worked or drank with. But I'm so damn happy. Happy doesn't even seem like a big enough word to describe what I'm feeling. I have this perfect baby, right here in my arms. He coos at me in little baby noises I thought only existed in sound effects on television shows. He sleeps on my chest, his tiny weight calming my heart.

He doesn't care that his dad knocked me up after a hot-and-heavy week where we did very little except drink wine and fuck. He doesn't care that, a few months before that, I had taken to stocking my purse with airplane bottles of vodka just in case life got too stressful. He doesn't care that it took a positive pregnancy test for me to realize that my relationship with alcohol was problematic. He doesn't care that I have no idea how I'm going to support him and me and keep this New York City apartment on gallery commissions alone.

He just wants to eat, sleep, and make precious baby noises. And I just want to be here for all of it.

Baby Mason's eyes started gray but have been slowly shifting closer to hazel. They're his father's eyes, and it's jarring every time I see them. I don't have a lot of formative memories of my parents—they were either working or exhausted for most of my childhood—but I do remember my mom telling me I have my dad's eyes. I wonder if she felt a connection with my father every time she saw my eyes, too. But I can't ask either of them, since they both passed away when I was in college.

Mason opens his mouth for a big yawn, stretching his little arms and scrunching up his tiny face as he wakes up. I know without a doubt that he'll be hungry now because that's the routine. Sleep, wake, feed, be adorable, rinse, and repeat. Sure enough, he starts rooting around with his little mouth, looking for my nipple. I unclip my bra and oblige, settling into the surprisingly strong pull of his baby lips and the sound of him gulping milk.

Then, like clockwork, my apartment buzzer sounds. I open the lobby door with the keypad on my phone, then text Brandon that the door is unlocked. Every day after work, he brings us dinner and sits with the baby so I can shower or fold laundry or take a minute to myself. But recently, he's been staying longer. Last night, he watched a movie with me even though I fell asleep halfway through. Twice last week, he and

I stayed up late to talk—mostly about nothing important. We just lost track of time.

"You're not in the safest part of the city. I don't love you keeping this door unlocked if I'm not around," Brandon's voice comes from behind me as soon as he's inside. He sets plastic bags on the table. The smell of the food makes my stomach rumble.

He can't see my face, but I roll my eyes anyway. "What does you being around have anything to do with it?"

"I could defend my son if I were here," he insists, coming to sit next to me on the couch. "And you, of course."

"Of course." I raise an eyebrow. Mason, apparently satisfied or maybe recognizing Brandon's voice, pops off my breast and looks up at us. I clip my bra back where it belongs and pull my shirt down quickly. Brandon has seen it all, obviously, but it still feels a little weird. I hand him the baby and a burp cloth. He tosses the cloth over his shoulder and rests the baby on top of it, patting his back. Mason is growing quickly, but Brandon's huge hands still cover more than his entire back. It's a sweet sight, this gentle giant and his teeny baby. I settle back into the couch with a little sigh.

"You can go do whatever you need," he says.

I lean the back of my head against the couch cushion as I watch him burp the baby. They look so good together. So peaceful. Brandon looks happy, too, but he always looks happy. Even before Mason came along, he was a jolly guy. But, at five years younger than me, he still has a lot of youthful exuberance. I have to hand it to him, though; unexpectedly becoming a young father hasn't done anything to dampen his natural joy. Maybe having more money than he knows what to do with helps. I wouldn't know what that's like.

"I think I want to stay on the couch for a while with you two," I say without thinking. Then, I quickly add, "If that's okay?"

Impossibly, Brandon's expression turns even more joyful. I suppose I shouldn't be surprised. He's made it very clear he's not coming here every day just for the baby. In fact, every day he asks me to marry him, and every day I tell him I have no interest in a marriage borne of an accidental pregnancy. I assure him he can be in our lives as much or as little as he wants, but I'm not marrying someone just because I got knocked up, and that's that.

"Yeah, that's okay." His voice is eager. Mason lets out a loud burp. "Good one, buddy!"

I laugh, and Brandon's eyes light up. We hold each other's gaze for longer than usual, and I start to get warm and tingly. I thought that was something that happens only in books and movies, but apparently it's real, and it has been happening more and more. Maybe it's me coming down from the pregnancy hormones.

Yeah, that's probably it.

I clear my throat, grasping at anything other than the feeling between my thighs. "Can you watch Mason next Thursday at five? For an hour or so."

"Sure. Are you going out or something?" He tries to hide the jealousy in his voice, but the edge of it is clear enough.

I fight a smile at his envy. "Um, I thought it would be a good idea to see a therapist? I wasn't sure about..." I trail off, not sure how much I want to tell him. He turns to me, as if he's soaking up everything I'm saying, and that expression helps me continue. "Well, about the drinking. I want to stay sober. For Mason, I think. So, I guess I wanted to talk to someone about it?" My voice kicks up at the end like a question. It's the first time I've told anyone about this, and it feels awkward to say out loud.

Brandon doesn't take his eyes off Mason as he asks, "You really think you need to? You said you've been fine without it so far."

My mind wanders to the half-empty whiskey bottle stored in the back of a cabinet above the fridge. I haven't touched it since I found out I was pregnant, but I can't quite bring myself to throw it away either. And, lately, I've been thinking about it more and more.

"Yes," I say with a firmness I'm not quite certain of. Fake it till you make it, I guess.

His gaze meets mine. "I think that's great, Cat." He's so sincere. It immediately soothes me. My shoulders relax, and I let out a slow breath, nodding.

Brandon gently rests the baby on top of his thighs, then holds his fingers out. Mason grabs them, squeezing and relaxing his little fists over and over again. Brandon moves one hand to wiggle his fingers, and the baby is completely enthralled. His eyes are wide, taking in the pads of Brandon's fingertips dancing just above him.

The corners of Mason's mouth turn up, and I straighten to lean closer. I've seen him smile before, of course, but it's still so new. I don't want to miss a second of it. My cheek brushes lightly against Brandon's upper arm, and I don't move it away.

Then, a little bubbly giggle bursts out of Mason's mouth. I gasp.

"Holy shit. Did he just laugh?" I breathe, afraid to make too much noise and spook him out of this moment.

Brandon can't take his eyes off the baby, a smile spreading across his own face. "I think so."

"Do it again!" I insist. He does, and Mason giggles. This time, the sound is unmistakable. "He laughed!" I grab Brandon's arm, and his breath hitches. "Oh my god. Brandon! He laughed!"

"Was that the first time?" Brandon asks, still staring at the baby.

"Yes! I've never heard that before. That is, without a doubt, the best sound in the entire world."

"Close." Brandon turns his face so he's looking intently at me. "I still think yours comes in first."

I face him, our noses almost touching. My lips part gently as I search his eyes for even a drop of teasing. There's none. He truly thinks my laugh is a better sound than our son's.

Our son.

Holy shit. We made this baby together. We haven't been at it very long, but we are raising this baby together. The energy in the room shifts suddenly.

We're an "us" now.

He just made this baby laugh, and I got to hear it for the first time. And, in the midst of it all, he still managed to compliment me and make my toes feel curly and my belly feel tingly.

I can tell from the heat in his gaze that Brandon feels it, too. Suddenly, I desperately want him to kiss me. Right here. Over our giggly baby. I could move a centimeter forward and...

"Marry me," he whispers.

This feels different than every other time he's asked. It's never been unintentional before, but he's started getting creative in his comments, and most of them have turned into a joke—an obligatory part of every evening, on the off chance I've changed my mind.

This time, it's real. His desire is palpable. Even Mason is quiet, as if they're both waiting for me to realize what I've probably known all along.

I love him.

I love Brandon. I love our baby. I love this little life we've created together, even if it's not exactly how I pictured it happening. Maybe especially because it's not.

"Yes," I whisper back.

Brandon looks at me in silence for a long second, then reels backwards, eyes wide as if the word just hit him. "Wait. What? You said yes?"

I laugh, and his eyes brighten. "Yes, you idiot."

"Shit. I didn't expect you to say yes. Let me..." he trails off, looking around helplessly. He hands me the baby, then stands. "This wasn't how that was supposed to go." He runs over to his coat and pulls a box out of the pocket.

"What are you doing?" I rest the baby against my chest.

Brandon gets on one knee in front of me. "I'm doing this how it's supposed to be done." He puts one hand on top of the box and holds it from the bottom with the other.

"You just carry a ring box around with you?"

"No," he pouts. "I carry a *ring* in a ring box with me."

"On the off chance I'd say yes one of these times?" I ask, incredulous.

"Well... yeah." He says it as if it's the most natural thing to do.

"Isn't it supposed to be done in a fancy restaurant with candlelight and cheesecake or something?" I tease.

He stops, lowering his hands. "Is that what you want? We can do whatever you want. Anything. Just tell me, and I'll make it happen."

"No, Brandon, that's not what I want." I chuckle. "I want... you. And Mason. The three of us, together."

"I want that too, Katie." He raises the ring box again, this time snapping it open to reveal a beautiful, emerald-cut diamond on a silver band. Except, knowing Brandon, it's platinum or something out of my league. "Marry me."

The ring is too good for me. Hell, the man is probably too good for me, too. He's got more money than I could ever dream of. He could have had his pick of women if I hadn't kept him in my bed for a week, and if we both hadn't forgotten the condom several of those nights. He probably deserves someone who doesn't have a drinking problem, or who comes from a more solid family background, or a thousand other things I could name.

But, right now, I don't care. All I want is us.

"Yes."

Chapter 1
Brandon

It has been ninety-four days, seven hours, five minutes, and fifteen seconds since I last had sex with my wife.

And she is standing in the doorway of my home office in leggings that leave very little to the imagination and a sweater that hangs off her shoulder like some sexy 80s rom-com vixen. It's doing nothing to quell the seemingly semi-permanent stiffness between my legs.

The next thing I know, she narrows her eyes, purses her lips, and puts her hands on her gloriously full hips, and I've more or less lost track of this conversation.

Katie in a state of calm is perfection, but Katie fired up is downright sinful. Unfortunately, at the moment, her ire is directed at me. I have a feeling my less-than-zero chance at breaking our dry spell tonight is plummeting with every word I say.

I pinch the bridge of my nose and squeeze my eyes shut as I take a deep breath. I need to regain some focus.

"I think this would be a good move for us. It'd be an upgrade," I say for the hundredth time this week.

"An upgrade for whom?" she asks through gritted teeth. When I open my eyes, her hands are still on her hips, and I can't think about anything but how supple her skin felt the last time I grabbed exactly where her palms are resting. I close my eyes again and take another deep breath. If I can't see her, I won't think about how long it's been since I've been able to hold her.

Except that's exactly what I'm thinking about. It's been the only thing on my mind since she kicked me out of our bed over three months ago.

I open my eyes but look down at the shiny surface of the mahogany desk in front of me. "For all of us. Mason has had a hard time making friends at school, Christine will have more space to play, and you hate it here—"

"I love it here." Her words are like daggers, each one punctuated just a little.

That's not what she said a few months before she kicked me out of our bedroom, but I'm getting the sense throwing her words back at her right now won't end well for me. Instead, I say, "I don't know what hold this city has on you, but you haven't been happy here for a long time."

She mercifully drops her hands from her hips as she leans back slightly, her mouth making an O-shape and her eyebrows pinching together. Her nostrils flare slightly as her brow furrows even deeper. "How would you know if I'm happy here or not? You're never home."

I press my palms into the desk in front of me and push myself to standing. "Because I've been busting my ass as a senior architect for years, working for a promotion that won't ever come because my parents thought handing the firm to their very qualified son would look like nepotism. The guy they did give it to is too young to retire, and it's too good of a gig for him to ever move on to a different firm. I can head up the Chicago branch like my parents want, and that will free up more time for me to be available for you and the kids."

She scoffs at this and folds her arms in front of her chest. This pushes her perfect breasts up a little higher, and I curse my past self for thinking standing up was a good idea.

"I don't think you understand how promotions work, Brandon. When has more workplace responsibility ever resulted in more family time?"

"I can set some boundaries as a stipulation of moving my entire family halfway across the country to do them a favor," I insist. My parents had been worried about anything that looked like nepotism a few years ago when a rival firm was dealing with allegations of their own. Now that that's blown over, they know they need me if they ever want to step back. Some boundaries would be the perfect compromise.

Apparently, Katie doesn't see it that way. She eyes me warily. "I also don't think you understand how boundaries work. When was the last time you set any with your parents?"

Without thinking, I run my hand through my long, rust-colored hair. I didn't go into the office this morning, so it's loose and falls to my shoulders. Katie catches the movement and rolls her eyes so far back I'm surprised they don't continue for a full three-sixty.

"Your hair is not a boundary," she says drily. "And neither are your tattoos."

"Considering it pisses them off every time they see me, I think it is." My parents have long held the opinion that their son shouldn't have long hair or ink, and that clients wouldn't trust me if I look like a "vagabond"—their word, not mine—but as of yet, my hair hasn't put anyone off.

Katie raises an eyebrow and, thankfully, drops her arms to her sides again. She sighs slightly but doesn't say anything. She's softening.

"Listen." I need to switch tactics here to capitalize on this shift. I come around the desk and sit on the edge of it, facing her. "Chicago is great. You loved it when we were out there for Daniel's wedding. Mason really hit it off with Ben's nephew, so he'll have a friend waiting for him. This is a huge opportunity. I won't get a chance for a promotion in New York for a long time. My parents want to retire and leave the whole Chicago firm in my hands, which means I can delegate more tasks. I can be around more often. Plus, my parents will be looking for things to do, so they can take the kids whenever we need them to." As soon as the words are out of my mouth, I know I've made a mistake. To say Katie hates my parents would be a stretch, but my mother has a tendency to meddle. Katie was all too happy when they moved out to Chicago to open the Midwest branch of their architecture firm.

"That's not the flex you think it is." Her voice is hard again.

"You won't have to see them that often. They can take the kids and we can be—"

"Be what, Brandon?" She raises her arms and lets them fall again, clearly frustrated. "Be the kind of couple who lies to each other?"

I wince, and her self-satisfied expression tells me she saw it. "I didn't lie."

"You accepted this job without telling me. You took me out to Chicago for two weeks before Daniel's wedding to scope out the area, but you didn't tell me until we got there. I'd say that's a bunch of lies right in a row." Her hands are back on her hips, and I'm sensing my tenuous control of both this conversation and my libido slipping even further from my grasp.

"I hadn't accepted it. I wouldn't have if you weren't on board."

"What part of this"—she gestures wildly, encompassing the entirety of our existence the past few months—"suggests I'm on board?"

She said it. That's what made me think she was on board enough to agree to the move. But she was drunk at the time, and she's still mortified about it, so I don't dare bring it up.

"We're all miserable, but you can't see what's staring at you in the face." I want to be understanding. I really do. But her willful ignorance about the boon this could be for us is starting to slip beyond frustrating. And yet, as soon as I've said it, I know I've lost her.

"Oh, and you can? That's rich coming from someone who's hell-bent on ignoring their own family. You must be some kind of clairvoyant."

I push off the edge of the desk and stand. "I'm not ignoring my family. I'm working tirelessly to provide us with a good life."

She narrows her eyes at me. "Brandon, you have a trust fund and an inheritance your parents allow you to borrow from. You don't need to prove anything to anyone. The only reason for you to be at the office all the time is avoidance."

There it is. There's the real reason she's so upset. I mean, yeah, what she perceives as lying about the job and the move is upsetting her, but I think, deep down, she knows Chicago will be a better place for us. She's mad I've had my nose to the grindstone these past few years, with no end in sight. What I need her to understand now, though, is that this really is the end. It's finally in sight.

I take a step toward her but stop when she takes a step back. I try to ignore how much her retreat hurts as I say, "I'm not avoiding you." I hold my hands up to stop her before she can argue. "I know. I shouldn't have had to work this hard. My parents own the firm for crying out loud; I should have been a shoo-in for the position here. But I want to fix it. I want to give you all a fresh start in Chicago. Let me do this for us, Katie. I can be around more for you and the kids. And I can get this promotion I've been working for since I graduated. Please, give me a chance."

"No." It's firm, and she doesn't offer anything else.

"No? That's it? Just no?"

"That's it. I was ready to be a single mom to Mason, remember? I insisted on it for almost a year. I was ready then, and I'm ready now. You can go to Chicago, but I'm staying here, and so are the kids."

I gape at her. Never in a million years did I think she'd threaten me with the kids. It's not even an ultimatum for me to stay at this point. She upped the ante by suggesting I leave them, and it throws me for a second.

I press my mouth into a firm line. I will not lose them.

"You're forgetting something too, Cat." I'm pulling out all the stops here with my old nickname for her, one I came up with after a week of us hardly leaving her bed when she'd purr softly every time I touched her. I can see her cheeks turn pink. I smirk and step forward again. This time, she stays rooted to the spot. "You married me after Mason was born because you liked having me around. Me. You told me so yourself. I'm still the man you fell in love with, and I'm telling you I want to be around more again. This is the way to do it, and I think you know it."

She regards me for a moment, and then I catch it. Her expression relaxes the tiniest bit, and I do a mental fist pump.

"How long?" she asks.

"My parents want me to take over the project in Leade Park and phase themselves out in two months—until March."

"*Leade Park?*" she explodes. "Since when is the project in Leade Park?"

This was a detail I hadn't released yet. I found out shortly after I accepted the job, but when she continued to sink deeper into her anger about the whole move, I could never find the right time to tell her.

"Leade Park High School accepted the firm's bid to work on an addition. It seemed like the perfect project for me to take on to show that I can manage something large-scale with a lot of moving parts, so I volunteered for it."

Katie's expression turns to ice. "Are we living in Chicago, or are we living in Leade Park?" She pauses for a beat, then jumps right back in before I can respond. "Tell me the truth, Brandon. I'm sick of being in the dark on this. If you want me to give this a chance, you need to tell me what, exactly, I'm taking a chance on."

It's a fair request, and I'm kicking myself for thinking this bit of information would make her happy when she is irreversibly pissed off. I've been married to her for six years, and I pursued her for almost an entire year before she even agreed to marry me. I should have known better than to think I could snap my fingers with a surprise and turn this ship around.

"I put an offer in on a house in Leade Park." I spit out the words before I can overthink it.

She throws her hands in the air and turns away from me, leaving the office. I follow her out into the kitchen, where she starts opening and closing cabinets, seemingly at random. My heart just about stops as I wonder if she could be looking for a bottle she stashed somewhere out of sight.

She's making a hell of a lot of noise, and her movements are starting to turn frantic, so I reach out and press my palm on the cabinet door she's moving to open next. She stops, grunts in frustration, and looks up at me. Our bodies are close together, and I tower over her. I've always been tall, but she's also relatively short, so the top of her head barely reaches my shoulder. We are closer to each other than we have been in months, and I catch the sweet floral of her perfume. I try not to groan.

I have her cornered, leaning against the cabinet, and her eyes glimmer. I can't tell if it's a flash of indignation or if it mirrors my own desire. Probably the former.

"What are you looking for?" My voice is huskier than it was a minute ago, and from the slight upturn of one corner of her mouth, I can tell she registers it. She'll probably use it against me, but I don't care. I haven't wanted her this badly since she iced me out right after Mason was born.

"Food," she says, her voice flat.

"Food?" I try not to sound relieved.

"Yes. Food. My therapist told me yesterday that when I feel like punching you in the face, I should try a snack first. Something about regulating my blood sugar to help my mood."

I can't tell if she's being serious or not. My guess is this is somewhere between a joke and the truth, so I lean forward slightly. Playfully. She tries to hide the little rumble in the back of her throat at my proximity. At least there's some desire, then.

Emboldened by this realization, I let myself smile. Her gaze falls to my mouth, then meets mine and there's a flash again.

"I'd like to see you try to punch me in the face, Cat." Then, I lean slightly closer. "We can tumble around a little if it'll help you get some of that aggression out. Could be fun."

She furrows her brow and pierces me with a skeptical look. Dammit, I took it too far.

"You're in the guest room until I say otherwise," she almost whispers. If I'm not mistaken, she doesn't sound completely committed to this declaration, but I lean back slightly in deference to her.

"Am I in the guest room here or in Leade Park?" I consider for a moment, then add, "Or we can find a new place in Chicago, if you'd rather."

Her attention shifts to something over my shoulder as she considers the question. After a moment, she sighs. "This promotion means that much to you?"

I make a small movement so I'm in her line of sight, forcing her to meet my eyes again. "You and the kids mean that much to me. The promotion, the house, it's all means to an end, and the end goal is spending more time with you."

Her blue eyes bounce back and forth between mine, and I can tell from the look on her face that she's verifying my statement. I hope she can tell I'm being sincere, because even if it was stupid to try and surprise her with this move, I am telling the truth. I want to be a good husband and a good dad, and I want to get her away from this life that has left her a dimmed-down version of the woman she was when we met. I know this is the way to do it.

"When would we have to leave?"

I've got her. I know I do, but I also know she needs to draw it out a little longer. She's not going to start making this easy on me now.

"The house is empty, and the sellers want to close quickly. I thought we could go out there in a week or two. Spend Christmas there."

"Absolutely not. We're having one last Christmas here, in New York."

"I have to start January first."

"The first is a holiday. If you want to be around more, you can start by taking your holidays off."

"Fine. The second, then. But I want to get set up in the house before I start. We can have Christmas here, but not New Year's."

She folds her arms over her chest again, and I catch another whiff of her perfume. Being unable to kiss her is agonizing.

"I want to stay here for New Year's."

Now, she's just being difficult, but I don't want to lose her to her stubborn anger again. "You can stay for New Year's," I bargain, "but I have to go out there right after Christmas. I will take care of moving all the stuff out of this place, and I'll set it up there. It'll be ready to go when you and the kids arrive."

She chews on her bottom lip as she frowns at me. I'm sure she doesn't like this offer, but it's the best I can give. I don't want to have to deal with starting a new position, trying to prove to Katie I'll be around more often, and a cross-country move on top of it all.

"Fine," she says, resigned. "We'll move to Leade Park."

I almost fall to my knees in gratitude and relief, but I stop myself. "You're not going to regret this, Katie."

"You get two months, Brandon. Keep this place, too, because if I still hate the Midwest on March first, I'm coming back here with the kids. You can decide then if you're coming with us or staying there."

She begrudgingly extends her hand so we can shake on the deal. There's no way I'm going to let her come back here without me, and there's no way I'm giving up the opportunity to lead the Chicago firm. I'd better start thinking about all the ways I can make her fall in love with Leade Park. Hopefully, in the process, she'll fall so much more in love with me, too. I definitely have my work cut out for me, but I'm up for the challenge.

I take her hand and shake it firmly.

Chapter 2

Katie

LEADE PARK. LEADE-FUCKING-PARK. AT first, I thought he had to be kidding, but no. He showed me pictures of the house on the internet. He had me sign paperwork for the mortgage that he just *happened* to have in his desk drawer. He bought a real-life house, in a real-life suburb, near real-life Chicago.

I'm going to be one of those suburban moms in leggings and a sweatshirt with a messy bun. I'm going to be a suburban athleisure mom.

I catch a glimpse of myself in the mirror over the dresser, noting my leggings, sweatshirt, and messy bun. I grunt to myself. Fine. I'm already an athleisure mom, but at least I'm an *urban* athleisure mom.

For the next few weeks, anyway.

Of course he up and bought a house without me. *Of course* he did. That man buys and sells real estate investments all the time with his seemingly unlimited funds. He even bought two apartments next to each other and knocked down walls like some home renovation show to make this space perfect for our family. Well, he can treat this house like another one of his investment properties, because we're not staying. Even if I do have to admit that the house looks pretty cool from the pictures, and the kids will have lots of space to play and run around.

I dump the basket of clean laundry out on the bed and sigh through my nose, noting how wrinkled the clothes have gotten from sitting in the basket for two days. I consider spraying them down and throwing them back in the dryer for a while but ultimately decide against it. They'd just sit there for two more days, since Brandon sure as hell isn't going to fold them.

I start tossing clothes into four piles—one for Brandon, one for me, one for Mason, and one for Christine. I do it with more fervor than strictly necessary.

I'm hate-sorting clean laundry. On a Tuesday in November. This is what my life has become.

I used to be fun. I used to have a life outside of this apartment. I used to party all weekend and, sometimes, into the week. I used to have a job and friends.

I don't miss the partying. Well, I do, but I don't miss the hangovers and the incessant need to chase the freedom from my nerves that alcohol provided. There's drinking, and then there's drinking too much. When drinking at parties turned into too much wine with high-paying clients followed by slipping shots in my lunchtime soda, it became a lot less fun.

I suppose I kind of miss the job. Working in the gallery didn't leave me much time to paint, but neither does motherhood. At least I got paid to work in the gallery.

Since Brandon has so much money—both from his family and from his job—it has never been necessary for me to work. My parents both worked themselves to the bone. Dad had to work long hours to make ends meet, and Mom took on odd jobs while I was at school. They were both miserable and died relatively young. They never had a chance to enjoy me or each other.

So, once I finally decided to marry Brandon, he asked if I wanted to stay home and enjoy my babies. I did. I could have been a single parent.

My mom basically raised me alone all those years, and I was confident I could do it, too. But I fell in love, and that was that. Within a year, I became a stay-at-home mom and wife, all by surprise.

Though after seven years of motherhood, I'm starting to realize that having a job might not be all about the income.

I had started thinking about the possibility of going back to work part-time now that Christine is in preschool, but then Brandon dropped this bomb on me. It's a moot point now. There aren't any art galleries in Leade-fucking-Park.

I suppose a move to a suburb was always inevitable. We're a family, after all, and family living in New York City is difficult. But I wanted to be a mom more than anything. I was ready. It didn't matter to me that Mason was the product of a hot-and-heavy week during which Brandon and I only left my bed to use the bathroom, eat, or drink more wine. Come to think of it, we did most of the eating and drinking in bed, too.

I should have known my life was about to change the minute we met. It was at a party; I was with a woman I met at a club the week before. I smile lightly at the memory of her. She was incredibly good looking—all legs and sharp features. But she couldn't hold a candle to Brandon, who was there as the date of one of my work friends. We took one look at each other across the room and our fates were sealed.

I knew next to nothing about him. I didn't know he was wealthy. I didn't know he was a grad student studying architecture. I certainly didn't know he was five years younger than me, almost ready to graduate and take on the world. The only thing I knew was that the high I got from that first kiss when he pressed me up against the outside of a brownstone was better than anything I had ever experienced. Which was a fair amount, with both men and women.

That was one of the things I loved about Brandon from the start. He wanted to know about my past, but he's never asked me to label or define myself. With him, I've always been just... me. Which, I suppose, is still true. But the me I am now is a hell of a lot different than the me I was then.

I groan internally and start chucking clothes a little harder until I get to the bottom of the basket. Just the sight of the bed, even under piles of clothes, has me thinking about Brandon and me in it. He and I haven't been together since we were in Leade Park for Daniel's wedding. Before that, actually, because there's no sex when you're on vacation with two small children.

Sex had never been an issue with us. A lot of couples lose that desire when they add kids to the mix, but we've always craved each other. But if he thinks he's welcome in this bed after these most recent developments, he's got another thing coming.

So far, my willpower has been stronger than my libido. I just don't know how long I can hold out.

I grab his t-shirts and start laying them out flat on the bed, one on top of another. A low chuckle resonates behind me, and I whip around to face the bedroom door. Brandon is leaning against it, his shirtsleeves rolled up to expose the tattoo of a cat on his forearm. I love that tattoo. It's a black outline of a sleeping cat, curled up and happy, but it takes up almost his entire forearm. He wanted a tattoo of my name on his arm, but I told him that was too gauche, so he settled for the animal that he nicknamed me for instead. With his sleeves rolled up like that, he looks like a damn Adonis. I glare at him, certain that he's doing this on purpose to tempt me.

"Are you hate-folding laundry?" he asks with a smirk.

"No," I say sharply. Technically, I'm not folding anything yet.

He laughs again, clearly not buying it. "Okay. Do you want some help?"

I avoid looking at him by lowering my attention back to the bed and the piles of laundry laying there. I'm not surprised he wants to help now that he knows how upset I am, but where was he before this? How many times had I wished for a break from the drudgery of housework when Christine was a tiny baby and the piles of two kids' laundry felt overwhelming? How many times had I hoped he'd come home early and relieve me of some of these boring chores?

"No," I say again, though my tone is less convincing.

The room is silent for long enough that I'm pretty sure he left, but then he's next to me, grabbing Christine's tiny shirts and folding them. I stop what I'm doing and watch him.

He doesn't look up from his task as he asks, "What?"

I clear my throat. "Nothing."

He glances at me, then back to the shirts. "You know," he starts cautiously as he lays a folded pink shirt on top of the pile, "we could find someone to help out when we get to Leade Park."

This isn't the first time he's brought this up. We're probably the only people in our social circle who don't have hired help. At first, I balked at the idea. I didn't come from money, so I'd never considered hiring a housekeeper or nanny. And besides, I was obsessed with Mason when he was born. No one was going to care for him as well as I could. By the time Christine came along, I was determined to give them as close to a normal upbringing as possible.

Now, both Mason and Christine are at school, and Brandon rarely works from home, so these chores are all that fill the hours between drop off and pick up. And yet, they never seem to end.

I scoff and turn back to Brandon's stack of laundry. "What would I do with my time if we hired someone?" My tone is no-nonsense, but it's a cover. I genuinely have no idea how I'd fill the hours.

Brandon rests his huge hand on top of the tiny clothes and slides his gaze to me. "Anything you want."

I try not to let my surprise show on my face. It's not him telling me to do whatever I want that's shocking. I'm more taken aback that, given the opportunity, I don't actually know what I want to do.

I shut down my expression and shift to Mason's pile of clothes. "I can't do *anything* I want," I grumble. "What I *want* is to stay in New York."

I can see Brandon's shoulders sag. From the corner of my eye, he looks crestfallen, and I feel bad for saying it, even as I press my lips into a firm line and laser-focus on the laundry.

"Katie—" he starts, but he's cut off by my phone ringing. I grab it off the nightstand and answer it without looking at the number.

"Hello?"

"Hello, is this Mrs. Conley? This is Riverside Premier Preschool calling," a woman's voice comes through the line, and she already sounds apologetic.

I know where this is going. I close my eyes and pinch the bridge of my nose, trying to keep the frustration out of my voice. "Yes, this is she."

"I'm so sorry to call in the middle of the day, but your daughter, Christine, vomited after her snack today and is running a low-grade fever. You'll have to come get her as soon as possible. She won't be allowed back until she has been fever-free for twenty-four hours," the woman says.

"Yes, of course." I glance at Brandon, who has stopped folding to look at me, his brow furrowed. "I'll be there as soon as I can." I hang up, sliding the phone into the pocket on the side of my leggings and grabbing my purse from the top of the dresser.

"What's going on?" Brandon asks.

"Christine is sick. I have to go get her, and she can't go back to school until she's better for a whole day, so I get to be home with a sick toddler tomorrow." I check to be sure my wallet is in my purse. "I swear, we're only paying them for a new virus every other week," I grouse as I throw my purse over my shoulder and move to leave the room.

Before I can get out the bedroom door, Brandon gently catches me, his hands curling around my upper arm as he turns me to face him. He's so tall; I can't help but tilt my chin back to look up at him.

"Let me," he says softly, the warmth from his touch seeping through the layers of my sweatshirt. The feel of his hand on my arm is so distracting, and his offer to help is so foreign that, for a moment, I'm confused.

"Let you what?" I breathe. The sensation of our bodies so close together has me thinking I'd let him do pretty much anything right now, which sends a wave of heat directly between my legs.

My willpower might not be as strong as I thought it was.

A corner of his mouth tips up as his eyes darken. Oh, he definitely feels this too. He leans ever-so-slightly closer to me, his hand tightening on my bicep. For a second, I'm positive he's going to kiss me, and even though I'm angry and frustrated and disappointed, I desperately want him to.

But then he blinks a few times and breaks the spell. "Let me go get her."

I blink a few times and take an involuntary step backwards. His hand drops from my arm to his side.

"Oh. Um…" I trail off, looking down at the ground. My instinct is to tell him no, to reassure him that I've got this because I always do. But if I'm going to demand that he's around more, then I should put my money where my mouth is. I look up at him, and his expression tells me he's eager to do this. "Yeah. Sure."

He nods once and brushes past me out of the bedroom. His keys jingle as he grabs them off the key hook by the door. I come out of the bedroom to stand in the hallway. He pauses when he sees me.

"Thanks, Brandon," I say, my voice hushed.

A hopeful smile plays at his lips as he slides his wallet into his back pocket. "This is the start of something better. I promise," he says, and then he's out the door.

I stare at the door for a minute, then look back at the mostly-folded piles of laundry on our bed. It could take him up to an hour to get her home, but it'll only take me about five minutes to get all of this put away. Dinner is in the slow cooker, and I cleaned the house top-to-bottom yesterday. Whatever will I do with my time?

A corner of my mouth tugs upward as I think about what Brandon said.

Whatever you want.

Whatever I want. The endless possibilities are daunting, but also a little exhilarating, if I'm being honest. I grab the piles of laundry and start putting them hurriedly away, not wanting to waste a precious second.

Chapter 3

Brandon

CHRISTINE'S PRESCHOOL ISN'T FAR, but on a bad day with traffic, it can take a good thirty minutes to get there. As soon as I pull out of our parking space, I know today is going to be a bad day.

I groan and tap the steering wheel. I'm definitely looking forward to leaving New York City traffic. I wasn't sure Katie would agree to this move, so I haven't thought too far ahead about where to enroll the kids in school out in Leade Park. I wonder if the neighborhood public schools would help to avoid the hustle and all the driving.

When we were younger, we took the subway everywhere, but that's a lot harder with two kids. Katie and I both grew up in the city, though we lived in different worlds. She used the subway out of necessity. I used it because it offered freedom from my parents. I learned how to navigate the subway system at a very young age with my older brother, Shane. After I realized he was getting into a kind of trouble I didn't want any part in, my best friend, Daniel, and I would use it to explore the city.

The thought of Daniel has me smirking. I should give him a call soon. It's been a while since we talked. We used to get into trouble, sure, but it was the harmless kind of trouble kids get into. We were good kids. We met when we were around Mason's age. But Mason has had such a hard time making friends. I have a sneaking suspicion it's because we don't have the same lifestyle as his private school peers. Katie has been determined that the kids live a life not steeped in financial privilege; it was one of the conditions of her agreeing to marry me. But it means Mason can't relate to kids who live in penthouses, have lavish birthday parties, and sport their own no-limit credit cards.

All of two cars make it through the stoplight ahead of me, and I hit my brakes again. I glance at the time—eleven on a Tuesday. Daniel's new wife, Mac, is a teacher at their local high school—the one I'm going to be working on—so she's probably at work. Daniel is probably also working, but as a now-famous writer, he gets to make his own hours. I shrug and press his name on my phone to start a call. He answers in two rings, his voice coming loudly through the car speakers.

"Katie forgive you yet?" he asks, and I hear a distant, rhythmic pounding as he speaks.

I reach to turn the volume down. "Hello to you, too."

"I'm trying to prepare for the firestorm I'll inevitably get in the middle of when you all move out here." The pounding continues, though it slows down and becomes more erratic.

"You seem very certain that this move is happening," I grumble.

"She's not going to let you come out here alone."

"Don't be so sure about that. She gave me two months to convince her to stay. She told me to keep the place here, and if she still hates the idea of living out there by March first—" my voice breaks a little, and I clear my throat. "If she still hates it by then, she's bringing the kids back here, with or without me."

The pounding stops, and Daniel's chair squeaks lightly as he shifts. "She said that?"

"Yes."

He lets out a low whistle. "Is this promotion worth it for you?"

"You've asked me that before."

"Yeah, but that was before Katie threatened to leave your ass if she hated it here. The stakes have changed."

I hit the gas as the light turns green. I make it through the intersection just as the light is turning yellow again. Now that I'm through this light, I should be able to move a little faster to Christine's school. I sigh, coming back to the conversation. "There's not a job in the world that means more to me than Katie and the kids," I say.

"Sounds like there's a 'but' at the end of that sentence," Daniel prods.

I rub my palm against my jaw, a few of the rough hairs of my beard catching on my wedding band. "But..." I start, then let out a humorless laugh. "It's complicated. I'll never move up here. If I start over at a new firm in the city, I'd have to hustle even more than I'm already doing. My parents want to step away. It's the perfect opportunity."

"But?" Daniel asks again.

There's a pit in my stomach I can't shake. "But what's the point of any of it if Katie is miserable, or if she takes the kids and leaves me?"

Daniel is quiet for a long minute, and I drum my fingers on the steering wheel. He hums softly—a sound that means he's getting ready to say something he's not sure he should say. "Isn't she already miserable?" he finally asks.

I let out a puff of air through pursed lips, my mind flashing back to a month ago when Katie came home from a fundraising event for Mason's school. She had the smell of wine on her breath, and her words were slightly slurred. Almost eight years sober, and she gave in. *I just want to leave this place,* she had said when I laid down in bed with her and held her as she started crying. *I just want to be fun again.* I held her through all of that. The next day, I told my parents I'd take the job. It had been perfect timing to leave for Daniel's wedding a few weeks early, both to scope out the area and get her away from New York for a while. At the time, I thought I couldn't have scripted a better opportunity, but now, after watching her slam cabinets looking for something to take the edge off her anger—food, she had said, but I don't know if I can believe her—I'm worried I made things worse. Talk about a catch-22.

"Yeah, I think she is," I finally respond. The pit in my stomach grows heavier.

"Do you think bringing her out here is going to make it worse?"

"It could," I muse. "I have to come out right after Christmas, but she wants to stay here until New Year's with the kids." I leave a lot unsaid there, but Daniel knows.

"Are you worried about leaving her alone? You think she might—"

"Maybe," I cut him off. "I don't know. I trust her; I really do. But she's human, too, you know?"

Daniel is silent again before he says, "Well, don't forget you've got us out here. Mac and I want to help. Katie and Jenny seemed to hit it off when you were here for the wedding, too. Maybe having friends and some support will move the needle."

"Thanks," I say quietly, and then when a car cuts me off, I hold down my horn and yell some expletives I'm not proud of.

"Are you driving?" Daniel asks, unphased. When you learn how to drive in Manhattan, you also learn how to yell at asshole drivers.

"Christine is sick, so I'm picking her up from school."

"I bet Katie appreciates that," he says suggestively. The pounding resumes over the line, and, just like that, the tone changes completely.

"Having trouble with the book?" I ask. Whenever Daniel is working something out with his writing, he bounces a tennis ball against the wall. I'm surprised Mac hasn't hidden them all yet.

He chuckles. "Yeah. I don't want to rub it in, but it turns out being really fucking happy isn't great for my signature angst."

Despite my domestic issues, I can't fight my smile as I finally pull into a visitor parking spot at the school. Daniel deserves all this happiness and then some. "Well, good luck with that. I'm here, so I have to get going."

"Let me know what your plans are, okay? We'll come out and help with the house or whatever you need."

"Will do. Thanks," I say, and we both hang up.

I make my way inside the school. I'm not usually the one to pick her up, so it takes a second for me to find the front office. The secretary leads me to the nurse's office where Christine is laying on a cot, her thumb in her mouth and her eyes almost closed. She's sick and it's almost naptime, which is a brutal combination for a toddler.

I take a knee next to the cot and brush her dirty blonde hair away from her little face. She feels warm, and her eyes are a little glassy as she looks up at me. As soon as she sees me, though, she pops up and wraps her little arms around my neck.

"Daddy!" she exclaims in surprise.

I wrap my hands around her tiny body and lift her so I'm carrying her as I stand. "Hey, Chrissy-pie."

"I got sick," she says into my shoulder, then burps a little.

I allow myself to grimace since she can't see me. This could be a rough ride home. "I heard." I rub my hand up and down her back comfortingly. "Let's get you home, baby girl."

On my way out, I nod in thanks to the school nurse who, in turn, shoots me a sympathetic smile. I get Christine secured in the car seat, and as soon as I've pulled out of the parking lot, I glance at her in the rearview mirror. Her eyes are closed, and her head is tilted to the side, her chest rising and falling slowly. I shift in my seat, trying to stretch away the lingering soreness in my back from the less-than-optimal guest room mattress. I envy her ability to comfortably fall asleep anywhere.

It takes less time to get home than it did to get to her school, and when I gently lift Christine out of her car seat, she barely even stirs. She sleeps with her warm cheek pressed into the crook of my neck as I carry her inside.

When I enter, Katie is nowhere to be seen, so I make my way back to Christine's room and gently place her down on her mattress, my back protesting at bending over so far with her added weight.

As soon as I cover her with the blanket, she squirms a little before putting her thumb back in her mouth. She's sound asleep in a few seconds, so I creep out of the room and shut the door behind me. She'll probably wake up cranky and hungry from skipping lunch, but it doesn't seem worth waking her just to make her eat something that might come right back up.

I turn to head back toward the front rooms when I catch sight of Katie in our bedroom across the hall. She sits cross-legged on the far edge of the bed, nearest the French doors that lead out to our small balcony. Her back, which is half-facing me, is ramrod straight. She's wearing her huge headphones that go over her ears and block out most of the sounds of the house. I bought them for her when she mentioned getting overwhelmed by all the noise the kids tend to make when I'm home.

In front of her is a large sketch pad sitting on the portable, folding easel I bought her for her birthday a few years ago. Her pencil case is open next to her. One of her pencils is stuck in her bun, and one is in her hand as her fingers tap against her knee. She's studying her work intently, completely unaware of me watching her. Her head bobs slightly to a rhythm I can't hear, and she narrows her eyes critically.

I haven't seen Katie with her art supplies since... Honestly, I can't remember the last time she had her art supplies out.

The window in the bedroom faces West, and the golden, afternoon light is coming through the bedroom windows. It illuminates her and the sketchbook in a way that makes her appear as if she's lit up from the inside out.

She's absolutely breathtaking.

I take a few steps inside the bedroom, and that's when she notices me. She slides her headphones off so they rest around her neck, letting the soft music escape into the room. She taps her phone a few times and the music stops.

"You're drawing." My voice is quiet. I don't mean to sound surprised, but I am.

She quickly flips the sketchbook closed. Her eyes fall to her hands, and if I'm not mistaken, her cheeks flush slightly. Is she embarrassed I saw her?

"Oh," she says, and when she raises her eyes to me again, that steely look I've become so accustomed to over the past few months is back, but it's lost some of its edge. She stands and comes around to the side of the bed toward me. "You said I should do whatever I want, and the light here was perfect today, so I thought..." She trails off, looking back toward her easel. She shakes hear head, avoiding my gaze. "Anyway, I'm done now."

I study her for a moment, willing her to look at me again. I take another few steps toward her, but she won't meet my eyes. "You don't have to stop on my account. Christine is sleeping, and I can take care of her when she wakes up."

She shrugs but doesn't say anything, so I reach out my hand to gently cup her cheek. Her skin is so fucking *soft*.

"Hey," I say, drawing her jaw up gently so she'll look at me. "Is this what you want? Time to do your art again?"

She swallows, her eyes finally meeting mine. "Maybe? I don't know. It was just the first thing I thought to do with my time."

I nod slowly, my mind racing. I can do this for her. I can give her the time and space for her to do whatever she wants, whatever makes her happy.

"It feels a little pointless, though," she continues.

I pinch my eyebrows together, my hand still on her cheek. I'm heartened that she hasn't pulled away yet. "Why?"

Her gaze falls to something over my shoulder. "Who's even going to see it?"

"Do you want people to see it?" I ask, my voice still quiet. This is the most intimate conversation we have had in a long time, and I'm trying really hard not to say the wrong thing and blow it.

She shrugs, still not meeting my eyes. "Maybe."

I press my palm into her cheek a little more, and she finally looks at me, allowing me to see the uncertainty in her eyes. I fight against a soft smile, not wanting her to think I'm mocking her. "Art now, audience later," I say. It's something she always used to say to the artists at the gallery where she worked when they were feeling particularly vulnerable. She parroted

it to Mason last year when he decided to enter an art competition at his
school.

Ever so slowly, a smile starts to spread across her face and *holy shit*,
it's so bright and beautiful that I can't breathe. Seeing her dazzling face
makes me realize how long it has been since I've seen her truly smile like
this, and my chest physically hurts with the desire to make her smile more
often.

She leans almost imperceptibly closer to me, and my fingers brush a
few tendrils of her platinum blonde hair that have fallen out of her bun.
I reflexively curl my fingers around the back of her neck, and her eyelids
flutter closed.

After months of the cold shoulder, I'm going to kiss my wife. *Do not
screw this up*, I tell myself as I lean in close enough to feel her sweet breath
on my lips.

The moment our lips brush against each other, a retching sound
comes from Christine's bedroom followed by a miserable wail.

"Mooooooooommy," she cries. Katie's eyes snap open, and she backs
away, moving around me toward the door.

"I've got her," I say, but Katie shakes her head and wordlessly opens
the door to Christine's room, disappearing inside.

I hear their muffled voices, and I know I should go to help, but before
I can grab a towel and get in there, Katie's sketchbook catches my eye.
Confident that they won't be coming out any time soon, I flip it open to
the page she was working on.

It's a familiar scene of a man holding a small child in his arms. The
child is holding a pumpkin, and there's another, older kid reaching for
it. It looks strikingly similar to the scene we encountered when we found
Daniel and Mac's friend, Ben, in the pumpkin patch with his nephews

last fall. We were on our way to "help Jenny with her grand gesture," as Katie put it. The kids hit it off after that, which made me even more certain this move would be good for all of us. But why would she be drawing Ben and his nephews?

I take a step closer, squinting at the shape of the man's body. Real-life Ben is jacked and spends an inordinate amount of time at the gym. This man doesn't even come close to him. He's got a little bit of a dad bod, to be honest, and the kid he's holding is clearly a little girl, not a boy.

Then, it hits me. She was drawing me and the kids. That little light in her eyes that she tried to hide from me was brought on by her drawing us playing and having fun together.

It doesn't escape me that she had to put me and the kids in a fake scene because I'm gone so often, but I can work with this. I can be around more and have fun with the kids. I can give her time to create this art if that's what is going to make her happy. I can make her smile like that again.

"Brandon," she yells from Christine's room. "Can you get a bath started?"

"Sure," I call back, making sure to flip the sketchbook closed again. "Whatever you need."

Chapter 4

Katie

THE WEEKS BEFORE CHRISTMAS fly by, like always. Brandon may have vowed to be home more, and that first day seemed promising, but that's all it was. One day, and then he's back at the office, leaving before the kids wake up and coming home just in time to put them to bed. This is a particularly difficult time for it, too, since the kids are done with school for the semester and have been home on winter break. All day. With me.

I fight the breakdown for so long. I keep my cool while I watch complete strangers start to pack up our bedrooms in huge boxes—watch, because I refuse to lift a finger to help in this charade. Brandon is too busy packing up his all-important office to help pack up our less-important home, so he hires people to do it for him. I only allow them to start packing the bedrooms because I want our living room to maintain some semblance of family comfort through the holiday.

So, on the day before Christmas Eve, when Brandon is sitting at the kitchen island drinking coffee and he tells me he has to go back into the office yet again to finish getting everything ready to move to Chicago, I lose my shit.

"We always take the kids to Rockefeller Center the day before Christmas Eve," I say under my breath.

"This year is a little different, don't you think?" He seems completely unfazed as he sips his coffee, which only irritates me more.

I eye him from the stove where I flip a pancake. "That was the point, though. We were going to spend a normal holiday here before we had to move." My tone is clipped. I can almost see him scheming ways out of this conversation. He must know I'm not too far from an explosion.

He tilts his head to the side slightly. "I'm leaving in three days. You're leaving in a week and a half. Did you really think this holiday would be normal?" His voice is carefully bland.

I slap the spatula on the hard countertop and glare at him. "I *thought* you'd be on board with our family traditions. I already bought the tickets."

"Mom?" Mason's voice drifts from his bedroom. "What was that noise?"

I take a deep breath and let it out slowly through my nose, never breaking eye contact with Brandon. "Nothing, buddy." I force my voice to remain sweet. "Just dropped something in the kitchen."

"Oh, okay," he says, then his head pops out from the hallway into the living area next to the kitchen. "When are we going ice skating?"

"Eye-skating!" Christine calls from her seat at the little table next to our dining table. She almost drops the purple crayon balled in her little fist in her excitement.

I eye Brandon, trying to keep my expression neutral and probably failing. "We'll leave after Christine's nap."

"After her nap? That's forever," Mason whines.

I glance at him over Brandon's shoulder. "It'll pass before you know it. Didn't you have that book you were excited to read? Super dog or something like that?" It's a thinly-veiled attempt to get him to go back to his room so I can continue talking to his father, but it seems to work. Mason's face brightens as he remembers the book in question, and he pivots on his heel to go back to his room just as Brandon stands to bring his coffee mug to the sink.

"Oh, no you don't. We're not done here." I start to put my hands on my hips when I remember the pancakes. I scrape them off the pan and onto the kids' plates on the island.

"Cat—"

"Don't call me that when I'm mad at you," I spit out as I bring a plate over to where Christine was sitting a second ago. She's no longer there, and I look up to see her shock of blonde hair pass through Mason's doorway. I mentally calculate that I have about two minutes before the fighting starts.

"You're always mad at me," Brandon is mumbling as he rinses his mug.

"You're always doing something to make me mad," I counter. "How am I supposed to *not* be mad at you when you throw our lives into disarray and ignore our traditions in the process?"

The only indication of his frustration is the bang of his mug hitting the bottom of the sink louder than is normal. He hangs his head between his shoulders and holds on to the edge of the counter as his back rises and falls slowly. "I'm getting a little sick of being the one to shoulder all the blame for this." His words are barely audible, but as he turns around to face me, I swear I see pain burn in his hazel eyes. He presses his lips together into a thin line, as if the simple clenching of his jaw could keep more words from tumbling out of his mouth.

Spoiler alert: it can't.

"I'm not the one who came home drunk after eight years sober and begged to leave this place, Katie."

I take an involuntary step back, my mouth gaping for a second before I close it, my nostrils flaring. There it is. The real reason he's been so adamant about this move. But I'm not letting him have this one. He doesn't get to swoop in and save me. I don't need saving. "People say things they don't mean all the time when they've been drinking." I try to keep my voice flippant, but I can hear the edge in it. I take a deep breath before I add, "Besides, I didn't realize I wasn't allowed to have fun anymore."

He tilts his head, and his expression almost looks as if he feels sorry for me, which stokes the ever-burning flame of anger in my belly even further. "It didn't seem very fun for you."

It hadn't been. It had been a desperate attempt to drown out the fake, tittering laughter of the PTO moms at a fundraiser for Mason's school. For three years now, they've made ignoring me an art form. I knew it was a mistake at the time, but they were all sipping their champagne and chatting, and I wanted to feel like I was on the inside rather than the outside for once. Drinking that champagne had felt like a way to show them all I was like them, at least in this small way. But one glass turned quickly to four or five—I can't remember—and I ended up slinking out and taking a cab home.

Brandon's expression turns apologetic, and I take that to mean my own is showing all the hurt I've been trying to keep locked away. I take a shaky breath, not exactly sure how to respond, but I don't have a chance to.

"Chrissy!" Mason's thin whine comes from the hallway. "Get out of my room!"

"I want that dinosaur!" Christine wails.

This seems to snap Brandon into action. "I have to get going." He grabs his coat off the coat rack by the door, lifts his keys from the hook next to it, and pulls it open. He pauses with his back to me, almost as if he's going to say something else. He must decide against it, because the next second, he steps out, and lets the door slam behind him.

"Chris*tine*. NO!" Mason shouts, and Christine lets loose an ear-piercing cry.

I tip my head to the ceiling, sighing. "Give me strength," I mumble to no one in particular, then make my way to the bedrooms to deal with the kids.

Between mediating two more arguments before lunch, making said lunch, having said lunch knocked on the floor multiple times, wrestling Christine down for a nap, and cleaning up from a morning of children-created chaos, I don't have much time to think about what Brandon said until hours later. I finally get a chance to eat my own meal—a sad peanut butter and jelly sandwich—standing at the kitchen island at around one in the afternoon, which is about when the full weight of our argument this morning presses on me.

I had been surprised he brought up that night, but I would be an idiot not to admit that my choices didn't haunt me a little.

My sobriety isn't a huge deal in our lives, or it hasn't been until now. For most of my twenties, I didn't think I had a drinking problem because I didn't have a Hollywood drinking problem. I wasn't in desperate need of alcohol to function. I wasn't strung out. I just needed it to take the edge off the stress sometimes. And in social situations. And sometimes at work if someone was spending a lot of money; it said something about you if you knew which wine to pull out for which occasion. And then sometimes we pulled out more if we were working late and bored. Working at the gallery, I was surrounded by it. I started carrying tiny bottles of alcohol in my purse, just in case. It always felt like something adults did, and after my parents passed, I didn't exactly have adult role models lining up to show me the way.

But when I found out I was pregnant with Mason, my first reaction was to grab a bottle of whiskey from the top of my refrigerator and take a long pull directly from the bottle. Just to calm my nerves. It tasted almost like ammonia, and I spit it out into the sink. It was at that moment that I realized two things: one, pregnant women aren't supposed to drink shots of whiskey at ten in the morning on a Tuesday, and two, maybe no one is supposed to drink shots of whiskey at ten in the morning on a Tuesday. It was a quick realization: If my first reaction to a stressful situation is to take a pull of liquor straight from the bottle, I might have a problematic relationship with alcohol.

It was relatively easy to stay away from the booze when I was pregnant. Most people were accommodating, or cautionary—as if it was any of their business what I did with my body. But once Mason was born, it got a little more difficult. Babies are stressful, and people started inviting me out again. I'd turn them down, ostensibly because of the baby, but mostly because I didn't want to be tempted to drink. I had this tiny baby who depended on me and only me, even though Brandon had been showing up every day after work to do what he could. I couldn't be tipsy with a baby to care for. It was around that time that I started seeing my therapist, and she helped me stay the course. Brandon and I got engaged, my maternity leave ended, and I didn't want to go back to work. He suggested I stay home if I wanted. The temptation was gone. But, with it went my friends and the life I had before Mason, too.

If I'm being completely honest, the whole city changed for me after that. The throngs of people and smashed-together buildings used to be manageable with something to take the edge off, but with a baby and no booze, it all started to feel claustrophobic. It was still magical. There's an energy to New York that you can't quite get anywhere else. But the energy felt more electric and less invigorating.

I suppose it had been out of character when I came home from the fundraiser a little tipsy. This morning, I had snapped at him about being allowed to have fun, but he had been right. It hadn't been about having fun. It had been about desperation to feel like I fit in. I drank that champagne out of misery and kept drinking it all night, which is what I've spent the past eight-ish years trying not to do.

I pick at about half of the sandwich and push the rest around on my plate, eventually glancing at the clock. I had been hopeful that Brandon would make it back before we have to leave for ice skating, though I'm not surprised when he doesn't.

By the time I dump the remnants of my sandwich in the trash and load all the dishes from lunch into the dishwasher, I can hear Christine singing to herself from her bedroom, and I finally come to terms with the realization that I'm going to have to take the kids by myself this year.

I draw out getting ready as long as I can, but when Brandon hasn't shown his face by the time Mason comes out dressed in his ugly Christmas sweater and fleece pants, I know I can't stall any longer.

We take the subway to get as close as we can to Rockefeller Center, which the kids always think is a treat. I think it's awful, but the subway has always been a reminder of harder times. And, as with most things around the holidays, this is for them and not for me. When we get off the train, I lift a wriggling Christine into my arms and balance her on one hip while clutching Mason's hand with the other. I'm as comfortable in the city as anyone else, but it's crowded with holiday shoppers and tourists, and I'm alone with both kids.

By the time we climb the stairs out of the subway station, my right bicep is burning from holding Christine close to me, and I can barely feel the fingers of my left hand from Mason holding on tight. The pinch of my wedding band between the fingers he's squeezing is starting to make me antsy.

It's going to be a long night.

We slowly make our way across the couple of blocks to the giant Christmas tree and ice rink while pointing out decorations and light displays on the buildings we pass. Even while clutching two kids through throngs of people, Christmas in New York is magical. The millions of fairy lights twinkle all around us, and faint music plays over the hustle and bustle of the tourist crowds. Mason must feel it, too. As soon as we can see the outdoor ice rink, he speeds up, practically dragging Christine and me with him.

I let go of Mason's hand and let him run a little ahead of me, then Christine starts wriggling to break free, so I put her down, as well.

"Hey!" Mason yells, his voice muffled by the wind and the crowd. "Is that Dad?" He stops in his tracks and points his mittened hand somewhere vaguely in front of him.

I don't bother to look where he's pointing. "Oh, I don't think so, honey." I come up next to him, holding Christine's hand. "Your dad had to work today."

The crestfallen look on Mason's face kills me. I know disappointment is a part of life, but I hate it when my kids get their hopes up only to be shattered later, especially by their father. My own father disappointed me so many times I eventually became numb to it. I don't want the same to happen to them.

Mason's bottom lip starts quivering. I hadn't realized he was looking forward to seeing Brandon as much as he was excited about the ice skating.

"But who is going to skate with us, then?" A big tear threatens to fall down his cheek.

I squat down in front of him so we're eye-level. "Oh, kiddo. I'll skate with you and Christine, okay?"

"But you hate ice skating." His voice shakes, and then that tear does fall. It breaks my damn heart.

"I do," I admit. There's no sense lying to him. He's old enough to remember the past few holiday seasons. Usually, Brandon skates with the kids while I get hot chocolate and watch from the side. I put a gloved hand on his cheek, brushing his tear away. "But I'll do it for you. It'll be fun, okay?"

Mason nods, but he continues to look down at his shoes as I stand and take his hand so we can make our way toward the line for skate rental. He squeezes it tight, pinching my fingers painfully around my wedding band again. I shift his hand in mine to stop the discomfort.

"Why the long face?" a man's familiar voice booms from next to us. Mason's entire countenance changes, his shoulders lifting and his face lighting up. Despite myself, my heart skips a beat at the sound.

Christine jumps up and down. "Daddy! Daddy!" she screams, then tears her hand free of mine, running toward Brandon, who is just a few feet away from us. As soon as she's close enough, he grabs her under her arms and lifts her up, twirling her around. She giggles. Mason stays next to me, gripping my hand and smiling.

He settles Christine on a hip as she puts her arms around his neck and buries her face in the shoulder of his jacket. He crosses the distance between us, then reaches out to muss Mason's hair. "What's wrong, little man?"

"Oh, I just didn't want Mom to have to ice skate with us because she hates it," he says.

"Good looking out for your mom, bud." He meets my eyes, his smile softening. "I'm here now, though. Let's get on the ice and give your mom some time off, huh?"

He holds my gaze for another moment. I think he probably wants to say something, but whatever it is, he won't say it in front of the kids. His eyes drop from mine to my lips, and my tongue flicks out to moisten them. He huffs quietly, then drags his eyes back to mine, his grin brightening ever so slightly.

Brandon's smile has always been relaxed and genuine, which is easy for someone who walks through the world knowing he has enough money and privilege to solve most problems that come his way. There was a time when his laid-back nature rubbed off on me, and I could feel the tension leaving most situations, but whatever standoff we've found ourselves in recently isn't going to be fixed by him showing up to ice skate and flashing me a grin.

Nevertheless, I relax a little as he studies me. He must see it, too, because his smile widens and his eyes sparkle like the Christmas lights around us.

It's short-lived, though, as Mason starts tugging on his hand and pulling him toward the skate rentals. Brandon lets himself be led by his son, but he looks over his shoulder at me. "Enjoy your hot chocolate," he calls. "We'll see you in an hour."

I watch the three of them as they walk away from me, Brandon in the middle with a tiny Christine perched on his hip and a bundled-up Mason holding his hand on the other side, both kids' vibrant, puffy coats contrasting his black, wool one. If I had any time, I'd sketch this scene, with the massive Christmas tree lit up behind them. For now, though, I'll have to settle for tucking the picture into a pocket of my brain and hope I can hold on to it forever.

They get in line, then Mason turns to say something to Brandon, who leans closer to be able to hear. After a moment, Brandon straightens, then tips his head back and roars his laughter into the darkening sky. I can hear his booming guffaw from where I stand, and I feel a corner of my mouth pulling up at the sound.

Brandon calms, though Mason is still beaming with pride at having made his father laugh. Brandon ruffles Mason's hair again, then he notices me still watching them. He tilts his head at me as he shifts Christine higher on his hip. His expression seems to say, *Go. I've got this.*

I nod once and turn to get myself some hot chocolate so I can set up next to the ice rink and watch this little trio of mine.

Chapter 5

Brandon

THINGS DON'T GET MUCH better between Katie and me after ice skating, though we both do a good job of keeping the tension to a simmer so the kids don't suspect anything is up. Between last-minute gift wrapping, our Christmas Eve and Christmas morning traditions, and my packing to leave, we can't even get two seconds alone to talk. It's possible she's inventing things to do to avoid me, too, but I'm not sure.

I haven't tried to move back from the guest room, either, so I'm as much to blame as she is. Still, I get the eerie feeling that I'm watching my family slip between my fingers before my very eyes.

As soon as my flight lands in Chicago, I text Katie to let her know I arrived safely. She texts back right away, but it's just a thumbs up emoji. I don't know how to read that, so I don't bother trying. Instead, I message Daniel to let him know I'm here and that I need to get my suitcase from baggage claim. Daniel offered to pick me up from the airport, saying it was so I could save money on a taxi, but we both know neither of us need to worry about paying for a cab. I get it, though. Despite having seen him just about three months ago, I'm excited to see my best friend again, too.

I grab my suitcase off the carousel and pop the handle up so I can wheel it out the doors to the roundabout where passengers catch their rides. As soon as I emerge from the airport, Daniel's car pulls over and stops right in front of me. He opens the trunk, so I stash my suitcase and climb into the passenger seat just as I hear a whistle sound from nearby.

"Yeah, yeah. I'm going," Daniel mutters under his breath as he pulls back out into the street. "You think New Yorkers are in a hurry, and then you visit a Chicago airport." He glances at me and back to the road. "How was the flight?"

I press the button to lean my seat back a little more as I stretch my legs out in front of me. "Lonely," I say. It's not sad or a ploy for sympathy; it's simply a statement of fact. Daniel and I have known each other long enough and been through enough shit together that we are always honest with one another.

He snickers as he changes lanes. "You'd rather have a toddler crawling all over you while you're trapped in a metal tube for three hours?"

"Well, yeah, actually, but I was mostly thinking about Katie." Katie and the almost-four-months since I've seen her beautiful smile, touched her, felt her body under mine. I swallow hard against the ache in my chest.

Daniel merges onto the highway toward Leade Park before he glances at me again. "Still bad, huh?"

"Bad is probably an understatement." I pause as I rhythmically tap my foot. "I might have confronted her about the drinking."

Daniel cocks an eyebrow, but otherwise, his expression betrays nothing of what he's thinking. We're both silent for long enough that I pull my hair back, frustrated. "I might have jumped the gun on this move," I admit.

"What makes you say that? You were pretty sure about it a few months ago."

"I got spooked. I mean, yeah, I want this promotion. And I wouldn't mind leaving the city for good. Living in the city with kids is just different, man. I don't know how our parents did it."

Daniel snorts. "They didn't. They hired people to do it for them."

I angle my head at him, conceding that point. "Yeah, well Katie never had any money growing up. She has always been adamant that she doesn't want me throwing our money around where the kids are concerned, and she still is."

"Aside from that massive apartment," Daniel mutters.

I chuckle. "Right. Well, her argument there is that the kids don't know what real estate costs in the city, but they do know if they're being raised by a nanny or driven around by a chauffeur. And, if they had to share a room, she'd lose it with all their arguing."

Daniel tilts his head back and forth. "She's probably right."

"Anyway, I met them at the ice rink downtown the other day, and Katie looked like she was clutching the kids for dear life. The older they get, the harder it seems for one of us to keep the two of them close by. And, you know, parenting is different now than when our parents did it."

He's quiet for a long moment, which is usually his tell for when he's formulating something to say. His gray eyes slide to me, then back to the road. "Why was Katie alone downtown with the kids in the middle of the holiday rush?"

"I had to finish packing up my office," I say, but even I know better than to believe that entirely.

Sure enough, Daniel shoots me a skeptical look. "You've known about this move for months, and you had to pack up your office a few days ago instead of helping your wife do your holiday tradition stuff with the kids downtown?"

I frown. "When you put it that way, I sound like an asshole."

Daniel shrugs. "If the shoe fits."

"You know, it's really good to see you, man. I love having my balls busted by my best friend and my wife at the same time." I fold my arms across my chest and stare out the passenger-side window. The trees and grass fly by us as we speed down the highway. There are no hills to speak of. Illinois is so *flat*.

Daniel chuckles. "I'm going to go ahead and guess that you brought up what she said when she was drunk that night and bailed."

"That is not at all what happened." I eye him sidelong. "I had been avoiding her in order to *not* bring up that night because I thought it would make things worse."

"And then you brought it up anyway?"

"It slipped out."

"Did it make things worse?"

I dip my chin and glare at him. When he doesn't respond or take his eyes off the road, I purse my lips. "I don't know. The kids started antagonizing each other, and I left. I did really have to pack up the office," I say quickly before he can give me any more shit. "But I saw her face, and it looked like she felt just as bad about the whole thing as I did. That was not the face of a woman who is going to start drinking again."

"But you thought she might, and she let it slip that New York isn't as great for her as it once was. Which was why you ultimately decided to make the move out here."

I sigh deeply. "Yep." I pause, then decide to continue. "She told me once, about a year ago, that she had considered drinking again. That she wanted to because of all the stress and boredom. She started seeing her therapist more often, which seemed to help."

"Until she came home drunk," Daniel says pointedly.

"Until she came home drunk," I confirm.

We sit in silence for a while, the sound of the cars around us on the road the only noise between us. Eventually, Daniel signals to exit the highway. When he slows to a stop at the light, he turns a bit in his seat to look at me. "If you think you made a mistake, then why are you here?"

I take a deep breath, staring at an oak tree that has twisted itself around some power lines. "The night she came home drunk, she cried. I held her all night and she just cried and cried." I rub my fingers over my temple, the memory of that night bubbling up, clear as day. The sobs wracked her body as I held her in our bed, not knowing what else to do. "She's the most stoic person I know, Daniel. I don't think that woman even shed a tear when she was in labor. Either time."

"You cried, though," Daniel snickers as he hits the gas when the light turns green.

"I sure fucking did. Even if her vice grip hadn't almost broken a few bones in my hand, those babies brought me to my knees." I flex my hand at the memory. "You did too, you asshole."

"Yeah, but I'm the brooding, emotional writer. I'm supposed to cry." He smirks, clearly trying to lighten the mood.

I chuckle lightly, then my face falls. "But that night broke something in her. I saw it. I saw that little extra piece of emptiness in her eyes the next morning. I figured she meant what she said, and I made the decision. It was supposed to be a happy surprise."

"And you didn't think that the stress of the move might have the opposite effect from what you intended?"

"I did," I answer immediately. "I absolutely did. But it felt worth the risk." I look at him out of the corner of my eye. "We don't have anyone out there anymore. My parents are in Chicago, you're here, my college friends are spread across the country, all the other guys we went to high school with moved out of the city..." I trail off and shrug.

"Have you heard from Shane?" It would make sense that I'd be able to lean on my older brother, but Daniel knows better than that. Shane has been in and out of rehab for the past ten years. I don't even know where he's living right now. Daniel's probably trying to gently lead me to some connection between my past with Shane and my present with Katie. But, joke's on him, because I've already been over this a million times.

"No," I say simply.

Thankfully, Daniel drops it. He pulls up to the curb of my new house and puts his car in park. "We're here for you, Brandon. Whatever you need, Mac and I want to help."

I look out at the house. It's a sprawling, cream-colored house with a three-car garage and a manicured front lawn. A fence surrounds the back yard, and deep green shutters line the second-story bedroom windows. It should look cheerful and suburban, but instead it looks dark and empty, even from the outside. Not for the first time today, a pang of loneliness hits me square in the chest. Loneliness and overwhelm. I suddenly realize how much work there is to do to get the house ready for Katie and the kids, and I want it to be perfect when they arrive. I need to impress Katie with this, and hopefully earn my way out of the guest room.

"I need to get her back," I say quietly. I know, technically, she's not gone, but she might as well be. I look at Daniel, his steely eyes already on me and his brow furrowed slightly. I swallow heavily. "I have this feeling of dread. Every morning I wake up with it, and every night I fall asleep with it. She threatened to leave me." I have to fight for my voice not to break, and I almost lose.

"Do you think she really would?" Daniel asks.

I nod. "I do," I say, resigned. "She's stubborn. But, more than that, I'm worried she's starting to think the life we have was never the life she wanted. I knocked her up, and she thought I wanted to marry her just to do the right thing. She never believed me when I told her how head-over-heels I was about her. I was thrilled about Mason, but she was it for me. I knew it the minute I met her."

"You spent a year chasing her. You don't think she believed you even after all that?" His eyebrows push further together.

"I hope so, but I don't know. Between the chase and the wedding and Mason, and then Christine..." I trail off and shrug helplessly. "It's not like we've had a ton of time to spend on our relationship. We were just sort of dropped into the middle of it. We had to build the plane while it was already in the air."

Daniel's expression smooths out and he nods knowingly. "You never got a chance to date your wife."

"Not really."

A smile slowly cracks across Daniel's face, his dimples on full display. "You need to get her to fall hopelessly in love with you. Again."

I narrow my eyes at him. "I don't like whatever that look is."

"I happen to know a thing or two about wooing women."

"You were in a shitty relationship with a manipulative gold digger for years. She wouldn't even believe you when you broke up with her," I remind him. "Or did you forget when she showed up here and Mac almost—rightly—left your ass high and dry because, for a writer, you are a terrible communicator?"

Daniel raises a finger in the air. "Ah, but she didn't"—he points the finger at me—"because I know a thing or two about wooing women."

"I had to come out here to tell you to get your head out of your ass so you could see how miserable she was planning the wedding," I counter.

He's quiet for a moment, biting the corner of his mouth. "Okay, that one's fair. But our newly-engaged friend, Ben, can help, too."

I narrow my eyes skeptically. "Ben, the man who took nine years to get the girl?"

"Ben, the man who understands the art of patience," Daniel corrects. I shake my head incredulously.

As if on cue, a black sedan pulls up and parks behind Daniel's car on the curb. I glance in the rearview mirror and catch a shock of red hair dipping below the dashboard. Mac rights herself, then exits her car holding a tray of something covered in aluminum foil. Daniel's grin turns from mischievous to almost giddy. Seemingly forgetting about our conversation, he practically leaps out of his car to greet her.

I get out of the car more slowly, but as soon as Mac sees me, she smiles warmly and balances her tray on one hand so she can wave. "Hi, Brandon. Welcome to Leade Park," she says, and she sounds completely genuine. Despite my sour mood, I can't help but grin at her hopeful nature. She was like this when my family was here for their wedding, too—warm and welcoming and eager to please.

"Hey, Mac. It's good to see you again. Can I help you with that since your useless husband hasn't offered?" I indicate the tray she's still trying to balance in her hands.

"This is for you, actually." She holds the tray out to me, and I take it. I flip up the corner of the foil to see what looks like a huge lasagna. I look at Mac questioningly, and she shrugs. "It's kind of a Midwestern thing to bring a casserole to the new neighbors. I'll bring another one when Katie and the kids get here, but I didn't want you to go hungry."

I'm so touched that I don't have words for a moment. Mac's shoulders start to drop a little as she starts to speak again. "I asked Daniel if you had any food intolerances, but if you don't like lasagna—"

"It's perfect, Mac. Thank you. Truly." I try to give her a genuine smile. I don't want her thinking I don't appreciate her gesture.

Luckily, she straightens at the compliment, the smile returning to her face. Daniel suddenly claps a hand on my shoulder, startling me enough that I almost drop the tray.

"Let's see this place," he suggests.

I nod and lead us to the front door where I pull a key out of a lockbox on the porch. I swing the door open, and we all step inside.

The place is practically empty; Katie felt it was better to leave most of our furniture in New York so, in her words, it'd be there when we came back. I've been tasked with furnishing this place as well as setting up our belongings when the truck comes later this week on top of putting my new office together downtown. I take a deep breath and let it out. It'll get done. It has to.

Daniel lets out a low whistle. "This place is huge."

"That's an understatement," Mac whispers.

I didn't think it was that big when I bought it, but it was furnished in all those pictures. Now, the front room is empty, and the cavernous living area and kitchen look vacant. Everything is sterile and lonely, and I don't think that's just a reflection of my state of mind.

As if reading my mood, Daniel squares his shoulders and nods with determination. "We'll get this place looking like home in no time."

Mac looks between us, catching on. "Oh, totally. Daniel's deadline isn't for a while, and Jenny, Ben, and I are still off for winter break. We'll get everyone here to help."

"Thanks," I give her a thin smile. "I'm just going to put this in the refrigerator." I indicate the tray I'm still holding, then quickly leave them behind on my way to the kitchen.

I put the lasagna in the refrigerator, then close the door and lean my forehead against it, letting the cool steel calm me. I don't cry frequently—though I do so more than Katie, apparently—but the absence of my family and the threat of their loss is pressing on me. I wouldn't at all be surprised if Katie decided to stay in New York without me. It was easy to ignore while we were all together through Christmas, but now that we are truly apart, I know this is what it would feel like to be without them, and it's crushing me.

I sense more than hear someone enter the kitchen. I glance over to see Daniel's shoes, and I let out a puff of air through pursed lips, not bothering to lift my forehead from the refrigerator door.

"Hey," he says quietly, coming over and putting a hand on my shoulder. "We'll fix this."

"I have to," I murmur, pressing myself off the refrigerator door and meeting Daniel's gaze. "There's no other option for me."

Daniel takes a breath as if to speak, but Mac's voice floating from another room interrupts him. "Hey, guys? Come here for a minute."

We follow her voice through the living room to a smaller, adjacent room. There are huge windows along one wall, and light is streaming in, illuminating the empty space.

"This is a great room," Mac is saying. Her hair looks like it's on fire from the natural afternoon light, and I wish Katie were here to see it. It's something she'd love to paint.

"It is," I agree, looking around the room again.

"Daniel built me a library in a room kind of like this. It's my favorite room in the house." She smiles at him, and he looks back at her so intensely, I almost ask if they want me to give them some privacy. She shakes herself out of it, though, and looks around the room again. "I was thinking, maybe you could build her a library, too, or something else she might like. It might help for her to have a space that's just hers. Something from you."

I take in the room again, with its perfect light, high ceilings, and blank walls.

Daniel is still looking at Mac like she hung the stars, but right now, I have to agree with him. It's a brilliant suggestion. I knocked down walls between apartments in New York. Setting this space up would be a piece of cake.

"I don't think she'd want a library," I start slowly as they both look at me. "But I can think of something else she might like."

Chapter 6

Katie

THERE'S LIVING WITH THE workaholic father of your children and thinking he's no help, and then there's living eight hundred miles away from the workaholic father of your children and *actually* having no help.

By the time New Year's Eve rolls around, I'm about ready to change our flights and meet Brandon early. It's sheer stubbornness that keeps me from doing so, but I'm tempted. Very tempted.

I'm tempted to take a drink more than once, too. The only reason I don't is because I don't want the kids to see me like that. But it feels like a losing battle with each passing day.

It wouldn't be so bad if everything wasn't working against me. The kids are home on winter break. The cars and most of our important belongings were shipped out early so we would have them there without having to drive halfway across the country with two small children—the only thing that seems like more of a nightmare than the single-parent life I'm currently living. And the weather is garbage. It's not even pretty snow; it's brown slush as far as the eye can see and just on this side of too cold to spend any length of time outside.

Thank goodness for screen time. Though, if I have to watch the toddler version of super dogs one more time, I'm going to lose my mind.

To Brandon's credit, he calls twice a day like clockwork. The kids miss him and look forward to talking to him, and he never lets them down.

He calls in the morning before he leaves for the office, and then he calls at night to read them a bedtime story. The kids take that evening call from Mason's bed because it's big enough for both of them. Christine is usually adorably asleep before the end of it, and Mason and Brandon like to spend some time quietly chatting. I usually try to make myself busy elsewhere, and Mason has always already hung up the phone by the time I sneak in to carry Christine to her room.

I don't ask if Mason is hanging up because he doesn't understand that the grown-ups should talk, or if Brandon doesn't want to talk to me at all. I don't know if I want the answer.

It doesn't matter, anyway. I have so much work to do to get the kids and myself ready to leave that I don't have time to dwell on it for too long.

By the time we've boarded the plane to Chicago, I'm left with no choice but to admit two things to myself: one, my threat to leave Brandon and come back to New York on my own might have been empty, and two, I miss him. A lot.

Before long, we're in the air, and I'm staring off into space. I'm holding a sleeping Christine in my lap and contemplating my life choices when the flight attendant taps me on the shoulder.

"Anything to drink, ma'am?"

She could be talking about any liquid I could put in my mouth, but my brain goes straight to how great a mimosa would taste right now. I shake myself a little, trying to jostle that thought out of my head. This is why I try not to leave the house. It's everywhere, and I can't escape it.

I paste on a fake smile. "No, I'm good. Thanks."

"Can I have an apple juice?" Mason asks, too loudly. Christine shifts at the sound, but thankfully doesn't wake. I nod, and the flight attendant writes it down, then moves to take the next order.

Christine mercifully sleeps through the whole flight while Mason watches a few movies on his tablet with his headphones on. She's still groggy when we land, so I carry her to baggage claim to wait for our suitcases. Just as I'm trying to mentally calculate how I'm going to wheel my suitcase while carrying a half-sleeping toddler and keeping an eye on a seven-year-old, a young man steps into my line of sight.

"Excuse me, ma'am?"

I attempt to sigh inconspicuously, but from the smile plastered on his face, I can tell I'm not hiding my annoyance very well. I had heard this about Midwesterners, that they are personable and willing to talk to strangers. Strike one, Midwest. I prefer cold, hard, anonymity in large crowds, thank you very much.

I shift Christine a little higher on my hip to hopefully draw his attention to the fact that I have my hands full and need to keep this conversation short. "Yes?"

"Are you Mrs. Conley?" he asks, still smiling.

It's at that moment that I notice he's holding a sign that says *Conley* in big, black letters. He must be the driver Brandon sent to pick us up when we realized the truck delivering our cars got stuck in a snowstorm. I sag with relief. If Christine wasn't getting heavier and clingier by the minute, I'd hug this man for coming all the way into the airport to find us.

"I am. How did you know?" I ask.

His grin becomes impossibly larger. "Your husband did an excellent job describing you. I'm Tom, and I'll be driving you to your house. He also mentioned you might need some help with your bags. If you can just point them out for me, I'll get them for you, and we can be on our way."

I indicate our bags as they come along the carousel, and Tom lifts them off when they're within reach. Once we have everything, we follow him out to the parking garage, where he leads us to a sleek-looking van. When I open the door, there is already a car seat and a booster seat installed. Mason gets himself buckled in, and I secure Christine, then sit beside her.

The drive to Leade Park isn't terribly long, but Christine fully wakes up about halfway through and starts begging for a snack. I stupidly stashed all our bags in the trunk of the van, so I spend most of the drive singing toddler songs about busses and spiders, trying to keep her mind off how hungry she must be.

"Mom?" Mason asks, lifting his headphones off his ears to hear my response.

"Mmm?"

"We're going to be living in a real house, right? With a yard?"

"We are." I smile at him, trying to be excited for the kids' sakes.

"Do you think we can have a swing set in the back yard? And a fire pit where we can roast marshmallows? Oh, and a sandbox?" he asks.

"I want a sandbox," Christine says thoughtfully.

"Oh, kiddo. It's a little cold for all that stuff right now," I say gently, trying to let him down easy.

Mason rolls his eyes. "Not now, Mom. In the summer."

I don't want to tell him I don't know where we'll be this summer. For all my bravado a few weeks ago, I don't know if I could be a single mom after this past week. But as I look at all the cookie-cutter houses and manicured lawns passing by us, I'm having a hard time picturing this life for my entire future.

"Maybe, sweetie. We'll see," I say, which seems to appease him.

He looks out the window, and instead of matching my melancholy disposition, he starts kicking his legs back and forth and bouncing with excitement. "Mama!" he exclaims. He only calls me Mama when he's really thrilled about something. "It's Daddy!"

I twist in my seat to look out the front window and, sure enough, Brandon is standing outside, his hair in a bun high on the back of his head, and wearing my favorite sweater he owns—a forest green, cable-knit sweater that hugs his torso in all the right places and makes him look like he walked out of a pub in Ireland.

I'm not certain about a lot of things right now, but I am one hundred percent sure he picked that sweater on purpose.

But after not laying eyes on him for an entire week, I can't exactly say I'm complaining.

His hands are shoved in his pockets and his shoulders are hunched against the cold, but when he sees us approaching, his face lights up. He pulls a hand out to wave. Mason already has his seatbelt undone by the time the car pulls into the driveway and parks. I put my hand out to hold him back until the car stops completely, but as soon as it does, Mason is up and out, running toward his dad. Brandon leans down and scoops him up, swinging him around like it's no great effort to lift his seven-year-old son. He sets Mason on his feet and buries him in a hug.

The scene tugs at my heart, and I can't look away. Brandon and Mason have always had a special relationship, and even though I missed him this week, I don't think it quite registered how much Mason missed him, too.

"Daddy! Daddy! *Daddy!*" Christine's yelling pulls me from the little moment I'm having. I snap open the buckles of her car seat in a rush and pull her over my lap to set her on the ground outside, stepping out just behind her. Brandon kneels on the cold ground and opens his arms for Christine to run into them. He practically crushes her, then plants a bunch of kisses on her chubby cheeks.

He's still on his knees and holding her when he looks up at me, his hazel eyes heating. I feel the warmth of them as he rakes his gaze over my body as if he's taking a long drink. I'm suddenly impervious to the cold. My body is on fire.

Holy shit. That didn't take long.

"There's my girls," Brandon says quietly, and though he's referring to both me and his daughter, I can tell his words aren't for her. "I missed you."

I drag my bottom lip through my teeth, and his eyes darken.

"Dad," Mason groans, drawing the word out. "I'm not a girl."

Whatever spell Brandon is under is broken at that. He stands and reaches out a hand to ruffle Mason's hair. "My girls and my guy. I'm so glad you're finally here." There's an edge of emotion in his voice that I can't quite place, but whatever it is disappears as he pays our driver and takes our bags, the kids on his heels as he enters the house.

I stand outside a little longer, staring up at the massive structure in front of us. It is clean and well-designed, but it looks like every other house on the block. And it's hard for any building to look inviting and warm in the dead of winter. I wrap my arms around myself, rubbing them. Now that Brandon isn't staring at me like I'm an oasis in the middle of the desert, I'm feeling every degree of the Midwest cold.

"Okay, kids. Go find your new rooms. I'm going to help your mom." I hear Brandon from the other side of the threshold before I see him come out. He stands on the massive front porch, his hands back in his pockets. He stops and leans against the railing, studying me.

"Hi." His voice rumbles through me.

I swallow as my hands go still. "Hi."

He comes off the porch and closes the distance between us. His tongue darts out to moisten his lips, but he doesn't touch me. He only stands close enough for me to see his breath in the cold air and to feel the warmth radiating off his body. All at once, I want nothing more than for him to fold me into the same kind of bear hug he just gave the kids.

"I missed you," he says again, his expression one of yearning.

I take an instinctive step toward him, my chin tipping up so I can look at his face. I see his hands twitch out of the corner of my eye, as if he's holding himself back from touching me. I wish he wouldn't hold back, but I'm also not going to make the first move here. I may have missed him this week, but I am not delusional enough to believe this move is going to magically fix everything.

"It's been a long week," I practically whisper.

His eyes soften, and then his broad hands cup my elbows. "I know. I'm sorry. I..." he trails off, then his Adam's apple bobs as he swallows hard. "You're here now. I'm giving you the entire night off." I scoff at that, and his brow furrows slightly. "I'm serious, Katie. Everything is ready for you in the house. Come on in and see. There's nothing for you to do but relax."

I raise an eyebrow. "Nothing?"

He dips his chin, his face coming closer to mine. "Nothing." For a second, I think he's going to kiss me, but instead, his face breaks into another of his bright smiles. "Can I show you?"

He sounds proud, but I'm skeptical. "You set up this entire house. In one week. By yourself." It's a statement, not a question, because I absolutely do not believe it.

His eyes turn toward the sky as he tilts his head back and forth. When his gaze meets mine again, he's smirking more than smiling. "I didn't do it by myself, but it is done. Come on. I think you're going to like it." He tugs at my elbows while walking backward toward the house. I follow, if only to make sure he doesn't run into anything.

Once we are both in the house, he drops his hands from my elbows and closes the door behind me. I stand in the entryway and take it all in.

It's absolutely huge, which, given Brandon's non-stop desire to spend his money on us, is not surprising. What *is* surprising, though, is how much it feels like *home*.

There is a long table against the wall of the entryway where he's already set out a lamp and a bowl for our keys. Underneath, there's a mat for shoes. Above us, from the vaulted ceiling, hangs a beautiful chandelier that casts a warm glow in the room. Ahead of me, I can see the edge of what looks like a massive, plushy sectional. Across from that is the kitchen island with a bowl of fruit and a tray of snacks that it seems the kids already found.

To my left is a dining room furnished with a long table that could easily seat ten people. There's a tall cabinet with glass doors showcasing all the crystal glasses his mother bought us for our wedding.

Everything we brought from our home in New York has a place. It all looks like it has always been here. Like it was meant to be here.

I shift my gaze to Brandon, who is watching me, his hands in his pockets and his eyes wide in expectation. I realize then that my mouth is gaping. "Have you slept this week?" My voice is incredulous.

He chuckles and smooths a hand over the top of his hair. "A little." He smiles sheepishly and shrugs. "I didn't do it alone."

"No way you and Daniel did all this. Did you hire people?" I look around the entryway again, my eyes catching on a framed painting hanging near the hallway.

"Mac and her friends helped, too."

I take a few steps toward the painting, squinting at it a little. "Jenny and Ben?"

"Yeah," he says, following me. "They just got engaged."

That stops me in my path. I raise my eyebrows at Brandon. "That was fast. They only got together, what, three months ago?"

"When you know, you know." His expression turns soulful, almost nostalgic. He regards me for another moment, then takes a deep, audible breath. "To hear him say it, it's been almost ten years in the making." He shrugs, then his eyes shift to the painting I had been looking at. He nods toward it. "I thought that would be a good thing for people to see as soon as they walk in."

I step up to it and, as soon as I can see it through the glare of the chandelier, I gasp. It's a painting of the New York skyline out of a window from the point of view of a bed. My window. My bed. I painted this while Brandon watched me during the week after we met. I wanted to immortalize the feeling I had lying in bed with him for a week—that feeling of being on the inside of something, looking out.

After I finished it, I had rolled it up and tossed it in my closet. We had been too busy exploring each other for me to care too much about it.

Later, when Mason and I moved in with Brandon, I don't remember packing it. I was so overwhelmed with being a new mom and planning our wedding that I hadn't even thought about it.

"You were in the shower." Brandon is standing directly behind me, and I don't know when he moved so close, but the temptation to lean back into him is staggering. He doesn't touch me, though. His voice is low and smooth. "I was over at your place, hanging out with baby Mason. Maybe a week or so after he was born? I brought you Pad Thai, from your favorite Thai place on First Ave. I don't think you had ever been more grateful for a shower and a meal. It seemed wrong that you had to be grateful for those simple things. Mason spit up, so I went into the closet." I can hear the smile in his voice at the memory. Only this man would be smiling about baby spit-up. "I saw it rolled up, exactly where you left it when you finished it. I thought it needed to see the light of day, so I took it. One thing led to another, and I didn't get around to framing it until just before I came out here. But I thought the first piece of art people should see when they enter our home should be something you created."

I drag my eyes away from the painting so I can turn to face him. He's still wistfully studying it over my head as I watch him. Finally, he looks at me, his eyes searching mine, suddenly uncertain. "Is that...okay?"

I don't have words. This might be the sweetest, most thoughtful thing he's ever done, and I'm not sure how to express how touched I am. I huff out something close to a laugh, and he looks pleased at the sound.

"Yeah, Brandon," I breathe. "It's okay."

"I love you, Katie. I always have." His voice is husky, and it does things to my insides I'm not proud of.

"That's not fair," I choke out.

This was clearly not the response he was expecting, because he frowns at me. "What's not fair?"

I find a little more confidence as I continue. "I haven't even been here for five minutes, and you're pulling out all the stops. You said I have two months to decide."

His knitted brows pull apart as a corner of his mouth turns up into a wicked grin. "I'm hoping you won't need two months, Cat." I shiver at the nickname, which makes his expression turn even more sinful. He leans in close as he says, "And you ain't seen nothing yet."

My eyes widen in surprise. "What do you mean?"

"You'll have to keep exploring the house, I guess."

I hum skeptically as I hear the pitter-pat of little footsteps running through the house. "Dad, this place is awesome!" Mason yells as he runs past us in a blur to the kitchen. Christine's shorter steps sound behind him, but she stops to clutch Brandon's legs.

He picks her up and tosses her toward the ceiling, catching her as she squeals. "What do you think, Chrissy-pie? You like your room?"

"It's a princess room!" She giggles.

"Only the best for my princess." He taps her nose, and she squeals again.

"Mom! My room has a slide in it!" Mason yells around a mouthful of snacks.

I arch an eyebrow at Brandon, who has the good sense to look sheepish. "It's a loft bed with a ladder on one side and a slide on the other."

"Sounds like a death trap," I mutter.

Brandon chuckles. "It's fine. I built it myself."

"That isn't as reassuring as you think it should be."

He opens his mouth and lowers his eyebrows in mock affront. "I'm an architect," he insists.

"You're not a builder."

He shrugs. "Potato, po-tah-to." He tilts his head to beckon me further into the house. "Come see the rest."

Before I can walk through the kitchen and living room area, Mason grabs me by the hand and drags me up to see his new bed. I have to admit, it is pretty cool. He and Christine start racing up and sliding down, so I leave Brandon to supervise them while I look at the rest of the house.

Christine's room looks like a princess threw up sparkles and pink tulle all over it. Her bed is huge and has a canopy with gauzy curtains hanging all the way to the floor. Her stuffed animal collection sits, well-organized, by the pillows, and there's a little table in the corner with two more animals having an imaginary tea party. It's no wonder she loves it.

The kitchen and living room are expansive. The windows are huge and let in a lot of natural light. I could see myself setting up my little easel in this room and painting while the kids play.

I open and close a few doors, all of them leading to closets. This place has plenty of storage, that's for sure. There's a half bathroom off the living room, which is good since Christine still needs a toilet close by. Next to the bathroom is a door that I assume is to another closet. When I open it, though, I see it's a good-sized room with the same large windows featured in the living room. I step inside, and that's when I notice what Brandon has set up.

There is a desk under the bank of windows with an adjustable top that can tilt up or lay flat. Right now, it's tilted up and a new sketch pad rests on top of it. On a rolling cart next to the desk, there are pottery cups full of pencils, colored pencils, brushes, and paints. My easel is set up in the corner, a larger canvas balanced on it and a new stool in front of it.

The walls have strips attached in a cross-hatch pattern, and on the strips are hooks and clips that will make it easy to hang pictures to see in the light from the window. A drying rack also sits to the side. There's already a page torn out of my sketchbook on display. I take a few steps toward it before I can clearly make out what it is. When I do, I gasp as my hand flies to my mouth.

Hanging in front of me is the drawing I started a few weeks ago of Brandon and the kids at a pumpkin patch. I haven't looked at this piece since I sketched it out a few weeks ago. I love it, but it pains me to look at it. Brandon hasn't had much time to spend with the kids lately, so I had to make up a scene for them. Despite my pride in my work, I wish it were a real scene.

"The room isn't finished." Brandon's voice is soft behind me, and I whirl around in surprise, my hand still covering my mouth. He is leaning against the doorframe, his arms crossed over his chest as he looks around as if seeing the space through my eyes. "I tried to get most of the basic supplies, but I'm sure you have others you'll need. There's an art supply store in the strip mall just up the road. And I wasn't sure exactly where to put the desk or the easel. But we can move them. Just tell me where." He indicates a large basin in the far corner. "I'm going to have a plumber put a sink in over there, but the ground is too cold for that kind of work right now. Maybe this summer." He glances at me, then at the wall. "If we stay."

"This whole room is for me?" My eyes are wide, and my hand is shaking slightly, so I shove it under the opposite arm and squeeze it.

"You were always setting up that easel in different places around the house. We never had space for a studio, and I know you didn't want to rent one and spend the time travelling there and back."

How had he known that? We never talked about it. It seemed silly to rent an entire space for a hobby I didn't have time for on top of driving back and forth in unpredictable traffic.

"Then, you set up the easel less and less," he's saying, still looking around the room. "I always wondered if it was because you ran out of time, or if it was harder with two kids once Christine came along. Maybe it was just a pain in the ass to set it up and take it down over and over again. Or maybe you worried that the kids would get their hands on it if you left it out. But now you can use this room and then close the door." He pats the door with his hand to emphasize it.

My gaze lingers on him for a second, then I turn around to see everything again, my eyes snagging on each thoughtful gesture in turn. When I face him, he's staring at me, looking like a kid waiting for approval.

I should tell him I'm overflowing. I should tell him between this and the kids' rooms and the painting in the entryway, my heart is wrung dry. I should tell him how I've always wanted a space exactly like this, but never had the money to do it for myself when I was single, and then never could find the time after the kids were born.

But the truth is that there's a huge part of me that's also skeptical. I don't know if I'll be able to make use of this space as much as he thinks. He promised me he'd be around more often a few weeks ago when we settled on this two-month trial period in Leade Park and then proceeded to disappear just as much—if not more—than before. Or, what if he actually is going to be around more often, but I end up hating it here in this quiet suburb anyway?

He breaks the silence. "Do you like it?"

I remain silent for a moment, then my gaze lands on him. "You said I could have the entire night to do whatever I wanted?"

His smile is tentative, though a little relieved. "I did."

"What about dinner?"

"Pizza."

"Bedtime?"

"You saw those beds. I'm not going to struggle to get the kids in them."

I hum, looking around the room again, then I eye him. "Head-phones?"

He walks past me to a small set of drawers I hadn't noticed earlier. He opens the top drawer and pulls out my black headphones and puts them over my ears for me. His fingers run gently along my jaw and come to rest on my chin, tipping it up.

When he speaks, his voice is muffled by my headphones, but I can hear him plainly all the same. "Enjoy it, Cat. You deserve this and more."

I can't help the soft smile that plays at my lips. His eyes drop to it, and I could swear he soaks it up greedily, cataloging it for later.

We stand like that for another minute, until a crash sounds from the upstairs bedrooms followed by a wail that sounds like it could come from either child. I grimace, but Brandon plants a chaste kiss on the tip of my nose.

"I've got it," he says, and swiftly leaves the room, making sure to close the door behind him.

Chapter 7
Brandon

THE KIDS AND I are both shocked to find the thin crust pizza cut into squares rather than huge triangles, and too crisp throughout to be folded in half, like proper pizza slices should be. Luckily, neither kid is picky enough to turn down any combination of cheese, sauce, and crust, so dinner goes pretty smoothly.

I consider knocking on Katie's door to see if she wants to eat but decide against it. Her desire to be uninterrupted is implied by the absolute silence coming from the room and the fact that she hasn't shown her face in hours. It's also possible that she discovered the drawer of her favorite snacks I stocked last week. I plan on keeping that shit stocked, too. If her therapist says snacks help, she can have as much as she wants.

I make a mental note to ask her if she's planning on finding a new therapist out here, too. I forgot about that little detail.

While the kids are eating their pizza and laughing at the stringiness of the cheese falling off the slices, my phone rings. It's probably Daniel calling to see how things are going, so answer it without looking.

"B," my brother's voice comes over the line. He sounds strung out, and I groan internally, wishing I had checked the caller ID before answering, though I know I would have answered all the same.

The kids are occupied and talking to each other. I use the opportunity to quickly cross the room so they can't hear me. "Shane." My voice is clipped.

"Hey, man. I kinda hit a rough patch. I lost my job," he says. He had been working at a convenience store last we talked.

"How did that happen?" I ask.

"Oh, you know…" he trails off, not willing to give me any more detail than he has to.

The truth is, I do know, just like I know he's calling to ask for money. He probably missed work one too many times because he was high. It's always the same story with him. Our parents cut him off a while ago, after his third or fourth stint in rehab didn't take, and every once in a while he reaches out to me because I have a soft spot for him.

"I'm sorry to hear that," I respond.

"Right. Yeah. Well, I was kind of wondering if I could borrow some money. Just a couple hundred to hold me over until I can get another job. I could swing by and pick it up tomorrow—"

"Shane, we moved," I cut him off. "We aren't in the city anymore. I told you this was happening the last time we talked."

"Shit, really?" He pauses as if he's doing some calculations. "Well, I could take the train—"

"To Illinois?"

"You moved to fucking Illinois?" It's an explosion, and I startle at it.

"Yes. I'm working to take over the firm from Mom and Dad," I remind him as patiently as I can. "And we are tapped out from the move."

"Of course you fucking are," he says, the hurt clear in his voice, though I'm not sure which statement he's referencing. Suddenly, the line goes dead.

I pull the phone away from my ear and stare at it. I don't know why I'm surprised he hung up on me, knowing what I know about him, but somehow I am.

But Christine, with some impeccable timing, chooses that moment to fling her pizza crust at Mason, who whines that his sister is being mean to him, and I tuck the entire phone call away to unpack later in order to intercept more flying pizza before there's a full-on meltdown.

As predicted, the kids are eager to get to bed. Christine scrambles into her huge canopy bed and climbs right in the middle of all her stuffed animals. Daniel and Mac's friend, Jenny, counted them all as she cooed over how cute they were when we were setting up the house. This room has Jenny's signature all over it—from the feminine, gauzy canopy to the sparkly gem stickers all over the walls. There's even a dress-up corner in her walk-in closet with princess dresses hung at three-year-old eye-level. Part of me regrets giving Jenny access to my credit card to pick out all this stuff, but hearing Christine's giggle of pure joy makes the future bill worth it.

She sinks down into the fluffy pillows, practically burying herself into the bed. I sit on the edge of it, smiling at how tiny she looks.

"Daddy! Dad! I'm a princess!" she exclaims.

I chuckle and tap her nose, which is about all I can see of her. "Can you feel the pea I slipped under the mattress?"

"Dad," she moans. "There's no pea."

I shrug. "I guess you're not a princess if you can't feel it," I tease.

Her little head pops up from the nest of blankets and stuffed animals she's made herself. She pouts. "You're kidding."

I lean in and kiss her forehead. "I am." I stand, then bow with a flourish. "Good night, Princess Christine. I'll see you in the morning."

She giggles again at the bow, then snuggles back down into her comforter. I flip the light switch off on my way out of the room, but as I am closing the door, I hear her little voice again.

"Daddy? You *were* kidding about the pea, right?"

"Yes, baby. Good night." I pull the door closed before she can ask any more questions and head down the hall to Mason's room.

"Hey, dude," I say as I enter.

"Don't call me 'dude.'" His voice sounds pouty, even though I can't see him because he's high up in his loft bed. I grab the step stool I left to the side of the room and drag it over so I can stand on it and see him. Sure enough, he's curled up in his bed with his back to me, facing the wall.

"What's going on?" I ask, folding my arms and leaning them against the guard rail.

"Nothing."

"Doesn't sound like nothing. Talk to me, buddy," I urge him.

He doesn't speak for a long while, and I almost give up waiting, but when he does finally speak, his voice is small and unsure. "I like it here," he says.

That's not what I was expecting.

I blink rapidly to collect myself. "Uh, I mean, that's good, right?" I ask.

His head nods slightly, but then he shrugs. "I know Mom doesn't want us to like it here."

Mason is an incredibly perceptive kid, but I thought Katie was above dragging the kids into this fight of ours. I don't want to blame her outright, though. I opt to gather more information instead. "How do you know that?"

He shrugs again, then sighs and rolls over to face me. There's an uncertainty in his eyes that I hate seeing. "She seemed so sad on the airplane. I asked her why she was sad, but she just smiled and said change is hard even if it's good."

I reach out and clap a hand on his shoulder in what I hope is a comforting gesture. "It was good of you to notice your mom was sad, and even better of you to ask her about it." It seems Katie didn't purposefully involve the kids in this, and I'm not going to, either.

"She was sad, though, wasn't she?" He's persistent, I'll give him that.

I can tell I'm not getting out of this without at least a little explanation. "Yeah, maybe a bit. She loved New York."

Mason bristles at this, scrunching up his nose. "Why? It was always so loud and smelly."

I chuckle. "I'm with you, buddy. I think she liked the hustle and bustle. She had her first job there, you know."

"At the gallery?"

"Yep. And she liked working at the gallery. That's where we became parents, too. And where we met and fell in love and got married." I turn my eyes to the ceiling as my tone goes jokingly wistful.

"Ew. Stop. I get it." He scoots up to the head of the bed and fakes a gagging noise over the side.

I make a mental note to figure out how people handle having their sick kids in loft beds if they really do puke off the side—something I did not think of before this very moment.

I laugh, bringing myself back to the conversation. "It's hard to leave a place that has so many good memories."

Mason comes back from hanging over the edge of the bed and flops back down, his hands folded under his cheek and his eyelids drooping ever so slightly. "Why did we leave if it made her so sad?"

"You can be sad and happy about something at the same time," I try.

He's not buying it. "She didn't seem happy."

I sigh again. "Well, I think she wants to give this a try, to see if it's better for our family. With my new job here, I'll be able to be around more often, and I think that'll make Mom happy, don't you?"

He nods, then yawns.

"It's admirable of you to worry so much about your mom, but why don't you let me do the worrying? I promise to tell you if there's anything you can help with, okay?" I ask.

"Okay, Dad. I love you," he says, closing his eyes.

"I love you too, bud. Good night." I climb down from the stool and turn off his lights on my way out of his room, closing the door behind me.

When I come downstairs, Katie is still in her studio, though I notice there are a few pieces of pizza missing from the box I had left open on the counter. I smirk at the thought of her scurrying out and squirreling away pizza to eat while we were all upstairs.

By now, it's completely dark outside, and the lights in the living room cast a warm glow about the space. I walk around, pulling the curtains closed, then settle on the couch with my research on past Leade Park High School additions and the wish list for this new student center from the school board. It doesn't seem like an overly complicated project, but it will take some creativity to extend the building in a way that's aesthetically pleasing. No one wants an addition that looks like it was slapped onto the side of a building.

It's not long before I have blueprints and sketches strewn about the coffee table. I grab the packet of research the district put together about other area schools' student centers and flip through it. It's all helpful, but I know I won't be able to get anything solidified until I tour the space and talk to some people about their priorities for the building. Everything I'm looking through is speculation and wishful thinking.

I lean against the couch cushions, resting my head back and looking up at the ceiling. I roll my head over to see what I already know: Katie's door is still closed. I didn't exactly intend to wait for her to come out, but it seems I'm poking around at all of these papers for that very reason. I've been working in this spot while the house was empty, but I have an office in the basement I can move into. I probably should, actually, so the kids don't grab the papers and tear them or start coloring them when they wake up tomorrow morning.

And yet, I stay right where I am. Knowing Katie is just on the other side of that door, I can't seem to pull myself away. It's been a week since I've even seen her, and I find myself wanting to see her again before I go to sleep. I wasn't able to get nearly my fill of her before she closed that door.

I grab the book I'm reading instead. It's Daniel's latest, which he doesn't know I haven't finished yet. I open it to where I left off. The reviewers all called this book a love letter to teaching and learning, but I can pretty much pinpoint the exact chapter he was writing when he fell in love with Mac. He wasn't kidding when he said being happy was detrimental to his signature angst. I'm not much of a reader—obviously, it's taken me two years to get around to reading my best friend's novel—but even I can see the shift in his writing with this book.

But I can't concentrate. My mind is shifting back and forth between Katie and my earlier conversation with my brother. I'd have to be an idiot not to see a connection between the two of them.

I pinch the bridge of my nose and close my eyes, tipping my head back against the couch again. I don't like making him angry, but I'm not sure how much more I should give him. I should set better boundaries, not enable him. But I'm not sure how else to help him from here. I take a few deep breaths and try to forget about it.

The next thing I know, I'm being lightly shaken awake. I grumble a little, but when I finally open my eyes, Katie is looking down at me, her face inches from mine. Her cheeks are slightly flushed, and her blue eyes are quite literally sparkling in the warm light from the lamp next to the couch. Her sweater is hanging off her shoulder, showing a hint of lace underneath. I catch a glimpse of her arm, her paints splattered over it like colorful tattoos. Her full lips are pink and parted just slightly, and her brow is furrowed while her hand rests unnecessarily on my left shoulder. Maybe I'm imagining it, but it seems like she's not moving her hand because she *wants* to be touching me.

For a second, I think I might be dreaming because my wife has never looked more beautiful than she does right now. All I want is to pull her close and kiss her.

She blinks a few times, and her eyebrows shoot up her forehead, her eyes widen, and her mouth goes round.

I raise my left hand to cover her right one still resting on my shoulder, and she makes that little purring noise in the back of her throat as her eyelids flutter ever so slightly.

Oh, fuck this. I have more willpower than the average man, but I have my limits. And after that shit with Shane earlier, I want her near me more than ever.

I grab her lush hip with my left hand and pull her to me. She lands on my lap and our lips collide. It's urgent and hungry. I'm practically devouring her mouth, but I don't care. It doesn't seem like she does either as she presses her chest up against mine. She threads her fingers through my hair and tugs. I can't help the moan that escapes my mouth, but she swallows it, parting her lips and allowing my tongue to explore.

It has been far too long since I've kissed my wife, and it is just as Earth-shattering as I remembered.

I lift her shirt and press my hands into her back, spreading them as wide as I can to touch as much of her delicate skin as possible. She breaks the kiss to breathe, and I take the opportunity to trail my lips along her jaw and down her neck to that exposed shoulder that has been terrorizing me for weeks.

"Brandon." She's breathless. The sound of my name on her lips has me lifting my hips so my hardness meets that perfect soft spot between her legs. She gasps, then shifts her hips on top of me, and I swear I almost come right there. But then she groans and tightens her grip on my hair—which is really fucking hot—and makes me stop to look at her.

"Brandon," she says again. "No. I... we can't."

"What? Why?" My breathing is rapid, and I'm trying to wrap my head around this sudden shift.

She makes no move to remove herself from my lap, so I hold perfectly still as I watch about ten different, conflicting emotions pass over her face. "I didn't come out here to make out with you," she finally says.

Her voice is husky and sexy and about an octave lower than usual. If I had any common sense left, I'd say something sweet and understanding, but her voice and her body are doing things to me I'm not proud of.

Instead, the words that actually come out of my mouth are: "So what?" I immediately grimace at how demanding I sound.

Luckily, she notices my expression and, when she does, she laughs. It's not her normal laugh; it's breathy and husky, not in a sexy way, but in the way of a laugh that has gone unused for far too long. It breaks my heart and fills it in equal measure, and my hands tighten involuntarily around her back.

She leans backward into my touch, closing her eyes. I'm dying to kiss her again, but I won't if she doesn't give me the green light. I'm desperate for her, but I'm not interested in kissing a woman who doesn't want to be kissed.

She takes in a deep breath, then blows it out puffed cheeks up to the ceiling. When she lowers her gaze, her eyes are open and meet mine. She tilts her head, and a corner of her mouth turns up sadly. "I don't know what to feel about this, Brandon. Everything you've shown me today has been perfect. Beyond my wildest imagination. But I still feel tricked. You took this job without me. You bought this house without me, too." She motions toward the studio, then, and I can see she's already made herself at home in there with tubes of paints, papers, and pencils strewn about. "If you knew I wanted a studio back in New York," she continues, "you could have done this for me there. You knocked down walls when we moved in. A studio space would have been easy by comparison." She pauses as she chews on her lips, uncertainty crossing over her features. "Why did we have to move halfway across the country for me to get the best of you?"

I don't have an answer for that. I should be able to explain why I've failed her so often over the years, but I can't.

She must sense it or see it in my face, because she untangles her legs from around mine and flips around so she's sitting next to me on the couch. She leans forward and rests her elbows on her knees, putting her head in her hands.

I scrub my hand across my face as I have the painful realization that I can offer her space and time and a studio full of paints and snacks, but there's an emotional need I'm not meeting, and I'm not sure how I can.

"I'm sorry, Katie." It sounds so helpless and small, and it doesn't come close to encompassing everything I'm coming to understand, but it's all I have to offer right now.

She turns her face so her cheek is resting on her palms as she looks at me. "Me too."

The wall hasn't come tumbling down, but I can see a tiny crack, and I'll take it.

We are silent for another minute, both studying each other, but too shy to touch each other again. I scrape my palm against my beard, and her eyes follow the motion. "Shane called just before I got the kids to bed." I'm not sure why I tell her this, but it feels like a small weight lifted when I do.

She sighs and runs a hand through her hair, taking the change in subject in stride. She straightens, then shifts to face me, bringing her leg up underneath her and resting her head against the back of the couch. "What the fuck did he want?"

I give her a knowing, sidelong glance, then return to staring at the empty wall in front of me. "Money. He didn't remember we had moved. I told him we were tapped out right now."

"You didn't tell him we were moving?"

"I did. He didn't remember."

She rests her hand gently on top of the cat tattoo on my forearm, and that simple, comforting gesture suddenly means more than any of the kisses we shared a few minutes ago. I shift my head to look at her. She doesn't have to say anything; she's known about Shane for a long time and has watched him stumble in and out of recovery for years.

She cocks an eyebrow. "Are we tapped out?"

I laugh humorlessly. "No. Though not for lack of Jenny trying. That princess room is probably the most expensive one in the entire house."

She looks around, taking in the space again. "I figured she did that room. Mason's bed has Ben written all over it." She looks to me for confirmation, and I nod. She fights a smile as she considers more of the rooms. "Mac had to have a hand in the kitchen. I'm guessing Daniel was probably pretty useless until someone told him what to do."

I chuckle. "Mac kept him busy."

She smirks, too, still looking around at details she must have missed earlier. I can't tear my eyes from her.

"She's good for him," she says.

"I'm glad he found her," I agree.

Her eyes finally meet mine, and she tilts her head to the side. "Who did my studio?"

"Me," I say without hesitation. I spent more time on that room than any other, and Mac told me in no uncertain terms that I should not let on that the idea for it was hers. She insisted I would have gotten there eventually. I appreciate her faith in me.

Katie hugs her knees into her chest, resting the bottom of her feet on the couch cushion. She leans her cheek against them, still looking at me. "I love it," she says quietly.

"I'm glad," I whisper back, fighting the urge to brush a stray hair off her cheek.

We stay that way for a moment, then she shakes herself and looks out at the room again, resting her chin on her knees. "Do you have an office?"

"There's an office space in the basement."

"Guest room?" She doesn't meet my eyes when she says it, and the hard set of her shoulders suggests she's conflicted about asking.

"There's a guest suite in the basement, too," I tell her.

She nods, still not meeting my gaze. Suddenly, this normally imposing and self-assured woman looks small and uncertain, hugging her knees close with her shoulders hunched over them. I want to fold her into me and tell her everything is going to be okay. I'm not sure it is, but I'll make it so for her. I won't rest until I do.

I swallow hard, steeling myself. "Do you want me in the guest room?"

"No." Her answer is immediate, and she finally looks at me, her eyes shining. "Maybe? I don't know."

Her uncertainty should feel like a blow, but after months of her ire, it actually feels like a balm to my soul. I take a chance and reach my hand to cup her jaw. She lets me, and I pull her head to me, planting a kiss on her forehead, then pulling back to look at her eyes.

"I'll stay down there until you're sure," I say. "I want you to be sure."

Her gaze falls, and her body sags. I don't know if that's the answer she was looking for, but she drags her bottom lip through her teeth and nods, pulling her sleeve over her hand and wiping her eyes with the cuff.

"Okay," she says, standing. "Well, good night, then."

"Good night, Katie." I muster up a little smile that she doesn't return.

She walks slowly to the stairs, and I watch her the whole way. When she gets there, she pauses and rests a hand on the banister, though she doesn't turn to look at me.

"You did good, Brandon." She pauses, then says, "The kids like it."

She doesn't need to know about the conversation I had with Mason earlier. She clearly feels conflicted enough as it is, and she doesn't need the added weight that knowledge will bring, so I just say, "Thanks."

She nods once, and climbs the stairs, disappearing into the darkness at the top.

Chapter 8

Katie

"WHAT DO YOU THINK about public school for Mason?" Brandon asks as he sits at the island, sipping his coffee. He's holding the sticky note I left my to-do list on, his thumb pressing against the first item I wrote down this morning: *Register Mason for school*. There's also a stack of private school brochures sitting by his right elbow. We had enrolled Christine in a hybrid daycare/preschool situation before the move, worried we wouldn't get a spot for the new year otherwise, but Mason's school has still been up in the air.

I eye him over my shoulder as I scrape my spatula against the pan in front of me, scrambling the eggs that are just starting to cook. "Are we that destitute after you furnished this house?"

Brandon chuckles, and for a second, this feels almost normal. Settled. A little light banter, like we used to have over breakfast before this mess of moving and new jobs and lying awake at night wishing I could run my hands through his hair...

"No," he answers, interrupting that thought. He pushes the brochures around, not really looking at them.

I turn my back to the eggs to let them cook a little longer. I bend over to lean my elbows against the counter. Brandon's gaze drops to my chest and quickly corrects itself back to my face.

"I thought you were always married to the idea of private schools." I arch an eyebrow at him and lean forward just a little more. I'm a tease, and I don't even feel bad about it.

He presses his lips together, then sticks his tongue in his cheek as he clearly tries hard not to drop his eyes to my chest again. I fight against a smirk, and his eyes glimmer at the twitch in my mouth.

He clears his throat pointedly. "In New York, it made sense. But this is a suburb. From what Mac tells me, the public schools in this area are excellent."

"Mac is a public-school evangelist," I counter. I'm just being difficult, and he probably knows it, but this is a game we play often, and I'm feeling playful this morning.

"Daniel seemed impressed." Brandon tilts his head, his hazel eyes sparkling. I'm elated he seems willing to play along.

"He's biased, too. And don't bring Jenny and Ben into this, either. They're all part of the system." I push off the counter and turn the stove off. I grab the plates I had set out earlier and start loading them up with eggs.

"I thought you, of all people, would be open to the idea of public school."

I put his plate in front of him and slide a fork across the counter. "What is that supposed to mean?"

He shoves a forkful of eggs in his mouth and speaks around it. "It means, you have been nearly obsessed with the idea of the kids living 'normal lives.'" He uses air quotes around the last words, nearly dropping his fork in the process of his gentle mocking. "Wouldn't public school fit the bill?"

"I want to go to public school!" Mason appears seemingly out of nowhere and slides onto the stool next to Brandon.

"How did you hear that, but you didn't hear me tell you to move your stack of books off the stairs five times this morning?" I ask, placing a plate of eggs in front of him.

He grimaces at the plate, then looks at Brandon, opening his mouth to speak, but Brandon cuts him off. "No way. Your mom made eggs. Eat them."

Mason grumbles, then uses his fork to push the eggs around on his plate. I walk over to where Christine is playing at a kid table and put a smaller plate and a plastic fork in front of her. She reaches out her chubby toddler arm and shoves the plate away without even looking at it. I sigh deeply and walk back to the island. I'm not trying to fight losing battles this morning.

"What makes you want to go to public school?" I return to the previous conversation.

"It seems fun?" Mason phrases it as a question. I'm immediately suspicious, and Brandon's narrowed eyes and furrowed brow mirror my own.

Mason sinks into his seat and shoves a huge bite of eggs into his mouth. Brandon and I wait for him to swallow, which takes a painfully long time. When he does, he straightens on his stool. "Those private school kids back in New York were all jerks."

"Language," Brandon and I say in unison. He smiles lightly at me before turning his attention back to Mason.

"Well, they were," Mason grumbles.

"Pretty sure kids are kids no matter where you go." I stab my own eggs with my fork and eat them while standing. I eye Christine over

Brandon's shoulder. She is grabbing eggs with her hands, smooshing them in her fists, and then shoving the mangled pieces in her mouth. You know what? Whatever gets the job done.

"It's worth a shot," Brandon turns his attention to me. "Plus, the school is really close. If it weren't so cold, we could probably walk there."

"I'm not sure who you mean by 'we.' You're never the drop-off parent." I put my hands on my hips as I frown at him.

His lips part as he shakes his head slightly. "Do you want me to be the drop off parent?"

I raise my eyebrows in challenge. "I want you to be any kind of involved parent."

He smirks at that—challenge accepted. "If Mason goes to the neighborhood school, I'd have plenty of time to drop him off most mornings on my way to work."

Mason perks up, his face brightening. His eyes get wide like he knows we've already decided his public-school fate as his head swivels back and forth between the two of us.

"Okay." I nod slowly, and Mason squeals, wiggling in his seat. My face softens at his excitement. "We can go check it out today."

Having gotten what he wanted, Mason has the good sense to eat every morsel of eggs off his plate and stack it in the sink before he tries to surreptitiously exit the kitchen, but I'm on to him. "Pick up your stuff, or you're not going to any school."

He stops and faces me, a familiar challenge in his expression. He looks so much like Brandon when he does that; it catches me off guard every time.

"How will I learn anything, then?" he taunts.

"*I'll* be your teacher," I threaten.

Mason shivers dramatically. "That would be awful."

"I know." I eye him, tilting my head in his direction. "So you better pick up your stuff."

Mason salutes me mockingly, then makes a hasty exit.

"I have to get going, too." Brandon stands just as Christine knocks her entire plate of eggs on the floor. It's unclear if she did it on purpose or by accident. Based on how unbothered she is by it, my guess is the latter.

I groan. "When is her first day, again?"

"Next Monday," Brandon says, halfway out the door. At least he sounds apologetic, I guess.

"Next Monday," I grumble, grabbing some paper towels from next to the sink and moving to clean up the mess. "Great. Well, have a good day, then." I turn toward the door.

Brandon has his coat on and his keys in his hand, but he pauses, looking at me with such longing it takes my breath away. After a moment, he blinks, then looks embarrassed. "Yeah, you too," he says quietly, and then he's gone.

The thought of wrangling the kids into the car, driving all the way to the school, fighting to find parking, getting Christine in and out of her car seat, and then keeping her busy while also filling out registration paperwork for Mason has me reeling. After a long day of travel, then a late night in my new studio, this is not how I want to be spending my day. It might actually be my version of hell.

I call the school to make sure the administrative offices are open, hoping they all took the break off so we can say we tried and curl up on the couch to take naps and watch movies. Apparently, school administrative offices don't observe full breaks. No luck there, then.

Before we leave, I take a few of the boxes that arrived yesterday to their respective rooms. Most of Christine's stuff was unpacked immediately in hopes of avoiding a toddler meltdown if we couldn't find something she wanted. Mason's and my extra boxes sat in the foyer, though, under promises to "do it later."

Well, it's later. I drop his boxes in the middle of his doorway so he can't get around them until they're unpacked. I take one of mine to the bedroom—pictures in frames, mostly, and a few books which I set up quickly. Another box lands in my studio, and one that I'm not sure what to do with ends up stowed away under the kitchen sink. Neither of those are important, so I'll deal with them later.

I drag my feet getting the kids ready. By the time we're all dressed and in our coats with our shoes on, I mentally calculate that we have just enough time to get this done before someone is going to melt down from pre-lunch hunger. I grab a few granola bars from the pantry Brandon did a surprisingly excellent job of stocking and shove them in my purse on our way out the door.

Once everyone is buckled in, I plug the school's address into the car's navigation system. I have to do a double take when it says it'll only take seven minutes to get there. I guess when they say "neighborhood school," they really mean it around here.

When we get there, my jaw almost drops at the parking lot. Rows upon rows of available parking. I don't know what I expected, but this wasn't it. I guess I've been a city person long enough that I'm still surprised when I see empty parking spots.

We park and walk inside, finding the front office easily. A woman sits behind a desk, her chair twisted so she can chat with another woman sitting at a small table. The woman at the table is cutting various shapes out of construction paper, and it seems like she's concentrating very hard on her task because she looks up at us, smiles in welcome, then turns her attention back to her task. She looks vaguely familiar, but I can't place her.

The woman behind the desk swivels her chair to us. "Well, hi there." She winks at the kids as she blows a huge bubble from her bubble gum. It pops dramatically, and Christine squeals. The woman somehow gets all that gum back in her mouth, smiling at Christine the whole time.

She turns to me. "Hi, how can I help you?"

"Um, hi. I think we spoke on the phone? We just moved to the area, and I'm here to register my son for school."

"Oh, sure. I'll need to see a copy of his birth certificate, your identification, his medical records, and then it'll be a $145 fee." She looks to the ceiling between items of her list as if trying to remember which one comes next.

"I'm sorry, did you say $145?" I ask, leaning forward slightly.

The woman scrunches her nose. "I know. I'm so sorry. Public school should be free."

"Oh, no," I say quickly. "We're from New York City. Mason"—I indicate him, and he smiles broadly—"was in private school there. $145 is... well, it's nothing."

The woman sitting at the table snorts, and I shift my gaze to her. She mutters, "Wait till you see the school supply list."

"The what?" I ask.

ALLIE SAMBERTS

She looks up at me, her brown eyes twinkling as she smirks. "The
school supply list. You'll need to make sure your son has everything on
it before he starts. What grade is he in?"

"Second," I reply.

"Yeah, my son is in second grade, too. I'm pretty sure the list was a full
page long this year, and I know they haven't even used half of the stuff
we brought in." She pauses her rant for a second, then squints her eyes
at me. "I'm sorry, have we met before? You look really familiar."

"I was thinking the same thing about you—" I'm interrupted by a
shrill scream from an adjacent room.

The woman at the table barely has a chance to roll her eyes before a
boy about Mason's age comes running into the office, a devilish grin on
his face.

Mason immediately perks up. "Brody!" he exclaims, just as the woman
also says the boy's name, albeit more sternly.

"Brody?" I ask. "As in—"

I'm interrupted again as Ben follows the boy into the office, carrying
a toddler. "My bad, Ash. We were—"

The woman, who I now recognize as Ben's older sister, Ashley, holds
up a hand to stop him and glares. "Do I want to know?"

"Probably not." Ben shrugs, then wisely shuts his mouth. It takes a
few seconds, but he eventually realizes we're standing there, and by then,
my arms are crossed in front of me and I'm smirking.

"Did I interrupt a family reunion?" I ask, finally figuring out that
Chloe, Ben's younger sister, is the secretary I've been talking to. Ashley,
Ben's other sister, brought his two nephews to school today. Brody and
Caleb played with Mason and Christine when we visited a few months
ago.

Every pair of eyes in the room turns to me, and Ben's face splits into a huge grin.

"Katie! You're here!" He sets his younger nephew down on the ground and walks to me, arms open as if he's going in for a bear hug.

I put a hand out to stop him. "Not a hugger." I widen my eyes a little menacingly so he knows I'm serious. I don't know what it is about huggers, but they always think I'll cave if they can just get their arms around me. No thanks.

Ben, to his credit, immediately drops his arms. "Oh, right." He closes his fist, then pushes it toward me, his smile turning goofy. He stands there awkwardly for a second, until Mason reaches up and fist-bumps him. Ben looks relieved someone responded to him. "Mason! My man. How are you, buddy?"

"Good!" Mason beams. My heart softens at his obvious excitement at being folded into this little group. I noticed it at the pumpkin patch, too. He was so relaxed and happy—and much better behaved—when we were hanging out with everyone. At the time, I knew Brandon had accepted this job, but I was so clouded by anger I couldn't process a lot of what was going on. I sulked by myself or followed Christine around most of that day and wasn't interested in making new friends. That must be why I didn't immediately recognize Ashley and Chloe.

"How's that bed of yours?" Ben is asking.

"Oh, the death trap you picked out for him?" Ashley says sardonically. For it not being a small town, news still spreads fast around here.

"It's not that bad," Ben insists. "It's sturdy. Right, Mason?"

"Right," Mason returns firmly.

"Yes, trust the seven-year-old to know what's safe," I murmur. Ashley chuckles, and Ben shrugs.

"Mason, come play!" Brody interrupts, hopping back and forth from foot to foot. Mason doesn't need to be told twice; he follows Brody to the back room without looking back at me. Caleb comes over to Christine and hands her one of two cars he's holding. She takes it, and they both plop down on the floor right where they were standing and start crashing the cars into each other, giggling the whole time.

"Okay," I drag the word out. "So, why are all of you hanging out in the local elementary school office?" I look around at the three adults.

Ashley speaks up. "My kids are on break. I took some vacation time to hang out with them. My husband works from home, so I've been trying to get them out of the house for a while each day. I'm also a volunteer for the parent-teacher organization." She gestures at the shapes she's been cutting out littering the table.

"I work here," Chloe adds. "But you probably figured that out."

"It's the longest she's worked anywhere, and we're so proud." Ashley teases. Chloe rolls her eyes. Ashley looks knowingly at me. She's being sarcastic in that big sister way, and Chloe takes it in stride.

"I'm on break, too," Ben chimes in. "I told Ash I'd take Brody to lunch while Caleb naps." He lights up as if he's just had a great idea. "I can take Mason, too, if you want." Then, his expression sobers slightly. "Or, you know, you can come with if you don't want to hand your kid over to some man you've only met three times."

"Oh, um. Maybe. I really need to register him for school, though, so…" I trail off and look at Chloe. Ben nods, giving a dorky thumbs-up, and heads back to the other room with the older kids.

I produce the paperwork Chloe asked for, and she springs into action, running to make copies and giving me a few forms to fill out. Ashley clears off a space at the table for me to sit, so I do.

The office is quiet for a few moments while I write and Ashley continues cutting her shapes. As I'm trying to decide what to write down for our pediatrician's name, Ashley breaks the silence. "It seems like our kids are going to be friends," she muses.

I hum, considering. "What are the odds they end up in the same class together? That would be Mason's dream come true."

"Oh, I'm sure Chloe can find a spot for him in Brody's class," she says with a hint of mischief.

I eye her across the table. Is knowing people who can do you favors how people get things done around here? If so, it's not as different from New York City private school life as I thought.

"Oh, don't worry. It's not anything untoward or anything like that. There are spots in all the classes. Chloe will just make sure he's put with the same teacher as Brody. If you want," she adds.

"That would be great, honestly. Mason..." I trail off, not exactly sure how much I want to share. "Well, he had some trouble making friends at his old school. He didn't quite fit in."

Ashley nods knowingly. "We had the same issue with my daughter, Amelia. We couldn't get her to take her nose out of her book long enough to make friends. She's at an actual playdate now."

I smirk, thinking about the pile of books it took Mason less than twenty-four hours to sprawl around the new house. Sounds familiar. "What did you do?" I ask.

"Incidentally, we put her in private school." Ashley glances at me, then back to her work. "Mason is your oldest?" she asks.

I nod, then decide to just write down our old pediatrician in New York for now and move on to the rest of the form.

"I'd like to say it gets easier," Ashley says, then sighs. "It doesn't. But sometimes you just need to shake things up a little to get them moving back in the right direction. You know what I mean?"

I look at her across the table, and she meets my gaze, smiling as if this burden of parenthood has united us in some way. Maybe it has, but I don't know how long I'm going to be here, so I'm not sure how much energy I want to expend on friendships that may or may not continue past March.

I hear Mason and Brody giggling in the back room, and glance at Christine and Caleb happily smashing their cars together on the floor next to the desk. An unexpected pang shoots straight through my heart at the thought of my two babies working so hard to make friends here only to be ripped from them in a few weeks. I realize that in all my stringing Brandon along, I'm doing it to them, too. It almost physically hurts to think about it. But I also know that I deserve to be happy, and so far, the best I can say about this move is that I'm conflicted.

I glance at Ashley, who has turned back to her cutting. "Yeah," I say quietly. "I know what you mean."

"Do you work outside the home?" Ashley asks, still focusing on her task. Little stars about the size of my palm fall from the construction paper onto the table.

"No," I say tersely. "I used to but..." I trail off.

Ashley shrugs in a completely non-judgmental way. "Do you work inside the home?"

"Aside from parenting and housework? Not exactly. Though I've been trying to get back into painting recently." I'm not sure what makes me add the last part, but it's out there now. Like toothpaste from the tube, I can't suck it back in.

"You're an artist?" Ashley asks, looking up excitedly. "Oh, that's so cool! I always wanted to learn how to draw, but law school got in the way. Chloe does digital illustrations on commission sometimes."

Chloe comes in from the back room, eying her excited sister warily. "Why did I hear my name?"

"Katie is an artist! I was telling her about your drawings." Ashley grins.

Chloe turns to me. "Oh, nice. What's your medium?"

"Acrylic on canvas, usually. I never got into the digital stuff. Staring at the screen hurts my brain." I give her a self-deprecating smirk.

She nods in understanding. "It's not as relaxing as other media, but it pays better. Everyone wants digital art now. But I really started using the tablet when I thought about writing a children's book a while back. Thought it might be easier to start digital instead of transposing it."

"Writing and illustrating a children's book would be a dream." I'm not sure why I say it. I've never thought about writing one before, but reading the kids their bedtime stories always fills me with a sense of calm. It's an attractive notion, that someone might feel that way about something I created.

"Hey, why don't we get the kids together soon?" Ashley jumps into the lull in the conversation. "Brody and Mason seem to have hit it off." She ticks her head toward the back room as a fit of giggles floats toward us.

"Um... sure," I say. "Let me give you my number." I grab one of the scraps from the stars Ashley's been cutting out and write it down, then hand it to her. She smiles brightly, tucking it into her pocket.

Mason runs out of the back room, kicking Christine's car in the process. Christine howls, and Mason shrugs his shoulders up to his ears trying to shrink himself, his eyes wide. I rush over to pick up Christine, who puts her little arms around my neck and squeezes her legs around my torso. I rub her back while glaring at Mason, who leans over to pick up the car and tries to hand it to her. She just wails louder and shoves it away. Mason shrugs, having lost interest after his minimal attempt at rectifying the situation.

"Mom?" Mason asks, raising his voice to be heard over Christine's crying. "Can I go to lunch with Brody and Ben?"

"You think now is a good time to ask this?" I grind out between clenched teeth, still rubbing Christine's back as she calms slightly. She rests her head on my shoulder and puts her thumb in her mouth, a sure sign that she's both hungry and tired.

Ben comes into the room with Brody at his heels. "Seriously, Katie, I'd be happy to take Mason with us. We're just headed to a restaurant up the street. You can get Christine down for a nap and have a little time to yourself. I'll bring him home in a few hours." Ben somehow manages to stand just over the line between boyish charm and major dad energy. He looks almost as pleading as the younger boys do.

Back in New York, I would never have allowed Mason to go to lunch with a man I hardly knew, but the few hours I had alone last night in my new studio were heavenly, and I'm itching to get back to it. I look at Mason, who has his hands clasped together under his chin and is giving me his best pretty-please eyes.

I sigh, resigned. "Let me text your dad, okay?" He should at least have a say in this, I suppose. Or, if he says no, it can be his fault and not mine.

I pull my phone out of my purse with one hand and send a quick text to Brandon: *Long story short, Ben wants to take Mason and Brody to lunch. Okay with you?*

Brandon's response is immediate: *Yeah. Ben's good people.*

I'm not too proud to admit I'm relieved. I want to see Mason make a friend while he's here, and I would love a little quiet time to myself while Christine naps. I give Mason and Ben my best stern look. "Your dad says it's fine, but I need Ben's phone number. And Mason, you'd better behave."

All three of them high-five each other. I glance at Ashley, who looks amused. Ben takes my phone and enters his number, and the three of them leave quickly, as if they're worried I'm going to change my mind.

Caleb is now lying on the ground, vrooming his car around with far less enthusiasm. Chloe finds her seat behind the counter again, still popping bubbles with her gum.

"Okay," I say, knowing I want to get out of here quickly so as not to waste a minute. "It was nice to see you all again, but I'm going to get this one home."

Ashley waves. "It was great chatting. Hopefully, we'll see you again soon." She sounds genuine, so I allow myself to smile slightly as I grab my purse and leave.

Once I get Christine home, I feed her a quick lunch and put her right to bed. I leave the door of my studio open while she sleeps so I can hear when she gets up, and I stand there taking in the work I did last night. I was a tornado of activity for the hours I was left alone. I'm not sure if it was because I was so excited to get back to my art, or if I was worried someone would interrupt. Either way, I wanted to get as much done as I could.

By the time I decided I needed to get some sleep, my eyes were too tired to make heads or tails of any of it, but now I take it all in with fresh eyes. Most of it is garbage, but there are a few drawings taking shape that I really like. The ones I like the best are, unsurprisingly, of my kids doing various fun activities together. One is the view from our airplane window as we left New York. Another is the view from the same window as we landed in Chicago.

I select the one of the New York skyline from above and clip it to my easel, then open up a box of paints Brandon placed in here. I grab two paintbrushes, shove the extra one in my bun, and get to work.

Chapter 9
Brandon

I DREAMT ABOUT KATIE all night. Beautiful, sweet dreams about her lips pressed against mine and my hands raking through her platinum blonde hair. By the time my alarm goes off, I'm so hard that I have to do a lot of innocuous mental math and take a cold shower before I can go upstairs to the kitchen. Katie holds out a mug of coffee to me, our fingers touching briefly in the hand-off. Her eyes hide a secret longing as if she had been dreaming about the same things as me last night. A giddy sensation passes over me at the touch, and I have to sit down quickly at the island because I'm hard again.

My wife is fucking perfect. And we kissed last night. It's not everything, but it's *something*.

And then, she and I banter back and forth about Mason's school, just like we used to do. It's exhilarating. It's exciting.

It's like I'm falling in love with my wife all over again.

After all that, it takes far more effort than usual to leave her. As I stand in the doorway, studying her before saying goodbye, I vow to myself that I am going to leave work on time every day from now until the end of time. I've missed too many hours with her already, and this move is supposed to mean more time home with her. With them. I'm going to make sure that's the case.

The drive to Chicago isn't bad, though I have heard that traffic in and out of the city can be unpredictably awful. The firm is in the Loop—in the heart of downtown—on the tenth floor of an office building with a gorgeous view of the city streets. I was here when my parents were scouting out office spaces, and I've come out a few times since. I honestly never thought they'd retire, so when they called in the fall to see if I wanted a shot at taking over this branch, I was surprised. And excited.

When I arrive at the office, my mom and dad are both waiting for me in the lobby near the receptionist's desk. Nothing like having your parents greet you when you get to work.

I haven't seen them yet because they've been traveling for the holidays, but I was hoping to have at least a few minutes to settle in my office before being accosted by Patrick and Maria Conley. I smile, hopefully conveying excitement that I don't quite feel.

My mom comes up to me and brushes a speck of invisible lint off my shoulder. "Oh, Brandon, try not to look so happy to see us," she says sharply, but quietly enough for only my dad and I to hear. Seems like I didn't do a great job of pretending to be happy.

My dad reaches out a hand to shake mine, his expression a good deal warmer than my mother's. I grip his hand and smile.

"Good to see you, son. How are Katie and the kids settling in?" he asks, releasing my hand.

"They just arrived yesterday. They seem to love the new place," I answer.

Mom makes a disbelieving sound in the back of her throat. "Haven't you been here since just after Christmas? What took them so long to move?"

"We talked about this, Mom." I grit my teeth. "Katie wanted to stay through New Year's Eve, and moving two kids is a lot of work."

She waves this away. "I will never understand that woman's insistence on not hiring help."

I simply shrug and smile. It's not worth it to try to explain that Katie did, in this instance, insist on help moving because she adamantly refused to participate. It's also not worth admitting Katie isn't yet fully on board with the move here. If I can't get this presentation ready for the administrators by March, it may all be a moot point anyway.

"Well," Mom claps her hands once as if this is no matter to her. "When can I come see my grandbabies?" Her sharp, gray eyes soften at the mention of the kids. I've always admired my mother for her toughness and her ability to pull up a chair in a room full of men and have her own seat, but even this hardened woman has a soft spot a mile wide for her grandchildren.

My gaze flicks to my father's, and a corner of his mouth tips up slightly in knowing amusement. The woman will not be satisfied without an immediate answer, and she does not give a single shit that Katie would rather walk across hot coals than have her over any time soon.

"I want to let them all get settled a bit. Maybe next week?" I ask, inwardly cringing at yet another thing I need to prepare Katie for.

Apparently satisfied, Mom nods once, then turns on her heel to walk back toward my new office. Dad raises a ruddy eyebrow, still looking amused, and extends an arm, indicating I should follow her.

"Your team is meeting in the conference room in fifteen minutes," Mom says as she walks primly through the cubicles back to my office. She shuts the door behind us. "I think it's best if we are not there with you," she continues as soon as the door is safely closed. She glances at my father, who nods his agreement. "We want to be as hands-off with this project as we can, though we are available to help privately should you need. Most of the work you will be doing is administrative. You'll be listening to the ideas of your team, fielding their questions, checking their math"—she makes a face at this, and I make a mental note to figure out who is the weak link with whom she's clearly irritated—"and, of course, it will be your job to finalize the visuals for the presentation you'll be making in March. Shortly after that, as you know, it is our plan to step aside permanently." There is a tinge of remorse in her voice, but her countenance remains stoic.

"That sounds so grave," I mutter. My dad stifles a laugh behind his hand.

My mother levels a glare at me. "You need to treat this seriously if you are going to have a future here, Brandon. All eyes are on you."

I try not to sigh heavily. "You've made that abundantly clear, Mom. I apologize if I've given you the impression that I believe otherwise." I pause, then continue against my better judgment. "Have a little faith in me. I'm ready for this. I know what I'm doing."

She eyes me up and down, her steely gaze lingering on my hair which I made sure to pull back into a presentable bun this morning. I send up a little gratitude that I also opted for long sleeves today so she can't see my tattoo poking out. If she could cut my hair off right now, she would happily do so. But she can't, so she settles for pursing her lips and folding her arms.

My father, who has been watching this entire silent exchange, finally decides to jump in. "Of course you are, Brandon. Your mother and I are understandably nervous. We don't want you to have dragged your entire family all this way for nothing."

Little do they know, if I can't also make Katie happy here, it'll all have been for nothing, anyway.

I simply nod. "I'm confident in my ability to knock this project out of the park." Which is true, but I try to sound extra convincing.

Apparently appeased, my mother reaches out a hand to cup my cheek. "We are, too, Brandon." She drops her hand and moves it to the doorknob. "Ten minutes. Conference room. Don't be late." She pulls the door open and leaves.

My dad shoots me what I could swear is an apologetic glance before he follows her out.

In the silence, I am finally able to set my bag down. I sit in my desk chair, the large, outside windows at my back. In front of me are floor-to-ceiling windows that look out over the cubicles and other offices. I run a hand over the aged wood of the desk I had sent here from my New York office. This desk is a relic—the drawers only open if you pull them a certain way, and the wood has grooves in it from decades of past architects drafting by hand on it—but I love it.

I walk to the little kitchen area adjacent to the conference room to pour myself a cup of coffee before making my way into the meeting a few minutes early. I set up my things at the head of the conference table, signing into my laptop and putting my notebook and coffee to the left so I can write down whatever I need to.

It doesn't take long for the team to file in. I try to smile warmly at everyone as they shuffle to their seats, also setting up similarly. I eye the clock, and as the meeting is supposed to be starting, there is still one seat conspicuously empty. We should have one senior architect and three juniors, plus the engineer, but there are only four other people present besides myself.

I check my watch to be sure the clock isn't running fast. It's not.

The older man to my left sighs heavily. "You may as well start. Thalia couldn't be on time if her life depended on it," he says gruffly.

My eyebrows shoot up as I glance around the room. A younger man and woman avoid my eye contact, and a man who looks to be about my age leans back in his chair and twirls his pen between his pointer and middle fingers.

I check the clock again. "Right. Well, let's start with introductions and we'll see if she arrives then," I suggest. The two younger members visibly relax while the older man tries—but not very hard—to hide his eye roll. I make a mental note of this interesting power dynamic before continuing. "Good morning, everyone. Thank you for being here. I'm Brandon Conley. Yes, my parents own this firm. Yes, I am here to hopefully take over for them at the end of this project. I'm excited to serve as team leader on the addition for Leade Park High School." I glance to my left, nodding my head at the man sitting next to me.

"Jasper Bean, senior architect. I've been working here for fifteen years and have served on two different teams designing school additions." Jasper is curt and imposing. His back is rigid against the chair, and his jet-black hair shows a hint of gray at the temples. I can't tell if he's annoyed at my presence as team lead or if he's just like this.

"Marianne Barnes," the young woman sitting next to him says. She's blonde and extremely put together, though she looks like she graduated yesterday, her wide eyes taking in the room in the way of someone who is more than slightly intimidated. "I'm a junior architect. This is my first large-scale addition project."

"Orlando Key, another junior architect," the young man next to her says. He has not one single hair on top of his head, though is sporting a well-trimmed beard that does little to make him look older than about twenty-five. There is noticeably less space between him and Marianne than there is between him and the man sitting next to him, which I take to mean they are friends or possibly something more. I file that information away for later.

"Calvin Saunders," the man next to him says. "I'm the engineer for the project. I won't be at all the team meetings, but your parents"—he nods at me—"asked me to be here to meet you today."

Just as he finishes his sentence, the door bursts open and a woman around my age bursts into the room. She's almost cartoonishly disheveled, her black hair falling from her bun in curls around her face, her brown skin completely free of makeup, and her blouse half-untucked from her trousers. I think I see a stain on her thigh, as well, but she quickly sits down in the empty chair, hiding the spot and dumping an armful of papers unceremoniously onto the table. The papers fan out in front of her, and she scrambles to stack them.

Jasper makes a noise of disgust to my left. "And this is Thalia Gutierrez, our third junior architect." He isn't even trying to hide his disdain, which is not a dynamic I want between my senior and junior architects before we've even gotten started, so I hold up a hand to stop him.

"I assume Ms. Gutierrez is capable of making her own introduction?" I ask, directing the question to her.

She sets the stack of papers neatly on the table and takes a deep breath to steady herself. She eyes Jasper, her eyes narrowing slightly, then nods once to me. "Thalia Gutierrez, junior architect. This is my fourth year with the firm. Was there any other information you asked for?" Her voice is steady and not at all what I would expect from a woman who rushed in here in a cyclone of papers and an untucked shirt.

"You'd have known if you bothered to show up on time," Jasper says under his breath.

I shoot him a warning look as I say, "No, Ms. Gutierrez." I turn to her. "I'm Brandon Conley, the new team lead. Do you need a second?" I don't know why she was late, and I don't want to make any assumptions, unlike Mr. Grouch to my left.

Thalia folds her hands in front of her on top of the table and sits up straight. "No, sir. I'm good."

"Great. Let's get started. Where are we with the planning?" I direct this question to Jasper. He launches into the driest and least enthusiastic update about the initial meetings with school district and community officials, including space constraints and design preferences. It only lasts about ten minutes, but it feels more like thirty. Marianne and Orlando write notes to each other on a notepad that lies between them. They try to be stealthy, but the way they take turns writing on the same notepad and hiding smirks behind their hands is a dead giveaway.

When Jasper wraps up, Thalia jumps in. "My turn. I have been the primary contact with the school. They have billed this as a new student center, which encompasses a lot. The space needs a bigger cafeteria to house their growing student population. They would like to fit more students so they can have fewer lunch periods."

"How many lunch periods do they have currently?" I ask.

"Eight. They'd like to have six."

"And how many students attend the school?" I start making notes on my notepad.

"This year, they have an enrollment of around 3,300. This is up 300 from two school years ago, and enrollment is projected to reach 3,800 in the next five years."

I let out a low whistle as I scribble some notes. "They want a cafeteria that houses upwards of 600 students?"

"That's not all," Thalia dips her chin and looks at me as if the best is yet to come. "They also want the building to include a faculty cafeteria, lounge, plus something they are helpfully calling 'educational spaces.'"

I frown. "What does that mean?"

"Unclear," Thalia says.

"I think it's pretty obvious," Jasper intrudes. "Large rooms for multiple classes, reading areas. What more do students need?"

He says it like it's the simplest thing in the world, and I try not to outwardly bristle at his tone. Thalia, Marianne, and Orlando are less conspicuous than I am. Marianne and Orlando shoot knowing glances at each other. Thalia leans back in her chair and folds her arms, clearly irritated he's interrupted her part of the presentation. Calvin, the engineer, is utterly unfazed.

When Jasper doesn't add anything more, Thalia continues. "I have been trying to set up meetings with the teachers to get their wish lists, but the administration is being difficult for some reason."

I regard Thalia, impressed. The planning process shouldn't exclude any stakeholders, and who better to ask about the functionality of educational spaces than teachers?

"I'm not sure why the admin would drag their feet on that, but, as luck would have it, I have some contacts within the school. I can reach out," I offer.

Thalia smiles and takes a breath as if to speak, but Jasper interjects. "How are your contacts better than the ones we already have?"

Jesus, this guy. If it wasn't clear already that Jasper has an issue with me being team lead, it is now. It's also clear to me that he hasn't been pegged for a team lead position because his people skills are severely lacking.

"Well, my contacts are teachers at the school. Since we are trying to talk to teachers, I would think that would be helpful." I'm failing miserably at keeping the edge out of my voice.

Thalia snickers, and Jasper glares at her. This has the potential to go south quickly, so I address Marianne and Orlando. "Anything to add?"

"No, sir. We were enlisted to help draft blueprints once everything that needs to be included is decided," Orlando speaks for both of them, and Marianne nods in agreement.

"Once you have the final plans, I can work up the materials and budget," Calvin offers, gathering his things to leave. The others follow suit.

I guess the meeting is over, then.

"Great. Okay, I'll reach out to the teachers and we can reconvene tomorrow," I say as the team starts filing out of the room.

I close my eyes and rub my temples with the fingertips of one hand. I didn't plan on controlling the adults on this team, but I did think they'd at least afford me the courtesy of deciding when our meeting ended.

I hear someone clear their throat to my right. My eyes fly open to see Thalia standing in the doorway, her stack of papers in her arms.

"Oh, sorry, Ms. Gutierrez. I didn't realize you were still there. Is there something you need?" I lean my forearms on the table in front of me to give her my full attention.

A corner of Thalia's mouth tips up, then she furrows her brow as she forces her expression to look less amused at my distress. "I wanted to apologize for my tardiness this morning."

I wait a beat, thinking she's going to offer more. When she doesn't, I shake my head. "I'm probably supposed to care that you weren't here on time, but I have the feeling I have bigger issues with this team than you running in here a few minutes late."

She smirks again, then indicates the seat she had been sitting in. "May I?"

I wave at the chair, indicating she should sit. She does, setting her papers down. They fan out in front of her again. "If I might be so bold as to offer some advice, Mr. Conley?"

I wince. "Mr. Conley is my father. Brandon, please."

"Right. Okay. Well, I don't want to throw anyone under the bus, Brandon."

"But..." I raise an eyebrow, urging her to continue.

She checks the door behind her to make sure it's closed. Assured, she swivels back to me. "Between you and me, Jasper is a drag on every team he's in."

I nod slowly. This confirms my suspicions, but it's my job as team lead to keep this project running smoothly. I don't want to jump in the middle of whatever tension is between these two.

"He's always grumpy as hell, but he's extra pissy you're here." Her eyes widen and her hand flies to cover her mouth. "Shit, I'm sorry. I am not great at watching my language."

I can't help but chuckle at her discomfort. "No need to apologize. Thanks for the heads up."

She shoots me a grateful smile, then starts to get up from her chair.

"Actually, Ms. Gutierrez—"

"Thalia."

"Thalia. If I might ask, and you don't have to answer since I'm not technically your boss yet, but why were you late this morning?"

"Oh." She starts dog-earing a corner of the paper in front of her, folding and unfolding it and looking at it like it's the most interesting thing she's ever seen. "Well, I'm just coming back after my maternity leave. I mean, I've been back for a few weeks now. My baby is six months old."

That explains the disheveled appearance. "Congratulations," I say warmly.

"Thanks," she says, but she sounds less than enthusiastic. "Her father," she spits the words with ultimate disdain, "ended up being less than reliable, so I moved in with my parents so I could come back to work. They live closer to Leade Park than to the city, which is why I asked to be put on this project. To be honest, I forgot I had to come to the office today. I've been doing most of the leg work at the school to be closer to home."

I nod slowly. "Ah." I pause, considering. "You said you've been with the firm for four years?"

"Yes. And I spent two years with another firm before that."

"And you've been doing most of the in-person work at the high school? You're tasked with making presentations to the team about the functionality of the space?"

"That's correct." She ticks an eyebrow upward, urging me to get to the point.

"Why aren't you on this team as another senior architect?"

She huffs a humorless laugh and doesn't meet my eyes. "You know how it goes."

I do know how it goes, but I want to hear her confirm it. "Explain it to me like I'm five."

She winces and chews on the inside of her cheek for a second as if trying to decide if she wants to say it out loud or not. Then, she steels herself, having made up her mind. "Nothing against your parents or anything. I don't blame them. But people don't typically promote women with new babies who can't get their asses to work on time because their baby daddy can't be bothered to take responsibility."

I hum, considering. She finally lifts her eyes to mine, and she looks worried. I smile in a way I hope is comforting. "Your instinct to contact the teachers was a good one. And, this might be unorthodox, but your colorful language tells me you've got some energy. Those are things I want on this team. I don't want to do the same old addition for this school. I want to do something truly creative, so I need more thinking like yours. We need to be able to take some risks here."

Her eyes brighten as I'm speaking, and she sits up a little straighter. It's clear from her expression that she's excited about this change of pace.

"I can do risks," she says, her eyes gleaming.

I chuckle. "Something tells me you aren't lying. That's great. Thank you, Thalia."

She smiles and stands, understanding she's been dismissed, but if I'm not mistaken, there's a definite pep in her step as the conference room door closes behind her.

I make my way to my office, and as soon as I'm back at my desk, I remove my phone from where I left it in my desk drawer and open up my text thread to Daniel.

Working on the addition for LPHS. Hoping to talk to some teachers about what they'd like to see in the space. Know anyone?

Before my phone can even go dark, I get a text message from Mac: *I have about a million ideas for this space. Want to talk now? I can call. I can drive downtown.*

I laugh deeply. I don't know Mac very well, but Daniel has spoken often of her love for her school, and he wasn't kidding.

When I don't respond immediately, she texts again: *Too much? That was probably too much. I'm excited to help. Just let me know.*

I don't want her to feel like her enthusiasm is too much, so I text back, *I'm going to put you in touch with Thalia Gutierrez. She's been trying to contact the teachers for a while, and I want her to take the lead on this.*

Admin blocked her, didn't they? she sends back.

Your admin and a senior member of our team, I return, standing to make my way to Thalia's desk. My phone buzzes again when I get there, and I pause to look at it as Thalia waits expectantly for me.

Is he sexist? I bet he's sexist. Let me at him. I know how to deal with sexist assholes.

I chuckle and shake my head, raising my gaze to Thalia.

"I have a teacher contact for you, and I think you'll like her a lot. You ready to take down her info?"

The sun has already set by the time I'm ready to leave, but, to be fair, the sun sets at about 4:30 here in the winter, so I'm not feeling too late when I close my office door behind me at 5:15. As I'm walking out, there are many, many people still working at their desks. My parents, however, are long gone.

I pass Thalia's desk and am surprised to still see her there. When I pause next to her, she removes an earbud and smiles. "Mac is a riot," she says. "We're meeting next week, and I already can't wait. Thanks for putting us in touch."

"No problem. But don't you have a baby to get home to?" I ask.

She blushes deeply, looking around like she's worried someone heard me.

"Are you embarrassed to have a baby at home?" I frown.

"No, it's not that." Her voice is barely above a whisper.

"Are you at a point where you can leave your work for tomorrow?"

"Yes..." she says slowly.

"Then you should leave." I look around, then lean in a little closer and lower my voice. "Listen. Between you and me, my wife moved here more or less on the condition that I leave on time every night and am home more often. I'm not the type to assume more hours in the office means more work getting done." I tilt my head toward the exit. "You are obviously free to do what you want, but I'm getting out of here to spend some time with my kids, and you should too."

I walk to the elevator and push the down button. I get in, and just as the doors are starting to close, Thalia runs through them, smiling sheepishly at me as they ping open again, then close behind her.

"Between *you* and *me*," she grins as she catches her breath from her jog to the elevator, "I think you're exactly what this company needs."

The drive home is quick, too, and I smile as I pull into the driveway and see the warm light from the house spilling out through the windows. I can see into the living room from where my car sits. Katie and the kids are in there, huge smiles on their faces, as they sway and twirl to the beat of a song I can't hear. Mason reaches up to grab Katie's hand, and she twirls him. He's so tall, and she's so short; it won't be long before he's twirling her. Christine lifts her pudgy little arms above her head, and Katie picks her up, settling her on her hip as she sways back and forth.

God, her ass is so round and perfect. It feels wrong to notice it considering I'm a voyeur spying on an impromptu dance party she's having with our children, but I can't help but watch it as she sweeps it left and right.

Mason glances out the window, and when he sees my car, he starts jumping up and down and pointing toward me. Katie whirls around, her eyes round and her lips making that perfect O. The things I would do to those lips if she'd let me...

Before I can finish that thought, Mason runs out the front door with Christine stomping behind him. I quickly get out of my car, opting to leave my bag behind, and pick him up in a big hug.

"Me too, Daddy! Up!" Christine somehow commands authority in her little toddler voice, so I have to obey. She's so much like Katie, and there isn't a day that goes by that I don't thank the universe that this little girl inherited all her mother's tenacity.

I set Christine on my hip and put an arm around Mason's shoulders to lead him inside. By the time I close the front door and put Christine down, Katie has busied herself tidying up the living room. She's bent over with that perfect ass in the air, and I swear I try to look away. I really do.

But I can't.

"Mason," I say, trying to keep the roughness out of my voice. Katie immediately stands and looks at me. I cou and try again. "Mason, go help your sister wash her hands for dinner."

"Sure. Come on, Chrissy." He leads her down the hall and into the bathroom.

I don't waste a second. I cross the room to Katie in two long steps and slide my arm around her waist, pulling her toward me. Her eyes sparkle as she tips her head up to me. I lower my lips to hers. She opens her mouth immediately, allowing my tongue to slip in. I draw her bottom lip between my teeth and bite it lightly. She lets out a breathy laugh, and my heart just about stops.

That sound. That beautiful fucking sound. Like a wind chime. It goes straight to my chest, and suddenly I can't breathe. I love her so much.

This used to happen all the time. I'd catch sight of her when she didn't know I was watching, a soft smile on her face as she felt her growing belly. Or she'd come behind me when I was sitting on the couch looking at something for work and drag her hands over my chest, pressing her lips to that space between my neck and my shoulder. Or we'd be at a stuffy party full of rich idiots, and she'd catch my eye from across the room, but I'd already be looking at her, and she'd blush.

My love for her has always been all-consuming, but it has consistently been these small moments that knock the wind out of me.

I pull back and rest my forehead against hers, my eyes still closed while I breathe heavily.

"Dinner won't be ready for another half hour," she whispers, amused.

"Okay." The roughness has returned to my voice tenfold. Fuck it. I don't care if she knows how much I want her.

"The kids will have to wash their hands again." I can hear the smile in her voice, so I open my eyes and, sure enough, the corners of her mouth are curled up gently.

It knocks the air out of me again. Katie is a guarded woman. She doesn't smile often, and her smiles are precious. I take in the contours of this one, more than a little proud that I put it there, and bottle it up in my memory.

"Fine." I lean in to kiss her again, and she lets me. No, she doesn't just let me. She's as eager to kiss me as I am to kiss her.

"Hey Mom—oh. Um, Chrissy, let's go play upstairs." The sound of Mason's voice causes me to pull reluctantly away from Katie's lips again, but I hear two sets of little footsteps scurry upstairs. Katie glances over my shoulder, then back at me, and we both break into a fit of giggles.

"They're going to be scarred for life," she says between laughter.

"I can think of worse things for them to see than their parents madly in love with each other," I return.

Her clear, blue eyes flick back and forth between mine, and her smile fades slightly.

"'Madly in love,' huh?" she asks.

I swallow hard, then lift a hand to cup her cheek. She leans into it, and I feel more than hear that little purr of hers.

"Yes, Cat." I sound over-eager now, but I don't care about that, either. I want her to know how completely lost to her I am. I always have been.

Her smile is gone now, but she closes her eyes and rests her cheek on my palm. Her face looks peaceful. More peaceful than I've seen it in a long time.

She takes in a deep breath through her nose. "I'm glad you're here," she whispers.

Whatever pieces of my heart were left intact shatter. How the fuck did I miss this for so long? What made me think staying late at work was more important than these moments right here?

I lean in and press a kiss to her forehead in a silent promise that I'll never miss these moments again. I fold her into me so her cheek is resting against my chest, then lower my chin to the top of her head, breathing in the scent that is so uniquely Katie—her rose-scented shampoo mixed with the smell of art supplies she never fully gets rid of, no matter how long it's been since she's painted. I hold her close, and she finally wraps her arms around my torso.

"Me too, Cat." I squeeze her even closer to me. "Me too."

Chapter 10
Katie

WE MAKE IT TO the end of the week, and things have been going pretty well. It's late afternoon on Friday, and I'm feeling optimistic as I half-shut the door to my studio and sit at the desk. I unfold my laptop and open my email. I click on the link my therapist sent last night and do a quick check in the camera before connecting. My hair is mostly escaping its ponytail, and I'm not wearing any makeup, but I'm already a few minutes late so it'll have to do.

"Katie," my therapist's bright voice comes through, though it takes another second for her face to appear on the screen. She's a slight woman with dark skin and hair so black it's almost blue. Her eyes are a warm brown, and even through the screen, I can tell she is looking right into mine over the distance.

"Hi, Nora." I give her a half-smile and an awkward wave. I don't make a habit of doing video calls, but telehealth seemed like the best option to continue therapy until I found someone local. Luckily, Nora was more than willing to accommodate the request.

Her office is in full view behind her—a cozy space with a couch and an armchair. The walls are painted a welcoming gray, and I can just make out the corner of the nondescript piece of art I used to stare at whenever I wanted to avoid her eye contact.

No avoiding eye contact over the internet, though, it seems. I suppress a shudder at how eerie it is that she can see me through my laptop camera.

"How did the move go?" She opens her notepad to a new page and clicks her pen.

I sigh. "It was fine, I guess."

"Still not sold on the Midwest, I take it?" A corner of her mouth tilts up.

I dip my chin to glare at the flat image of her face. "I doubt I'll ever be sold on the Midwest."

She chuckles, clicking her pen again. Her eyes shift as if she's looking over my shoulder. She squints. "What room are you in right now?"

I look around. "Oh, this is my new studio." I purse my lips against a smile.

"Why that face?" The woman misses nothing, even over the internet.

"I'm pretty sure this room is a bribe."

"What makes you say that?"

I know it's a therapist's job to ask these types of questions, but sometimes I wish we could just have a normal conversation, at least for a few minutes. "Brandon wants me to stay here, so he set up a studio for me to do my artwork."

"From what I can see, it looks like you have been painting." She points her pen at the screen.

I twist around in the chair to look at the half-filled canvasses behind me. I swivel back in my seat to face her again. "Um, yeah. I have."

"I know you wanted to start doing that when you were still living here. How does it feel to get back in the swing of it?"

I bite the inside of my cheek to avoid groaning at her question. How does it feel? It feels fucking amazing. It feels like coming home. It feels like something has loosened just a tiny bit in my chest, and I can breathe again.

I don't know why, but I'm not ready to admit that aloud just yet. "It feels good."

Nora hums as if she knows I'm not giving her the full story, but she lets it slide. "I'm glad Brandon gave you this space to do what you love."

I nod, looking around the room again even as I can feel her eyes still trained on me. I sigh heavily and look back to the screen, clasping my hands tightly in front of me. It's a good thing she can't see my knuckles turn white with how hard I'm gripping them together.

She scribbles something in her notepad. Maybe she can see my hands after all. "I know you haven't been there very long, but have you gotten out at all? Met anyone?"

"I haven't had a chance. The kids are still home from school. They go back in two days."

I must sound a little too wistful with that last sentence because Nora chuckles. "Not soon enough. I remember those days," she commiserates.

"Definitely not soon enough," I say. As if on cue, a loud crash comes from upstairs, followed by a toddler wail. "Shit, hang on."

Nora nods sympathetically, and I quickly leave the room. "Mason! What's going on up there?" I yell.

Mason's head appears at the top of the stairs. "We were both laying in my bed watching my tablet, and Christine took it and threw it on the floor. It's okay, though! It didn't break," he adds quickly.

"Are you both okay?" I raise an eyebrow.

"Oh. Yeah. She wasn't mad or anything. She thought it was funny."

"Right. Well, keep it out of her reach. Your dad should be home any minute."

"Okay, Mom!" he calls as he bounds back to his bedroom.

I re-situate myself in my chair and give Nora an apologetic look. "Sorry. Christine threw Mason's tablet—"

"I heard," she cuts me off. "You know there's a mute button on the bottom of the screen, right?"

I wince. "I forgot. Sorry."

She smiles as if this whole thing is incredibly amusing. "It's fine. So, I want to help you develop a plan for meeting some new people. You should get out of your shell and settle into a group of friends there."

I immediately bristle at this. "I don't know how long we'll be staying."

Nora levels a glare at me. "I thought we had agreed you'd give this a chance with an open mind."

Nora and I had agreed to this. She, like Brandon, thinks a change of pace will be good for us and had got me to begrudgingly admit that I could see how things might be easier here, which had led to me promising her that I'd give our new setup a real shot.

"It's so quiet here," I say. "Not just the lack of city noises. There aren't any people anywhere."

"You're not living in the country, Katie. You have neighbors. Mason and Christine will go to school..." she trails off.

"I did meet some women when I registered Mason for school. One was another parent, and the other was the school secretary."

Nora frowns. "The school secretary does not count as meeting a potential friend."

"Oh, well, they're sisters. Remember I told you about our trip out here in the fall, how we met up with some people at the pumpkin patch, and Mason made a friend?"

Nora nods, scribbling something else in her notebook. *Thinks the secretary is a friend*, probably.

"Well, it was them. Apparently, we live in the same district. They're related to the people we came out here to see last fall. Sort of. It's a long story, and we only have half an hour left." I hear the garage door bang open and shut. "Oh, hang on a sec." I make sure to push the mute button before shouting for Brandon.

"Yeah?" he yells back.

"I'm on a call with my therapist. The kids are upstairs throwing tablets or something," I call without leaving my chair.

"I'm on it!" Before I can unmute the call, he pops his head in, waves at Nora, then fully closes the door.

I stare at the door for a second, my face softening. He knew I left that door cracked open so I could hear the kids, and he immediately took the hand-off when he got home, allowing me to have this uninterrupted time. That knot in my chest loosens a little more, and a small smile plays at my lips as I turn around to face Nora again.

"What's that look?" she asks as soon as I unmute the call.

My eyes widen in surprise. The woman misses *nothing*. "Um... Brandon just got home."

Nora looks impossibly amused as she raises an eyebrow and fights against a laugh. "You've been seeing me for years, and I've never seen you look at your husband like that."

"Well, he's been trying to be more present, I guess, and he's been really good this past week about making sure I have some time for myself and…" I trail off and shrug. I'm stumbling over my words like a schoolgirl with a crush.

"When was the last time you were intimate with him?" Leave it to Nora to not mince words.

My cheeks heat and my eyebrows shoot up my forehead. "Uh…" My eyes dart to the window over my screen to avoid her gaze.

She tries a different tactic. "You said before that it had been a while. Any changes on that front?"

"No." My voice is firm, but when Nora lets out a low hum, I'm sure she hears the disappointment.

"Why not?" she asks.

I bristle at her straightforward line of questioning. *Why not?* What does she mean, why not? Because I started avoiding him as some kind of punishment for his brash decisions, and we never got it together to get back in the same room. It's simple.

"I didn't want to sleep in the same room as him until we were on the same page."

Nora regards me for a moment, her mouth scrunched to the side. "What will it take for you to be on the same page again?"

I blink a few times but remain silent. I don't know what it will take, if I'm being honest. I thought it would take him coming to his senses and keeping us all in New York, but even a few days here has given me the sense that we are on the cusp of something different. Better.

When I don't say anything, she jumps in. "It appears that Brandon is trying very hard to ensure your happiness," she starts slowly. "I would never suggest any level of intimacy you're uncomfortable with, but it seems that recent events have taken a toll on your relationship as much as they've taken a toll on you. This studio, coming home and taking care of the kids so you can have this time for therapy, for yourself…" she trails off like she always does when she wants to phrase something just right. "You said earlier it was a bribe, but what if it isn't? What if Brandon is trying to repair what has been lost between you two? It might be a good idea to let him know how much you appreciate his efforts."

I lean back in my chair, my brow furrowing as I cross my arms. "Are you suggesting I reward his basic participation in family life with sex?"

"Oh, no." Nora laughs lightly, but I'm still frowning. "Not at all. I hear how that must have sounded. I do think intimacy is an important part of any healthy relationship, but sex in a marriage should never be in exchange for anything. Intimacy can mean many things, not just sex." Her eyes bore into me through the screen. "Maybe start by letting him sleep in your bed?"

I laugh harshly, dropping my hands to my lap.

"I admire your commitment to the decisions you've made, Katie." *Well, that's a nice way to say I'm stubborn.* "But we've talked about expanding your support system before. It would benefit you to start letting people in. This is not New York, and you are not surrounded by"—she consults her notepad—"'rich assholes,' I believe were your words. Start by opening the door for your husband. Just a crack. Maybe see if you can make a few friends while you're there. Try it out. See how it feels. Consider it practice for when you come back here, if you must."

"Feels like homework," I grumble.

Nora laughs deeply. It's a rich sound, one that makes me smile, too. She tilts her head at me. "If it helps you to think of it as an assignment, so be it. I want to hear about your efforts next time." She checks her watch. "We have about five minutes left. I wanted to ask—"

"I haven't had a drink," I cut her off. I hate this part, even though it's why I started seeing her in the first place.

Nora regards me for a second, then nods curtly, making a note in her notepad. *Not a total failure*, maybe. Then, she looks at me. "Anything else for today, Katie?"

I shake my head.

She pauses for a moment, then says, "Keep an open mind. You aren't doomed to repeat the past."

I consider her words, then meet her eyes on the screen and nod once.

She smiles, and we wrap up just as I hear Brandon and the kids come storming down the stairs, Christine and Mason complaining that they're hungry for dinner. I stare at my blank screen for a few minutes, giving myself some extra time to decompress after that session, then sigh as I snap it shut and get ready to be Mom again.

I open the door to the living area and exit slowly. I can already feel my shoulders slumping and my eyes glazing over. They always tell you self-care is important, and therapy is part of that. What they don't acknowledge is how everything still needs to get done after you take care of yourself. And, often, when you spend an hour on a video call with your therapist, dinner gets pushed back, then bath time and bedtime get a little later. Before you know it, you're just as exhausted as you were before you "took care of yourself" and are left with no other free time to do anything else.

In short, self-care is bullshit.

At least, that's what I always thought, even though I recognized the power that therapy had in my life. I was willing to sacrifice time for a conversation with someone who saw my issues and didn't shy away from them. Someone I could be completely honest with and who wouldn't judge me for my worst moments.

But when I leave my studio and see Brandon in black joggers and a faded old cotton t-shirt that says *Kiss me, I'm Irish* and the kids standing on stools around the island starting to prepare dinner, I think maybe self-care can work if you've got other people to get things started for you.

"What's this?" I ask, walking toward them. There is flour everywhere—and I mean *everywhere*—and balls of dough in front of each kid.

Brandon looks up at me and smiles tentatively. "I stopped at the store on my way home. I thought it'd be fun to make pizzas tonight." He looks hopeful and excited.

Mason grins at me, a dash of flour grazing his cheek. "I'm going to put green peppers on mine," he says proudly.

"You are?" I don't believe him for one second. This kid avoids vegetables like the plague.

He nods, though, his chest puffed out.

"I like cheese," Christine says, though she's still having trouble pronouncing her L's, so it comes out more like "I wike cheese." She takes the red plastic rolling pin she's holding and pounds it on the dough in front of her.

"Oh, honey, that's not how you do it. Here, let me show you." I move around to the side of the island to stand next to her.

"No! I do it," she yells, clutching the rolling pin to her chest. I raise my hands in surrender. Never mind, then.

Brandon chuckles, and I eye him sidelong. He has a strange look on his face, but when I pinch my brows in question, he just shakes his head and hands me a ball of dough.

"I know we just had pizza last week, but is this okay?" he asks.

I take the dough from him and squeeze it between my fingers. The feel of it is totally satisfying. Mason reaches over and helps Christine flatten out more of her dough, and she copies his motions exactly.

The whole scene is so damn *sweet*. It's a picture-perfect family moment. My heart almost bursts in my chest, and my fingers practically itch to paint it. I decide I'm going to, after the kids go to bed.

"The addition of green peppers makes it an entirely different meal," I tease.

I look up at Brandon, and I can't help the smile on my face from growing. It feels almost foreign, my cheek muscles engaging in a way they haven't in a while. He grins right back.

"Seriously," I say. "This is great."

Chapter 11
Brandon

WHEN I CAME HOME from the store with supplies to make pizza, I thought I was a damn genius. Turns out, that stuff only works on the internet. The kids' pizzas are a disaster. Mason insists on topping his with green peppers, and when he goes to take a bite, he freaks out about the vegetables being on it. He also won't let us pick them off. Christine demands more and more sauce on her pizza, going as far as a mini-meltdown on the kitchen floor when we try to tell her she won't like it. Katie shrugs, says she'll do anything to stop the screaming, and helps her ladle sauce onto the crust. It comes out of the oven a sopping mess.

I toss some sauce, cheese, and meat onto a pizza while helping the kids. It turns out okay. But Katie, of course, makes a fucking masterpiece. She artfully combines different colors of cheese and cuts pepperoni pieces into just the right shapes to create a pizza that looks strikingly like my face, complete with green pepper eyes and a dark, rust-colored beard.

When it comes out of the oven, it looks so much like me that the kids dissolve into fits of giggles on the tile floor, and everyone wants a piece of it. I hold the pizza cutter just above the pizza, ready to cut, when Katie jumps in.

"It's my pizza! Let me cut it." She grabs the cutter from my hands, and a slight jolt of electricity passes between us as our fingers touch. I think she feels it too, because her cheeks turn a perfect shade of pink.

She's smiling a wide, easy smile I haven't seen in a long time as she goes to cut the pizza. It's such a beautiful sight. But as soon as I file it away in my brain to bring back out later, it's replaced by a wicked grin. She cackles as she slices into the pizza.

"You know," she raises her eyes to mine, the blue in them glinting. "I didn't think slicing into your face would be so enjoyable, yet here we are."

I can tell from her tone she's teasing, but with Katie, there's always some truth behind it. I raise an eyebrow. "Did you create Pizza Brandon just to cut it up?"

"No." She adopts an innocent expression. "But I can't help it if the end result is deeply satisfying." Her voice drops a register as she ends that sentence, and it doesn't matter that she's talking about cutting up my pizza face. I still go hard at her tone.

I remind myself that the kids are in the room and grab a slice of my beard. I shove as much of it into my mouth as I can, never breaking eye contact with her. The kids start to giggle again.

"Daddy ate his *face*," Christine laughs.

"Ewww," Mason groans.

"It's delicious," I insist around my mouthful, which sets everyone off into more laughter.

The kids insist on eating "Daddy's face," so we load up plates and sit at the island with all the pizzas of varying levels of success in the middle. We end up polishing off my face pizza, then moving to the one I threw together. We pack Mason's away for Katie or me to eat later, and we toss Christine's right in the garbage when she's not looking.

What I thought was going to be a disaster of an evening turned out beautifully. Because of Katie.

I don't know how she does it. Actually, yes, I do. She's fucking brilliant, that's how. She's a stunning woman, an amazing mother, and a talented artist. She takes everything I try to do and makes it better. She makes me better.

After we clean up, I can tell Katie wants to go back to her studio. When we first met, she'd get this look about her when she wanted to paint something. Her fingers would start to tap the nearest surface ever so slightly, and her eyes would glass over. She had that look a few times during dinner, and now she's looking toward her studio door longingly.

I watch her for a few seconds and offer quietly, "I got baths and bedtime. Go paint."

She slowly shifts her gaze to meet mine. I can't read her expression, but she's so still. After a moment, she nods once and makes her way into her room, shutting the door behind her.

The rest of my night is filled with wrangling Christine into and out of the tub, attempting to persuade—then finally ordering—Mason to take a shower, and reading probably fifteen bedtime stories between the two kids. By the time I'm finished, I'm exhausted and happy the way you are after doing something gratifying.

I head downstairs. Katie's studio door is still closed. I grab a slice of Mason's green pepper pizza and take Daniel's book that I still haven't finished off the side table before heading down to the basement to read in bed.

The guest room is sparse. There's only a queen-sized bed and a dresser in the corner. I hadn't wanted to furnish it too much because I had hoped I wouldn't be in here for very long.

I strip down to my boxers and climb under the covers. I prop up the pillows behind me and settle in to read, feeling like a complete asshole that I still haven't finished this book. Literary fiction just isn't my thing. Still, I try.

My eyelids are starting to droop after about an hour of reading, when I'm suddenly startled to attention as Katie opens the door.

"Hi," she says tentatively. She stands in the doorway, her left thumb twitching over her wedding band, which glimmers in the dim light of the room.

"Hi."

"Can I come in?"

Fuck yes, she can come in. I sit up straighter and nod. She fully enters the room, and I can see she's wearing an oversized t-shirt that comes to about mid-thigh and hangs off her shoulder. Her hair is down and brushes over her shoulders. There's a smudge of red paint on her left cheekbone that she must have missed when cleaning up.

As her eyes trail over my bare chest, they snag on the tattoo over my heart—K, M, and C. It's simple, but I know she loves this design. Back when things were easier between us, she used to trace her delicate fingers over the lines or press her warm hand over it.

How long has it been since she's seen any part of me naked? Too long, that's for sure.

She hums, and it's an uncertain sound. I, on the other hand, have never been more sure that I want someone near me.

"What's up?" I ask.

"I was cold."

That's the moment I know that she's trying to shift something between us, because I know she's lying. Katie is an anomaly of a woman in a lot of ways, but specifically in that she never gets cold. She's like a hot box, and sleeping next to her is like sleeping next to a space heater under a thermal quilt.

She smirks as if she's daring me to call her on her bullshit. I gobble that smirk up.

"You want me to turn the heat up?" I arch an eyebrow at her. I know that's not what she wants. If it were, she'd have done it herself. She's trying to say she wants to sleep with me. Or, at least, I hope that's what she's trying to say.

Her blue eyes turn toward the ceiling, and her expression changes to one of exasperation. A second ago, she wanted to play, but now I know she's thinking, *He's going to make me say it.*

I smile expectantly. Yes, I am going to make her say it.

"No, I..." she trails off, then her gaze lands on me. It's as if the sight of me makes her feel sure, because she straightens her shoulders. "I was thinking maybe I could stay here for a little while?" When I'm silent, she adds, "With you."

I try not to read into the fact that she wants to stay in the guest room with me rather than inviting me back to what's supposed to be our bedroom. Katie is incredibly stubborn, almost painfully so. I found that out after almost a year of asking her to marry me. She lives on her own terms and takes a while to warm up to almost everything. Still, it stings a little. If she's not inviting me back to our room, this is temporary.

But, just like when I was trying to woo her that first time, I'll take what I can get. I scoot over on the bed and turn down the covers. She doesn't waste any time and jumps right in, but she flips over so her back is to me. I close my book and lay it on the nightstand, leaning over to turn off the light. I shift around a bit and settle on my back, one arm under my head and one hand resting on my chest, right where my tattoo is.

She is silent for a moment, then she shimmies backward so her ass is touching my hip. I chuckle softly.

"What?" she asks, but her usual bite is gone. She sounds defeated, actually.

"You really are like a cat. Pressing up against me for attention."

"I said I was cold." Now she sounds defensive. "What's the point of me being in here if you're not going to warm me up?"

"You don't have to pretend to need my body heat to be in the same bed as me," I practically whisper.

She's silent for a long time. I sigh lightly, trying not to wake her up if she's fallen asleep. Just as I'm closing my eyes, she violently flips over so she's facing me, taking half the comforter with her. I gently pull my side back over me, then roll my head to look at her in the thin light from the streetlight filtering in from the small window near the ceiling. Her blue eyes almost glow, and the comforter seductively hugs her curves.

"Why aren't you touching me?" she asks. It's not mean or confrontational. She sounds curious.

I know she likes the banter and the playfulness, but I'm suddenly too tired for it. "Honestly?" I ask, and she nods. "I've never wanted to touch you more in my life than I do right now, but this feels like a sudden change of heart."

"Do you need a personal invitation?"

She's teasing again, trying to get us back on more familiar ground, but I'm not going to take the bait. "Right now, yeah. I do. I want to do what's best for us, Cat."

"Including going back to New York?"

I study her in the dim light. It illuminates her almost-white hair with a slight halo that's mesmerizing. I thought she'd been warming up to the idea of this new life of ours this week, but maybe I've been reading her all wrong.

And, honestly, this project is not as straightforward as I had hoped. My parents are more hands-off than I expected. I anticipated the managerial work, but I did not think I would have such a heavy hand in the design. Leading this team is no walk in the park, either. I'm basically doing two jobs at once, and it's more than I bargained for. I don't want to give up just yet, but it might be easier to persuade me to go back than it was a few weeks ago.

I flip to my side so I'm facing her. Our heads lay together on the edges of our pillows, our noses about two inches apart. "Is that what you want?"

"I don't know what I want." She says it so fast, I don't think she considered the words before they tumbled out of her mouth. When her eyes widen slightly, I know she's surprised that the possibility of staying here isn't as abhorrent as it used to be.

When her eyes stay wide, something shifts in her face. She looks vulnerable, almost scared. Katie is normally so guarded, completely committed to the stoic façade she insists on keeping up. I haven't seen this particular expression since the night she told me she was pregnant with Mason. I had crawled into bed next to her, even though she had told me to leave. I could tell she was saying it to give me an out. She was terrified, so much so that she couldn't see how over the moon I was about the whole thing. I already knew that I was in love with her; it's why I banged on her door after a week of ignored calls. And I knew I wanted to be a dad long before that. I wanted to spend as much time with her as I could, and I wanted that baby in my arms. I certainly didn't care if it happened a little earlier than I had expected.

But, that night, she floated away. It was the strangest thing. She hopped from cloud of worry to cloud of worry, climbing higher and higher with each new concern. And what was stranger still was she told me everything that went through her mind. Every single thing she feared, both tiny and massive, came tumbling out as I saw her growing more and more adrift. Her eyes became glassy and focused on some point in the distance as she floated on her anxiety.

I didn't know what to do. I was twenty-four, idealistic, and stupid. All I knew is that I wanted her to stay with me, so I grabbed her hand and told her that. I said, "Stay with me, Katie. I've got both of you." And she started inching her way back to me.

Now, Katie's body might be ready, but I need to be sure her brain has caught up. So, I try to ground her in the moment, to not let her slip away again.

"Do you want to be in this bed with me?" I start small. Give her tangible things she can focus on.

Her eyes remain wide as she nods, and a piece of hair falls across her face. My fingers itch to touch it, then to drag themselves across the soft line of her jaw, over her full lips. I restrain myself, though. I need her fully here with me.

"Do you want the kids to start school on Monday?"

She huffs, starting to look a little more stable. "Fuck, yes. They need to get out of this house."

I chuckle, and she smiles. This is good. Smiling is good.

"Are you okay with them starting the semester here, in Leade Park?"

Another nod. Her eyes search mine, bouncing back and forth between them. Her eyebrows pinch together, and she almost looks pained. That must not have been something she wanted to admit.

"Do you want to paint more? Or maybe go back to work?"

"Yes, to the painting," she breathes. She sounds almost dreamy, but then her voice becomes unsteady again. "Unsure about working."

"I can't blame you for that," I mutter. "Work sucks."

I'm about to lay out everything that's been going on at the office, but I stop short when she giggles. It's so charming. She's gorgeous. I almost can't stand it.

"Do you want me to touch you?" I ask gently, though my voice is rough with emotion.

"Yeah," she breathes.

I study her for a minute, but she looks sure, so I gently brush the piece of hair over her cheek and behind her ear. I drag my fingers lightly down over her neck and collarbone, following her arm to her side and resting my hand in the curve above her hip.

Her eyes flutter closed, and a low rumble escapes from the back of her throat.

"Do you want me to kiss you?" I whisper.

Her eyes stay closed, and her lips part gently. I brush my nose against hers, and she tilts her head, angling her mouth to meet mine. I shift my body closer to hers as our lips and tongues meet. She tastes so sweet, like strawberry lip balm and toothpaste and all my hopes and dreams rolled into one.

The kiss is slow and tender. I press my palm into her side, pulling her closer to me. She slides a thigh between mine and must feel how hard I am, because she pulls away and gasps. Her eyes fly open.

"I'm sorry, Cat. I want you. Badly. But if you're not there yet—"

"I'm not," she cuts me off. "It's not that I don't want you, too. I do. I just…" She trails off, then her breathing starts to quicken like it always does just before she starts crying. I pull her into me as I flip on my back. I curl my arm around her shoulders and tuck her into my side, holding her close to me.

I kiss the top of her head, then I feel a tear land on my chest. She gently traces a finger over my tattoo. My heart aches just under where her finger loops in circles.

"I know it's my fault." Her voice is barely audible. She tenses beneath my touch.

"What's your fault?" I stroke her hair.

She sniffles, and another few teardrops hit my chest. "All of it. Don't get me wrong, you shouldn't have made this decision without me. But I think I know why you did, and it's because of me. Because I can't keep my shit together."

This is as close as she's ever gotten to talking to me about that night after the fundraiser, and I want to tread lightly. "Baby, you have your shit together more than anyone I know aside from my parents, and no one wants to be as boring as them," I assure her.

She sniffles again and wipes her eyes with the heel of her hand. "You know what I mean."

I do know what she means. I squeeze her even tighter. "It was my fault, though." My voice is almost a whisper.

"How so?" She nuzzles her head deeper into my chest, and I hope she can't hear my heart racing.

"If I had been around more like you asked, you probably wouldn't have drank that night."

She doesn't hesitate. "What? No." She turns her head so her chin is on my chest to look at me in the silvery light coming through the slits of the curtains. Her eyes are bright with unshed tears. "You don't get to take responsibility for my actions."

"Okay, then you don't get to take responsibility for mine." I look pointedly at her. "I chose to take this job. I chose to move us out here without telling you right away. I love you beyond reason, Katie, but there was more at play than one mistake you made one night."

"It feels like what I did was bigger than just a mistake."

"Of course it does. But it was a blip on your radar in the grand scheme of things."

"Did it factor into your decision to move us out here?"

She's not accusing. She's simply asking a question, and I want to answer honestly, so I nod.

Her face falls, and her eyes dip down, falling unfocused on my chest. "So, it is my fault, then. Our whole life changed because I made a bad choice."

I sit up, pulling her with me. She crosses her legs underneath herself and clasps her hands in her lap, looking down at them. I place my palms on either side of her face and tilt her head up until she's focused on me.

"It wasn't one night of drinking, Katie. It was everything that led up to it. I left you alone in a city full of people you didn't feel connected to. I convinced you to join that fundraising committee, knowing full well those people weren't your type. But I did it so I wouldn't feel bad about hustling even more at work. And, all the while, I was missing our kids growing up. I didn't want that life anymore, and I know you didn't either, because if you had been happy…" I trail off. I don't need to keep rehashing her drinking. I'm sure she's done it enough herself. "It wasn't anyone's *fault*, Cat. I was watching our life get away from us. I wanted to do something about it." When she doesn't immediately respond, I continue. "I'm not asking you to be glad about leaving New York. I'm asking that you give us a chance to be happy."

A tear snakes its way down her cheek, then another and another. They fall over my hands, and I kiss them, one by one, until she laughs darkly. "Okay, stop." She pulls away from me, chuckling. I drop my hands to her legs, running my hands up and down her gorgeous thighs.

"I don't think sex is on the table yet," she looks pointedly at my roaming hands. "I have too much to figure out, and I don't want it to be all muddled with that. But…" she trails off, then her eyes meet mine. "Truce? Maybe I can… I don't know… stop being so angry at you, and we can stop being so angry at ourselves?"

A wide grin stretches across my face. "That sounds excellent."

"And, maybe tomorrow, you can come back to our bed?" She raises her eyebrows hopefully.

"Why not tonight?" I don't care anymore if I sound over-eager. Now we're getting somewhere.

She, however, slides back down between the covers and tugs my arm until I'm lying next to her again. "Because I'm tired and lazy." She drapes an arm around my torso and rests her head in the crook where my arm meets my shoulder. "And I'm finally warm, so I don't want to leave."

I slide my arm under her neck and around her shoulders, squeezing tight. "I'm here for whatever you want, Cat."

Chapter 12

Katie

THE NEXT NIGHT, BRANDON moves back into our room. He's a perfect gentleman, like he always is, but I can see the unbridled desire in his eyes. I know it's only a matter of time before we go back to the way things were before. We were never that couple that had sex every day or anything, but I like to think our track record was higher than the average parents of small children. Especially after I got my IUD a few years ago. That thing is a godsend.

It's not that I don't like the sex we have. I do. I'm desperate for it, if I'm being honest with myself. But there's something about sex with Brandon that scrambles my brain and leaves me buzzing in the most delicious way. Which sounds great on the surface, but it has always made me make dumb decisions without concern for the consequences. Like "forgetting" the condom somewhere in that first week he spent in my bed. That was pre-IUD, obviously.

I think it's clear I need to figure some shit out right now, so I'm not taking any chances.

By the time Monday rolls around, Brandon has been in my bed—our bed, I suppose—for two nights, and I'm already sleeping better. I'm sleeping like a rock, actually, when his alarm goes off Monday morning.

"It was nice not having that to wake up to," I mumble as he shuts it off.

I'm not facing him, and I'm trying to burrow into my pillow, but he pops up over my shoulder and presses a kiss to my cheek. His beard scrapes against my skin with a perfect coarseness that spreads warm tingles all over my body. I shift to my back so he's hovering above me, and he doesn't waste any time moving his lips to mine. I snake my hand up his chest and over his shoulder, settling it into his hair.

God, I love his hair. It was the first thing I noticed about him. I prayed that one of our kids would end up a redhead, but no such luck. But more than just being a beautiful terra-cotta color, it's thick and soft and glides between my fingers.

His hand snakes up my thigh and under the threadbare tank top I wore to bed. It pauses on my hip, but I can't help myself. I pull his head closer to mine, deepening the kiss. I press my chest up into his so my breasts graze him. He moans into my mouth, and I swallow it. Our tongues tease each other back and forth.

He pulls away, but not too far. Our noses touch briefly before he backs away so he can see my face.

"Katie," he warns. "I'm trying here, but you're making this very difficult."

A corner of my mouth ticks up. "It's not easy for me, either, you know. Especially with you... here."

"You're the one who made the rule."

"Yeah, well, I don't know why you listen to me." I angle my head so I can catch his bottom lip between my teeth. I gently tug.

"I listen to you," he says between kisses, "because if I didn't, you'd be mad at me. And yourself. Again."

"You're right," I breathe into him, pressing kisses along his neck and shoulder. "But I'm having a very hard time giving a shit about that right now."

"Same," he says on a moan. Then, he pulls away to look at me again. "You say the word, Cat, and I will worship your body the way it's meant to be worshiped. You're a goddess, Katie, and I'm your devoted follower."

I laugh-groan, partly delighted and partly embarrassed. The comment references an old joke from a visit to the Met. I was feeling down about my body, but he stood me in front of a statue of a woman, naked in all her glory, her ample hips and breasts on full display. "That one," he had said. "You're a goddess, just like her."

Brandon huffs in a mix of nostalgia and frustration. "But as much as I *want* you, I *need* it to be right for you." He presses a chaste kiss to my nose. "I love you, Katie."

That's it. That's all it takes for tears to prick my eyes.

Why do I keep crying? I'm such a fucking mess.

I take a deep breath, then let it out. Mercifully, the tears don't fall before I roll out from underneath him. Just in time, too, because the door to our bedroom bursts open, and Mason comes barreling in, shouting.

"It's my first day of school!" He punches the air in excitement.

"Keep it down. You'll wake your sister," I hiss.

He just grins at me, practically bouncing on his toes, and that's when I notice he's already fully dressed in a t-shirt featuring his latest favorite superhero and ripped jeans.

Brandon must notice it at the same time, because he smirks. "Excited to wear something other than a uniform, bud?" He gets out of bed and walks past Mason to the bathroom, mussing up his hair on the way.

"Dad, don't! I just did my hair," he whines.

Brandon tilts his head, squinting at Mason. "Huh. Doesn't look like it."

"Well yeah, not anymore," he grumbles as he makes his way back to his own bathroom, presumably to fix whatever Brandon undid.

I half-make the bed and follow Brandon into our bathroom. "He's excited," I note, catching Brandon's reflection in the mirror. He puts his toothbrush in his mouth and winks at me. He brushes while I use the toilet in a little side room, then join him at the sink next to his. Our apartment in New York was nice, but I don't know if I'll ever get over the size of this bathroom.

Brandon spits out his toothpaste and rinses his mouth, then splashes water on his face. "I think you're excited, too. I can't remember the last time you were out of bed before Christine."

I give him the side-eye while squeezing toothpaste onto my tooth-brush. "I'm always out of bed before Christine when they have school."

Brandon tilts his head back and forth. "But that's because you had to drop them off. You don't budge from that bed when you don't have anything to do in the morning."

I pause with the toothbrush almost to my mouth. "Right. It's almost like I have to drop them off at school today or something," I say sarcas-tically as I start to brush.

Brandon frowns at me. "Pretty sure I said I'd do drop off from now on."

I brush for a while, then spit in the sink. "Oh, you meant that?" I put my toothbrush down on the counter.

He comes behind me, bending down to wind his arm around my torso. I lean my head back against his chest and look at us in the mirror.

We don't look like we fit together—he's so tall and I'm so short. He has his hipster man bun and beard, while I have an edgy haircut and hair that has been bleached so many times, I'm probably the only one who remembers what color it was originally. He doesn't spend much time at the gym, but his dad bod still has some edges, whereas I'm curvy and soft. He carries himself like someone who has never had to worry about money a day in his life. I was barely making rent on my studio apartment until I met him, and I still pour over our bank statements every month until he reminds me that we actually pay someone else to do that for us.

He's never cared about any of our differences, even though it still nags at me occasionally. It took him the better part of the year after we met, as my belly was growing rounder and rounder, to convince me that I could fit into his life. That *we* could fit into his life. His parents, of course, weren't as convinced as he was, but I think they were just so glad he wasn't in and out of rehab like his older brother that they were willing to let this transgression slide. Provided I could behave myself at their fancy parties, of course. They were even happier when we made it official. And legal.

He presses a kiss to my temple, watching himself in the mirror as he does it. "Where did you go?" he whispers in my ear.

"We're so different." I lean further into him.

He smiles indulgently, like he's thinking, *This again?* "Not that different." Another kiss. "Aside from you being grouchy as hell while I'm an absolute ray of light." He moves to kiss me again, but I swat his bicep and try to break away. His hold on me tightens, and I giggle.

"I am *not* grouchy," I insist, laughing and still trying to break free of his hold.

"You are the very definition of grouchy," he insists, puckering his lips and trying to plant more kisses on my cheek. "If I looked up 'grouchy' in the dictionary, there'd be a picture of you."

Finally, he releases me, and I spin around to face him, my face twisted into a frown. "I am not. I'm a delight," I insist.

He laughs deeply, and the sound lodges itself in my chest and spreads its warmth out into my limbs. "You are a delight," he agrees. "But look at your face." He turns me to the mirror, where I can fully see what he's talking about. I'm frowning so deeply, I'm probably etching new lines in my skin. But I can't help deepening the glare as he grins over my shoulder.

He leans closer to my ear and whispers, "That's a grouchy face."

I swat at him again, but he dodges out of my reach. "Dammit. Go get dressed or something."

He moves to the closet, but chuckles to himself the whole way, shaking his head and muttering something about Grouchy Katie, and I pray this isn't going to become a stupid new nickname.

I go out in the hall with the intention of gently waking Christine up, but Mason runs past me, bursts through her door, and yells, "School today! Get up, Chrissy!"

She bolts up in her bed, her eyes wide, and her blonde hair standing on end. When she sees us, she lets out a belated wail. I glare at Mason, who has the good sense to cower and slink backwards out of the room.

I go over to Christine's bed, sitting on the edge of the pink satin comforter. I pull her onto my lap, and she buries her head in my chest, still crying, but calming a bit.

"I know, baby. Mason scared you, didn't he?"

"Mason's a jerk," she says vehemently.

I pull her little face away from me and look into her green eyes. So much like Brandon's, those eyes.

I hold her cheeks between my palms. "Who taught you that word?"

Her tears stop on a dime, and she grins impishly at me. "Mommy's a jerk."

"Excuse me?" I use my best mom voice.

Brandon comes in, somehow already dressed for work in a thin, blue sweater and gray slacks. He picks her up and throws her over his shoulder. She giggles wildly. "Daddy's a jerk!" she yells.

He carries her out into the hallway, and I follow, leaning on her door frame with my arms folded. He sets her down in front of Mason, then takes a knee beside both of them.

"Mason." His tone is full of warning, though he's such a teddy bear it's hard to take him seriously. "Did you teach your sister to call people jerks?"

Mason, already sufficiently scolded once this morning, looks to me for help. I shake my head, and he turns back to Brandon, shrugging. "She could have learned it anywhere. Kids grow up way too fast these days."

Brandon's back is to me, but the twitch in his shoulders tells me he's trying to stifle a laugh. Mason's too old to miss it now, and he smirks. Then, he looks at me over Brandon's shoulder and schools his face into seriousness. I'm not one to break easily.

"I'm sorry, Dad," he says solemnly, then he puts a hand on Christine's shoulder. "Chrissy-pie, we don't say 'jerk,' okay?"

She smiles with glee. "Jerk, jerk, jerk! Jerk, jerk, jerk!" Her little head bobs back and forth each time she says it.

Brandon stands, pinching the bridge of his nose. He looks to me for what to do next. Of course he does, because that stern talk to Mason is the limit of the parenting he's been able to do for a long time.

I sigh. "Ignore it." I glare pointedly at Mason. "She's looking for a reaction. Don't give it to her."

"Yep," Brandon says, as if this was also his assessment. I bite back a retort as he grabs Christine and throws her over his shoulder again. "Okay, squirt. Time to get dressed."

Brandon takes a squealing Christine into her room, and I hastily throw on my ripped jeans and an old sweatshirt before ushering Mason into the kitchen to eat breakfast and pack his lunch.

Somehow, everyone gets out of the house in a relatively timely fashion without too much drama. They're excited enough to rush out, and I can't help but think Brandon didn't get the full drop-off experience with missing shoes, messy backpacks, a last-minute request from school Mason forgot to tell us about the night before, and a resistant toddler. I'm sure all that's coming. I guess this is a good warm up.

My inner monologue sounds skeptical, and maybe it is. He seems willing to follow through on the promises he's making to come home in time for dinner, to drop the kids off at school, to give me more time to myself. But it's only a matter of time before the honeymoon is over. The kids will get antsy, Brandon will start spending more and more time at the office, and I'll be right back where I started.

Well, not *where* I started. I started in New York.

I pour myself a mug of coffee and entwine my hands around it, warming them. I sit at the island, looking toward my studio door. I have to admit, things feel different between Brandon and me. Different, even, than they were before all of this started. And it's more than just him framing my painting, or setting up the studio for me, or coming home on time. It's almost like he's happier, too. Like we're enough for him. Like *I'm* enough for him. He doesn't want to keep chasing and hustling. He wants to be here.

I'm probably an asshole for thinking it, but I wonder if it's enough for *me.* The bustle and noise of the city, the fancy fundraisers and parties, even the acquaintances I didn't like very much, didn't make me happy, but they filled the time. It all made me feel like I had some purpose. I still don't know what my purpose here is. I know my family should be enough. Everyone tells you it should be, anyway. But I don't know if it is. It hasn't been for years now. Brandon has his work. I want something more, too.

I suppose I'm not going to figure this out today, though, so I take my coffee into the studio where I sit on my stool in the middle of the room and survey everything I sketched out over the weekend. Rough drawings line the walls. Brandon and the kids making pizza. Brandon reading them bedtime stories. Brandon ice skating with them in Rockefeller Plaza. And, of course, the first one I did back in the city of Brandon and the kids at the pumpkin patch. But also, Brandon the way he was the other night when I came into the guest room, shirt off and hair a little messy, looking at me like he wanted to bear hug me and devour me in equal measure.

I frown at that one. "One of these things is not like the other..." I intone, then chuckle. I knew that one would be out of place, but I sketched it anyway. I couldn't help it.

There's a story here, though, of a man who loves his family. Of kids who worship their dad. I sip my coffee and study them more, the little bud of an idea that started in the school office growing roots in my brain.

Before that thought can fully take shape, my phone buzzes a few times in rapid succession. I don't reach for it right away because I know that rhythm well. Brandon has bad news for me. Not bad enough for a phone call, but bad enough that he's trying to break it to me in pieces. I decide to finish my coffee before I have to deal with it.

It must not be too bad, because my phone only buzzes five times while I'm sipping.

Brandon:

So. Don't hate me.

My parents want to come for dinner tonight.

But it won't be that bad. They can occupy the kids.

You don't have to do anything special. Seriously. I'll grab meat and veggies on the way home. I'll take care of it.

Mom wants to bake cookies with the kids for dessert? So at least there will be entertainment for us, too.

I snort. Maria Conley is not the cookie-baking type to say the least, which means it'll be more work for me to keep both her and the kids from shedding tears. But I decide to take Brandon at his word about dinner. Normally, I'd immediately start cleaning and making some elaborate and impressive meal, but he's clearly trying here. It's not like he doesn't know his way around the kitchen. He just hasn't been home in time to showcase his cooking skills in a while.

I'm sure his mother will have a few jabs for me. She always does. But, if Brandon is taking care of everything else, maybe this will be tolerable.

I type back: *Okay.*

He sends: *Sorry about this.*

I frown, typing: *No worries. This is partly why we moved here, right?*

The three dots appear at the bottom of the screen, then disappear and reappear two more times. I raise an eyebrow, and my foot starts tapping against the bottom rung of my stool while I wait.

You're amazing, Cat.

I blink at the message, reading it over and over. I respond quickly with a kissy-face emoji, then lock my phone. But I think about that message all day. And every time, I smile.

Chapter 13
Brandon

MY MOTHER ACCOSTS ME immediately after I walk into my office. She does not suggest we should have dinner tonight; she demands it. I don't even have my coat off yet when she swoops in talking about seeing the house and her grandchildren. And cookies. There's so much talk of cookies, I'm wondering how long it has been since she's had a carbohydrate.

"Your kids are getting older," she explains. "I'm getting older. It's something grandmas should do with their grandchildren. And we all know Katie isn't baking cookies with them."

I dip my chin to give her a warning look. "Mom," I say sternly.

She looks at me pointedly. "Is she?"

"Not the point."

My dad swings his arm around her shoulders. "Generally, when you're trying to be invited to someone's house, you avoid insulting the hostess."

Mom looks indignant. "She's not the hostess. She's my daughter-in-law."

"That doesn't make it better." I scrape a hand down my jaw.

"Whatever. I want to spend time with my only grandbabies now that you're settled in. I haven't seen them in so long." Her addition of "only" is another jab, this time at my brother, but we all let that one slide.

I can't keep them away forever, and Katie has seemed to be in a good mood these past few days. My mom is who she is, but Katie can generally tolerate the backhanded comments when she's happy. Now might be as good a time as any to have them over.

"Okay." I sound more resigned than I mean to. "I'll text Katie."

My parents leave my office in an excited flourish, and I fire off several texts about the situation, trying to break the news into bite-sized pieces to make it all easier to swallow.

I wait for what feels like forever for her to text me back. I'm able to fire up my computer and respond to a few emails before her text comes through. I brace myself before looking at it, expecting the worst.

Okay.

That's it. That's all it says. Either she's pissed, or she's in a better mood than I thought. Assuming the former, I send another apology text, but she responds, *No worries. This is partly why we moved here, right?*

Well, that's not what I was expecting. She's never this laid back about a visit from my parents. Maybe this new situation is starting to relax her a little. I smile at the thought. This is truly what I wanted for her with this move. I wanted her to find some peace, maybe a group of people she could connect with on a deeper level than what she had in New York. I wanted her to find herself again.

A nagging little thought knocks on my brain. When we met, she was like this. Carefree and laid back. But when we met, she was relying on alcohol to make her that way. What if...

No. I shut the door on that thought immediately. That's not Katie anymore.

I start to type a message about how cool she's being, maybe hinting at this change in her. Then I delete it and start again a few times, but all of it feels like the way my mother might passively hint at something she wants to talk about but won't do it outright. So, I finally just send, *You're amazing, Cat.* Because she is, and that's what she needs to hear right now.

She sends back a kiss emoji, which makes me chuckle. It feels like we're more solid than we have been in months, and I'm so glad I didn't send any of those earlier messages. Katie is fine. We're fine.

But that's the last piece of good news I get all day. Thalia is having trouble finding a good time to meet with the teachers. Jasper comes in about a minute before I'm about to break for lunch with an update about the junior architects who, in his estimation, are slacking. I try to brainstorm a few sketches of what these "educational spaces" might look like even though I'm not supposed to be designing. I'm doing my best with it, but it has been so long since I've been in a high school. And when I was, it was a stodgy private school where the most cutting-edge learning material was a collection of works by Alice Walker our librarian purchased which caused a subsequent uproar amongst the parents. I'm having trouble thinking of what these spaces should look like, to say the least.

Toward the end of the day, I almost beat my parents out the door so I can stop by the grocery store to grab food to make for dinner when the junior architects, Orlando and Marianne, come off the elevator giggling. Jasper shoots me a pointed look from across the room, then looks at his watch. I hadn't realized they hadn't come back from lunch. So, I pull them into my office to deal with that, which puts me well behind my original schedule.

My parents beat me to the house, because of course they do. Not only that, but my mom insists on baking cookies before dinner so they're ready for dessert. When I finally get home, it looks like a cookie dough bomb went off in the kitchen. Katie's face is slightly redder than it should be, which tells me my mom probably said something backhanded two seconds before I walked in. My dad is sitting at the kitchen table, holding a soda and probably wishing it were a beer, watching it all. His eyes are wide and his knuckles where they grip the glass are white. He seems to be the only thing in the kitchen not covered in cookie dough.

"Hi, honey," Katie says through gritted teeth as soon as I walk through the door.

That's less than ideal. She only ever calls me "honey" when she's pissed.

I drop the grocery bags on the floor next to the stove, since every available counter space is either covered in cookie dough or trays of cookies that are waiting for the oven. I kiss Katie on the cheek. She's holding her dough-covered hands out in front of her, trying not to touch anything. I, however, have to resist the urge to lick the dough off her fingers.

Cool it, Conley, I chastise myself. *This is a disaster.*

"I got hamburgers," I announce.

Dad perks up, but Mom wrinkles her nose. "Hamburgers?" she asks.

"Best I could do on short notice." I smile pointedly. She's not the only one who can be passive-aggressive.

"Your mom loves hamburgers. Don't you, Maria?" Dad asks deliberately. Mom shrugs, which is probably the best I'll get from her.

"I. Don't. Want. *Hamburgers,*" Christine wails, each word punctuated to a crescendo. "I. Want. *Cookies.*"

"We'll have cookies after dinner, sweetie," I say gently.

"No! Cookies *now*!" she insists.

"They're not even baked yet," I point out.

Katie presses her eyes closed and lets out a slow breath. "It's no use reasoning with a toddler."

I take a mental step back and reassess. Christine is five seconds from falling apart. Katie might follow her from the look on her face. Mason is trying to wash his sticky hands in the sink. My mom is puzzling over the thermometer on the oven. My dad is sitting unhelpfully off to the side, as usual.

Time for damage control. Step one: deal with the toddler. "Okay, Christine," I say. "You can have cookies as soon as they're done, but you have to wash up first." I note the cookie dough sticking to patches of her blonde hair. Step two: get Katie out of here for a few minutes. "Katie, why don't you take Christine upstairs for a quick bath?"

Katie shoots me a grateful look as she lifts Christine from her underarms and swoops her to the bathroom upstairs. I give myself a moment to celebrate that success. Then, I clap my hands once. "Mom, Katie, and Christine baked, so Dad, Mason, and I will clean up the kitchen."

"I baked, too," Mason protests.

"Yeah, but this is a disaster. Grab a rag, buddy."

He does, albeit begrudgingly. My dad also springs into action as my mom pops two trays of cookies into the oven, then starts washing her hands and arms like a doctor prepping for surgery.

By the time Katie returns with a rosy Christine, the kitchen is clean, the grill pan is heating up, and I'm mixing ground beef and seasoning into burger patties. My parents are playing a card game with Mason that he invented with ever-changing and wildly unclear rules, and the first set of cookies are about ready to come out of the oven.

I catch Katie's eyes over Christine's damp hair. She gives me a half-smile before planting a kiss on Christine's head. They both look more relaxed, too. Katies shoulders aren't riding up to her ears, and Christine has her thumb in her mouth and her head is buried into Katie's chest.

If I could paint, this is the scene I'd want to capture. My two girls, all rosy cheeks and smooth skin, tucked into each other and at ease.

Christine abruptly tries to wriggle out of Katie's grasp. "Gamma! I sit with Gamma." She marches over to my mom, who scoops her up off the floor.

"Oh, come here you little angel," Mom coos. And, dammit, that's pretty cute, too.

The buzzer on the oven goes off. Katie puts on an oven mitt and takes the cookies out, then slides two more trays in. I come up next to her with burger patties and toss them on the pan.

"You okay?" I ask under my breath.

"Yeah." Her voice is terse.

"Sorry I was late," I offer.

She glances sidelong at me and shakes her head almost imperceptibly. We're not talking about that now, then. I know better than to push it.

"Mason," I call as I flip a burger. "Did you show Grandma and Grandpa around the house?"

"He sure did," my dad answers for him. I hate when they answer for the kids as if they can't speak for themselves, but Mason puffs up with pride.

"And how was your first day at school?" I flip the other burgers as I talk. Katie leans back against the counter, her arms wrapped around her torso, watching the scene. I also hate how she tends to feel like an outsider looking in on this family time with my parents, but I understand. She's always felt like my family is from a totally different world.

"It was awesome. Brody is in my class, and the teacher let us sit next to each other because I'm new. And we read a book about sea turtles. Did you know turtles don't have teeth?"

I chuckle, flattening the burger patties with my spatula. "I don't think I did know that."

"Oh, I bet you did." Mom bounces a giggling Christine on her knee. Then, she addresses Mason. "Your father had a turtle phase."

"What's a phase?" Mason asks.

"He was obsessed with turtles. Had turtle posters and stuffed animals everywhere. He wrote Grandpa and me a persuasive letter to ask us to let him get a turtle as a pet," Mom elaborates.

Mason's eyes are wide. "Did you let him?"

Mom shudders. "No. Turtles are creepy."

Katie huffs, and I look over to catch her fighting a smile.

"What?" Mason exclaims. "How are they creepy?"

"They hide their whole bodies in those shells. How do they do that? It's weird," Mom insists.

Mason scrunches up his face as if that's the silliest thing he's ever heard, then turns to Katie.

"Don't even think about it," Katie jumps in before he can ask.

"You don't even know what I was going to say!" Mason protests.

I chuckle. "You were going to ask for a turtle."

Mason harumphs. I take the burgers off the pan and add a few more patties. Mason perks up. "But, Dad, you always wanted one and never could have one. You could live out your childhood dreams!"

I make a show of considering the offer while Katie eyes me warily. "Hmm. Tempting, but no."

I put plates, burgers, buns, and condiments on the island before telling everyone dinner is ready and to serve themselves. My parents look a little put off by the buffet-style eating, but Katie jumps right in to help Christine make up a plate of food she'll probably just push around. She gets the kids settled at the dining room table, then serves herself.

Frankly the whole dinner is nice, which is unexpected. It's cozy and filling. My parents mostly focus on the kids, and Katie relaxes even further as we eat.

Once we've all had our fill, Katie announces that it's a school night and ushers the kids up to bed. My parents take the hint and leave earlier than they would normally, and I'm left thinking this whole evening was a success despite the rough start.

Katie comes down the stairs and flops on the couch. I finish cleaning up the kitchen, then move her legs so I can sit and rest her feet on my lap. She opens one eye to glare at me.

"You left me alone with your mother," she says tersely.

"I'm sorry. My team—"

"You were the one who set this up, and then you were late," she cuts me off.

I guess the evening wasn't as great for everyone as I thought. Sighing, I rub the bottom of her feet with my thumbs. "I know. I'm sorry. It won't happen again."

She opens both eyes and rolls her head to the side, staring at something in the distance. She's silent for a minute, then lets out a harsh breath through her nose. She doesn't look at me as she says, "You know, I was hopeful for a few days there that you'd really be home on time, every day,

from now on." She pauses and still avoids at me. "It just makes me so...
sad." She says it so softly, and her expression pierces my heart. It's one of
defeat, but it's also guarded. Like she let herself hope one too many times
and won't let herself do it again.

It was just one night, but I can't blame her for thinking I'm falling into
old patterns. I slide out from under her feet and sit on the ground so we
are eye-level. "I'm trying, Katie. I hope you can see that. I wish I could
be perfect for you. I want more than anything to be here for you and the
kids." I hope she can tell I'm being sincere.

It must work, because her expression softens. "You invited them, then
didn't show. They thought you had left the office right after them. You
didn't call or anything."

I didn't even think to call. I never called before, but I suppose that's
when coming home late was the norm.

I kiss her forehead. She doesn't pull away, which is a good sign. I return
to the couch. "I really am sorry, Cat. I'm..." I trail off. "It's been a lot. I'm
doing a lot more designing than I should, given I have a team. My parents
are constantly warning me not to fuck up. It's not what I thought it was
going to be."

"I suppose we have that in common." It's a jab, but there's not a lot
of teeth to it. If anything, she still sounds defeated.

Her phone buzzes from where she tossed on the table. She grabs it and
reads something, frowning.

She narrows her eyes, looking at me. "Did you give Mac my number?"

"I imagine Daniel gave Mac your number. Why?"

"She just invited me to some..." she trails off, checking her messages
again. "Pasta night? On Friday with her and Jenny."

The other day, I overheard her therapist suggest she meet more people. This would be a good start. "You should go," I suggest as casually as I can.

She groans. "If I had known moving out here was going to be a revolving door of dinner parties, I would have rethought our arrangement."

"So grouchy," I tease.

If looks could kill, I'd be a dead man. "Do you really want to start about my mood after that dinner?"

"It was nice," I insist.

She closes her eyes again. "It was exhausting," she says on a sigh. I regard her for a moment without her knowing. I hadn't realized how low she was feeling, probably because she does such a good job of shielding herself from everyone, including me lately.

"I don't think dinner with Mac and Jenny will be exhausting," I try again.

She scrunches up her face without opening her eyes. "They're young, energetic, and childfree. That's the definition of exhausting."

"You talk like you're twenty years older than them instead of five."

"Mac's younger than Daniel, which makes her younger than you."

"Fine, six or seven."

Her eyes fly wide open. "She was *twenty-two* when Mason was *born*."

I chuckle at her revelation. "You say that as if it's a lot younger than twenty-four."

She raises an eyebrow at me. "You were young, too," she says softly, and I detect almost a tinge of regret. "Wide-eyed and idealistic and barely out of school."

I lower my eyebrows, concerned. "I wouldn't have done this any other way, Cat."

"You can't tell me this is the timeline you would have chosen for yourself." She whispers. I sit up straighter, my hands going still on her feet.

I'm completely caught off guard by her statement, and I'm not even sure how to respond. I thought I made it abundantly clear while she was pregnant that I was thrilled. I mean, sure, I didn't expect to jump on the baby train at twenty-four years old. But I love this life and this family we have.

"It worked out okay." I squeeze her feet gently. Her gaze meets mine for a second, then falls.

My phone buzzes. I consider not answering it to continue this conversation, but I don't know what else to say. I shift to pull it out of my pocket.

"Daniel wants me to meet up with him and Ben on Friday while you're with the ladies," I say. It would be nice to hang out. Part of my reason for wanting to move out here was to have more friends. I haven't seen them since they helped me set up the house, and that wasn't exactly relaxing.

Katie screws up her face, still not looking at me. "Oh. I got a pity invite so you can hang out with the guys."

What is going on here? Where did my confident wife go? Is this how she feels all the time, and she's just never said anything about it to me?

I suck in a breath. "I don't think Mac and Jenny are the type to do anything they don't want to do. In fact, knowing what I know about Mac, I'd say this was her idea, not Daniel's."

Katie considers this as she twists a lock of hair around her finger. "Maybe." She raises her eyebrows as if she's considering something, then eyes me sidelong and smirks. "Mac is pretty cute," she says playfully.

I burst out laughing. That's definitely not what I was expecting, but it's an age-old game between us. She likes to try to make me jealous. If she wants to play, I'll take the bait. I pointedly run a hand thorough my red hair. "You certainly have a type."

She hums with amusement, then her expression turns serious as she meets my gaze. "Maybe I used to. Now, it's just you."

My heart cracks in my chest. I want to scoop her up and hold her close, but she breaks the moment by looking away.

"Nora suggested I expand my social circle at my last appointment. I guess this wouldn't be a terrible place to start," she muses.

"See? You should go." I start rubbing her feet again.

She sighs in contentment. "What about the kids?"

"This is why we moved closer to my parents, remember?"

She's silent for another moment, chewing on the inside of her lip. "Okay," she says finally. "If your parents can watch them, I'll go."

I don't expect relief to flood me, but it does. I can't help but hope that she can build some real friendships here, starting with pasta night.

Chapter 14
Katie

ON WEDNESDAY, BRANDON IS so late that he completely misses the kids' bedtime, which is a new low. At one point, in the middle of mediating a screaming match between the kids and then talking about our feelings afterward, I think wistfully back to the days when I could have had a glass of wine and settled in with a good movie. I'm so angry that by the time the kids are in bed, I leave Brandon's dinner in the fridge and a note on the counter. I tuck myself in, hoping he'll get the hint that he should try the guest room tonight.

He doesn't get the hint. He comes in and quietly undresses, then slips carefully under the covers while I pretend to be asleep. His breathing steadies, and just when I think he's fallen asleep, he sighs heavily.

"I'm so sorry," he whispers.

He doesn't just sound sorry. He sounds *devastated*, like it doesn't even matter how upset I am. He's already crushed himself far more than my disappointment ever could.

My breath catches at his tone, but I don't say anything. I'm sure he falls asleep, but I lie awake much longer, my head spinning. My emotions are playing a tug-of-war between anger and compassion. I drift off to sleep before I can decide which one wins.

On Friday night, I pull up to Jenny and Ben's house at seven. There's a black sedan parked on the street outside, and I assume it's Mac's car. It would figure they're both here already. They're the best friends, and I'm being allowed to tag along because Daniel wanted to hang out with Brandon and didn't want to feel bad about it. I don't care what Brandon said; this has to be a pity invite.

I sit in my car for an extra minute, taking a deep breath and letting it out slowly. Things have been better, but still not great. It's not Mac and Jenny's fault I'm sad and lonely in this soft suburb. It's Brandon's, and I shouldn't project my anger at him onto these women who are just trying to help. And I did genuinely like them the last time we were here.

I look over at the chocolate chip cookies sitting on the passenger seat. We made so many of them with Maria that I had to get the rest of them out of the house, so I brought them to share. In my youth, I would have brought a bottle of tequila or gin to take the edge off the sure-to-be awkward social situation instead.

I sigh. It's disconcerting how many times I have thought about alcohol in the past month. It doesn't make me feel great about myself, truth be told.

No sense in dwelling on it in Jenny's driveway. Chocolate chips will have to do. I grab the plate and get out of the car, walking slowly up to the door and ringing the bell. As the door opens, I'm greeted by Mac instead of Jenny, and I'm struck by a pang of jealousy. I've never had a friend I've been close enough with to answer their door for them. It's such a strange thing to be envious of that it catches me off guard.

"Hey," Mac greets me, pulling the door open wider. "Come on in. Jenny is just—" She's cut off by a crash from the second floor. She glances toward the ceiling. "You okay up there?" she shouts as I step past her into the house.

"Yeah, sorry!" Jenny's call comes just before a series of muffled curses.

Mac shakes her head in the way of the long suffering as she closes the door behind me. "Jenny is changing upstairs. She should be down in a minute. Or ten. Anyway, welcome to her house. I can take those from you if you want." She indicates the plate of cookies, which she relieves me of as she heads toward what I presume is the kitchen. I notice she's not wearing any shoes, so I kick mine off along with my coat and follow her.

Ben is sitting at the kitchen table, and when he sees me, he smiles broadly. "Hi, Katie. It's good to see you."

"Hi," I say skeptically. I'm pretty sure Brandon said Ben would be hanging out with him and Daniel. But, maybe he's like me—the outsider amongst two childhood best friends.

As if reading my mind, he responds, "I'm leaving in a minute. Jenny requested I make my famous pasta sauce for you ladies, so I'm just waiting for it to simmer."

"I can take it from here if you want," Mac offers.

Ben raises his eyebrows at her as he moves to the stove and starts stirring what I assume is the sauce. "I was also tasked with ensuring the house doesn't burn down."

Mac narrows her eyes in frustration. "That was one time, and it wasn't even me. Daniel is the one who can't cook."

"How do I know his culinary ineptitude hasn't rubbed off on you? What's his is yours and all that," he teases.

"You don't forget how to cook just because you get married to some-one who sets off fire alarms in the kitchen," Mac insists as Jenny floats in. She wraps her arms around Ben's torso and pushes herself up onto her toes to kiss his cheek.

"I've got it now." She takes the spoon from his hand. "You can get out of here if you want."

Ben checks his watch and smirks at Mac. "Well, you might not become a worse cook because your husband is incapable, but I'm becoming someone who is always late because of this one over here." He tilts his head to indicate Jenny, who shrugs.

"Stop yapping and leave, then," she jokes, setting the spoon on a rest next to the stove. He grabs her waist and spins her suddenly toward him. She lets out a small yelp just before his lips meet hers. I look away in deference to them, but my gaze lands on Mac. She's still staring right at them, a goofy smile on her face. It's a stark reminder that these three know each other well, too. They've all been teaching together for almost a decade.

Ben pulls away, and Jenny swats at his bicep. "Go. You wouldn't want to keep the boys waiting."

"Have a nice time." Ben tips a fake cowboy hat at the three of us in turn. "Save me some meatballs." He grabs his wallet and phone off the counter and waves at us as he leaves.

As soon as we hear the door close behind him, Mac plops into a chair at the kitchen table. "I do not plan on leaving him any meatballs," she says to no one in particular as she grabs a cookie off the plate and takes a huge bite.

"Absolutely not," Jenny responds, opening the oven to check the food. Apparently satisfied, she closes the oven door and slides into another one of the chairs, also grabbing a cookie and taking a bite. They both turn to me at the same time, and Jenny waves to another chair. "Do you want to have a seat?"

It suddenly occurs to me that I've been standing in the middle of the kitchen, awkwardly watching this entire exchange, and I feel like a complete idiot. I try not to scowl at my acute awareness of how out of place I am as I lower myself into one of the two remaining chairs.

"Cookie?" Mac tilts the plate to me.

I raise an eyebrow at her. "Those were meant for after dinner," I say tentatively.

She purses her lips against a smile. "What a mom thing to say," she says. I bristle a little, but there's no malice in it. A corner of her mouth is turned up and the corners of her eyes are crinkled playfully.

"Yeah," Jenny smirks. "Live a little."

I feel like this is some kind of challenge. I glance between the two of them, each now chewing on a cookie. I shrug, grab one, and take a bite.

Mac and Jenny both smile perfect, beautiful smiles, but it's contagious. I smile, too, then glance around the kitchen.

"No wine tonight?" I ask. The last time I was with them, they were both clutching glasses of wine as if that was the sole thing between them and a breakdown.

Mac shakes her head. "We're cutting back," she says noncommittally.

"Not on my account, I hope." I raise an eyebrow.

Mac looks at Jenny, who shrugs. "You don't drink, so we're not drinking." She says it so simply, as if it's the easiest thing in the world to defer to me.

"I can handle having it around. It wasn't a problem last time," I point out.

Jenny shrugs again. "We don't need wine to have a good time."

I narrow my eyes and look back and forth between the two women. Mac lets out a puff of air. "We figured you'd feel enough like a third wheel without us drinking on top of it."

"There it is," I mutter, leaning my elbows on the table.

"Are we wrong?" She gives me a pointed look I imagine she uses often in her classroom. "You've been stiff since you walked in the door."

I scowl at her even as I roll my shoulders slightly to release some tension. "You're not, but that's not your fault. It's Brandon's. I know Daniel wanted to hang out with him tonight without making me feel left out. I wasn't born yesterday." It comes out a lot poutier than I wanted, which isn't helped by the fact that I'm more or less folding my arms in front of me on the table like a toddler. I stand by it, nonetheless.

Mac and Jenny exchange glances, then burst into raucous laughter. My eyes widen as I lean back in my chair and watch them. Jenny smacks the table, and Mac draws her arms around her torso as she leans into her giggles.

"Did I miss something?" I ask, my eyebrows pinched.

They keep laughing, and Mac dabs the corners of her eyes with a knuckle.

"What's so funny?" I try again, the corners of my mouth turning down.

"It's hilarious that you think Evans has that much pull over us," Jenny chokes out between her laughs.

"You think we invited you here because Daniel made us?" Mac dabs at her eyes again. She's really selling it here.

"Didn't he? I mean, didn't he at least ask you to call me?"

The laughter has died out now, but Mac's eyes are still glittering. "He did," she motions between herself and Jenny, "but we were going to, anyway. We loved hanging out with you a few months ago. We were excited you moved here, though I'm starting to think you aren't as excited about the move as Brandon is."

I wrinkle my nose. "I am not," I say simply. It doesn't feel like there's a need to add more than that until they both look at me questioningly. I sigh. "The short version is that he didn't tell me we actually came out early for your wedding so he could scope out the area. He bought the house before he even told me about it."

Mac's jaw drops slightly. Jenny leans back in her chair and folds her arms. "He bought a house without you knowing about it?" Jenny asks, and I can hear indignation tingeing her voice.

I don't need her to be angry on my behalf, but it feels good to be heard and understood. It emboldens me enough that I continue. "I'm surprised you didn't know. He tells Daniel everything—more than he tells me, apparently." I sound sour, and I am. Jenny and Mac's faces mirror my own disgust. I grab another cookie off the plate and take a bite as Jenny stands to shut off the stove.

"We knew his parents asked him to take over their Chicago firm, but we definitely thought you consented to this move." She takes the meatballs out of the oven and puts them on a potholder she throws on the counter. That must be Mac's cue because she stands and opens a cabinet to get plates down. She hands one to Jenny and one to me.

"I suppose I technically consented." I make my way over to the stove and take in a deep breath, smelling the sauce and meatballs. It all smells divine. "But I was coerced. He had already bought the house, and he more or less begged me to give it a shot. He's confident he can convince me to stay here in the next month and a half or so."

I follow Mac and Jenny as they fill up their plates with pasta, meatballs, sauce, and cheese. Neither of them are shy about how much food is on their plates; they load up, so I do, too. It's refreshing to be around two women who aren't being shy about their love of food.

There is a beautiful dining room just off the kitchen with a long dining table, but we settle back at the kitchen table for a more casual dinner, which is also refreshing. The last time I was here, Mac had pulled out all the stops for a fancy dinner party, and I'm glad I don't have to be totally "on" right now. I can just relax with cookie appetizers and a huge pile of spaghetti and meatballs for the main course.

Jenny twirls some pasta around her fork and eyes me over her plate. "I take it Brandon talking to Daniel is his way of calling in the troops. He's pulling out all the stops to get you to stay."

I slice a meatball with my fork and pop it into my mouth. It practically melts on contact, and an explosion of flavor hits my tongue. It takes a lot of effort not to moan. "Jenny, these are easily the best meatballs I've ever had."

She smiles softly at the compliment. "Well, there's more where that came from, if Mac doesn't beat you to them." She eyes her friend with her eyebrow raised, but Mac is too engrossed in eating to respond.

I swallow before speaking again. "To answer your question, yes. I think Brandon is going to do whatever it takes to keep me here."

Mac nods thoughtfully. "He spent so much time on that studio for you. I was touched he was being so careful to set up a space you'd love, but now it feels disingenuous."

"That's just it." I point my fork at her. "I don't think it is entirely disingenuous. He desperately wants me to be happy. He just also thinks he knows what's best. And he's impulsive, which is not always a great combination."

Jenny and Mac both nod understandingly, and maybe with a little sympathy. "Men." Jenny rolls her eyes and shakes her head.

I smirk. "I don't think it's as easy as vilifying an entire gender, but in this case, he may have had some alpha shit going on, yes."

Mac has been studying me, and I have the uncanny sense that she can actually see right through me. She narrows her eyes and tilts her head. "So, what *is* going to make you happy? Going back to New York?"

I have a feeling from the way she thought about it before asking that if I say yes, these two will advocate for me in a way no one in the city would ever have. I busy myself twirling pasta around my fork, though I don't eat it.

It's not that easy. I want to be in a place where I feel like I belong. I want to have a purpose and friends. Friends who don't make me feel like I'm a downer because I'm not drinking. Friends who don't make me feel like I'm on the outside looking in.

I raise my eyes to the water glasses on the table. I'm positive these two don't have pasta without wine very often. It's not lost on me that they barely know me and are willing to have a night without alcohol. A tiny kernel of warmth starts in my chest.

"I don't know, actually," I admit, still looking at the water glasses and avoiding their gazes.

"Leade Park does have a way of worming its way into the heart of even the most hardened New Yorker," Mac says wistfully.

Jenny snorts, then grabs a napkin to wipe some sauce off her face. Mac looks at her in disgust.

"I have recently started to think about putting together a book of my art, though." I'm not sure what makes me share this with them, but now it's out there, and I can't take it back.

"Like a portfolio? Or a coffee table book?" Mac asks. She leans forward, genuinely interested.

Her curiosity emboldens me. "A children's book, maybe?" I shrug as if this admission is no big deal. "I like reading with the kids. I thought it could be cool."

"I was listening to a true crime podcast about a woman who allegedly killed her husband and then wrote a children's book about him," Jenny says, stabbing a meatball with her fork. When Mac and I stare, wide-eyed at her, she chuckles. "Right. Not that kind of book. Well, you're here until March no matter what, right? So, while you figure out what you want to do, let's have some fun."

Mac nods enthusiastically, and I can't help but let my grin spread wide. "What kind of fun?"

"For starters, we need another member for book club," Jenny offers.

Mac scoffs. "Jenny, you hiding erotica in my home library is not a book club."

Jenny shrugs as if this detail is inconsequential. I look between the two of them, wide-eyed. "You two are something else."

"We get that a lot," they say in unison.

I smirk and take another huge bite of pasta, chewing slowly. If I had met up with a pair like this back in New York, I would have felt completely left out. My body would start to itch for a drink—literally itch from the inside out. I would have instantly tried to leave to avoid picking up a glass of the nearest something.

But these two are so warm and inclusive. I don't know if it's a practiced skill from being teachers and welcoming all sorts of students into their classrooms, or if it is something about having lived in this sleepy, friendly, Midwest suburb for years. Whatever it is, I want to believe there's no ulterior motive for them here. Maybe they truly do want to be friends with me.

I feel my shoulders relax as we all eat in silence for a minute before Jenny uses her fork to point to a spot on the counter behind me. "If we aren't going to start a book club, we should include the newbies in the date jar."

I swivel in my seat to see a glass jar with slips of paper folded inside. "What's a date jar?"

Mac wiggles in her seat so she's sitting straighter. "We all add ideas for dates to the jar. We meet once a month to have dinner and pick our next date. We do whatever is on the paper later in the month."

"That's cute." I smile. "What was the last date you did?"

Jenny's cheeks flush, and Mac looks positively giddy. Jenny raises her left hand and wiggles her ring finger, where a gorgeous diamond ring sits.

I frown. "So, you picked his proposal out of the jar, and because it's the date jar, you had to do it?"

Jenny barks out a laugh. "Oh god, no. He did it that way so we'd all be together. He actually didn't even have the ring in the box. There was a note that said he was ready when I was."

"Turns out she was ready." Mac nudges Jenny in the side with her elbow. Jenny shoots a sidelong look at her.

I smile. "Well, then, congratulations."

Jenny nods her thanks, and Mac steps in. "But before that, we took a cooking class, went horseback riding—"

"Hold on," I interrupt. "You got Daniel to take a cooking class?"

Mac wrinkles her nose. "Yes. That was bad."

I hide a smile behind my hand. I've known Daniel for a long time, so this is no surprise to me.

I clear my throat, trying to get back on track. "Okay. The date jar sounds fun."

Jenny stands and takes the jar off the counter, then sets it in front of me. "You take it home with you. We all got to add stuff when we started it, so you can add some ideas, too. We'll come over when you're ready and draw a date."

"Yeah," Mac agrees, a mischievous gleam in her eyes. "And, you know, if you wanted to add some ideas to fuck with Brandon, we won't try to stop you."

My jaw drops. "Are you telling me you put the cooking class in the jar just to mess with your new husband?"

Mac is the picture of innocence. "I would never." Her tone turns defensive. "But they put the horseback riding lessons in there to mess with me."

Jenny pinches her eyebrows together as she sits again. "I put ballroom dancing lessons in there to trip up Ben. Turns out he's an excellent dancer."

I look back and forth between the two of them. "So, this is more about fucking with each other than about the dates?"

"It's about both," Mac says. "But no one has ever accused us of being mature adults."

"Yeah," Jenny agrees. "So, add whatever you want. If it happens to be something that'll embarrass your husband, we'll be along for the ride."

My smile stretches slowly across my face. I think these women and I are going to get along just fine. For as long as I'm here.

Chapter 15
Brandon

Once my parents arrive to watch the kids, I stop to grab a six-pack before heading to Daniel's. I hesitate in the aisle, wondering if I should be doing this. Katie never had a problem with me having a beer or two with Daniel before, but things might be different now. I decide she'd probably feel worse if she knew I gave this up for her and check out as quickly as I can.

I'm a few minutes late, but I'm still the first one there. Daniel grins as he holds the door open for me to enter.

"I'm glad Katie agreed to have dinner with Mac and Jenny." He shuts the door behind me and takes the beer out of my hands so I can shed my thick winter coat. I hang it in the hall closet and follow him to the kitchen, where he takes two drinks out of the carrier and puts the rest in the fridge.

"Me too," I agree. "I overheard her therapist talking about meeting people when she was on a video call the other day."

Daniel raises an eyebrow at me. "You eavesdropped on her therapy appointment?"

"I *overheard*," I correct him. He looks at me as if this detail does not matter. I continue a bit defensively, "I can't help it if Katie has everything at full volume all the time."

Daniel seems unconvinced, but he grabs a bottle opener and pops the top off the beers. He hands one to me as we make our way to the couch in the living room. We clink our bottles together and take a sip. I don't have beer often, and I never keep it in the house, so I enjoy it all the more on nights like these. I'm glad I get to share some time with Daniel, too. When he moved out here two years ago to write that damn book I still haven't finished, he stayed because he fell for Mac. I like that he's close by again.

"How are Patrick and Maria?" He changes the subject, probably giving me a minute to catch my breath. Then, as an afterthought, he adds, "Any word from Shane?"

"Shane called the other day asking for money. No surprise there. Haven't heard from him since." I shrug, not willing to spend any more time on that line of conversation. "Mom and Dad weaseled their way over for family dinner on Monday."

"Wasn't that the kids' first day of school here, too?"

I take another sip of my beer. "Yep."

"How did that go?"

"Well, I got hung up at the office, then I had to pick up something to make for dinner on the way home, so my parents beat me there. Mom insisted on making cookies with the kids before we ate, so I walked into an explosion."

Daniel narrows his eyes at me. "There are so many things wrong with what you just said."

"Mom making cookies?" I venture.

"Yes," he says slowly. He narrows his eyes at me, which is his tell that he's trying to decide if he should say whatever he wants to say next.

"Are you going to ask me about staying late at the office?" I guess.

"Only if you want to tell me why." He puts his beer down on the table in front of him and leans back into the couch cushions.

"I had an issue with my team I had to deal with. But I have been home on time more often," I insist before he can say anything about it. Daniel looks skeptical, so I admit, "Sort of. I was late again on Wednesday."

Daniel shakes his head slowly, then runs a hand through his dark, wavy hair. "I'm sure that didn't help."

"I know, man. She was really pissed. Frankly, I was pissed at myself, but I need to do a good job on this project, or everyone's going to think I got this job because of my parents."

"And Mac will hate you forever if you botch this addition." He winks.

I glare at him, but before I can retort, the doorbell rings. Daniel checks his watch. "No way that's Ben yet. Must be the food." He stands to answer the door.

"Didn't you say seven?" I call after him.

"Yeah, but he's with Jenny now, so he's incapable of being on time anymore."

When he comes back to deposit takeout containers, some paper plates, and napkins on the coffee table in front of me, I huff.

"I see you still haven't learned to cook anything."

"Not for lack of trying." He flops back on the couch, picking up his beer from the table where he left it. The doorbell immediately rings again, and Daniel groans.

I chuckle, standing. "I got it." I set my drink down and go to the door, opening it to find Ben on the porch, blowing warm air on his hands. I let him inside.

"Shit, it's cold," he says, shaking his body as if that would shed the outside temperature from him.

I eye him up and down. "You're not wearing a coat," I observe.

"Didn't think I needed one to walk from the car to the house." He shrugs.

I lead him into the living room where Daniel is opening boxes of tacos, nachos, and various toppings. He hands us each a plate. "Sorry it's not homemade," he jokes.

Ben chuckles. "We'll get you to cook something. Someday."

I eye Ben skeptically. "Hard disagree."

He grabs three tacos and a handful of nachos, topping them with a little bit of everything before setting his plate on the coffee table. "I have faith still. Beer in the fridge?"

Daniel nods, filling his plate. I do the same as Ben gets himself a drink and joins us on the couch.

"So, Brandon," Ben starts. "When I left, your wife was standing awkwardly in my kitchen looking like she'd rather be anywhere else."

I wince. "She takes a few minutes to warm up." I don't mean to sound defensive, but that's exactly how it comes across.

Ben raises his hand to stop me and shakes his head. "No need to explain. I know you were worried about her liking it here, so I thought I'd mention it. I'm sure the ladies will help her feel at home." His smile is so wide and warm, it disarms me for a second. Every time I see him smile like that, I think he's got the Midwestern charm down to a science.

I sigh deeply, and both men eye me over their food.

"I don't want to spend the whole night bemoaning the state of my marriage, but things aren't going as well as I would have hoped," I say. I had already filled them in on our agreement as they helped me set up the house, so it's not news to them that Katie and I are struggling. But we were all relatively optimistic after the furniture was set up and everything was unpacked.

Daniel's eyes go wide. "She's still icing you out?"

"What do you mean?" Ben's head swivels back and forth between the two of us.

I take a giant bite of my taco and chew it slowly. I've known Daniel for almost my entire life, but I've talked to Ben like three times before this. And, while he's well aware Katie and I are having issues, I'm not sure if I want to talk about my sex life with a guy I barely know.

They both look at me expectantly, neither of them making a move to eat or drink while they wait for me to figure out what I want to say. Both of them seem ridiculously happy in their relationships, so maybe opening up to them isn't the worst thing I could do. I could probably use some advice.

I swallow my food and take a deep breath. "It's been a while since Katie and I have been..." I trail off.

It takes Ben a second, but he nods in understanding. "Oh," he says simply.

"Yeah," I reply, raising my beer to my lips. Ben looks at me with a good deal of sympathy.

"Do we need to make tonight Operation: Get Brandon laid?" Daniel asks.

I just about spit out my drink. "Please, no." I cough.

"You gotta be patient," Ben offers. "It took Jenny nine years to give me a chance, but I don't think you'll have to wait that long. Katie will come around."

Daniel snorts, and I glare at him. He shrugs. "Oh, come on. Katie is stubborn as hell. Once she makes up her mind about something, you have to drag her out of it."

He's not wrong. "Okay, but I'm not going to drag her to bed."

Both men nod approvingly. I drain my beer and go to the fridge to get another, mostly to give myself some space. This is not exactly how I pictured this evening. Isn't there some game on or something? Daniel isn't the sports type, but I'm almost positive Ben is.

As I head back to the living room and transfer another taco from the box to my plate, I've decided to change the subject to something more neutral, like sports, when Ben leans forward suddenly.

"What is it that Katie wants?" Before I can respond, he waves his hand in front of his face as if to erase his words. "I mean, I know you said she wanted time to paint. She's got a space now since you set up that studio, and time with the kids at school, right? But if that were it, she'd be falling all over you. So, what does she want?"

I stare at him dumbly for a second because I'm ashamed to admit I don't know. Daniel gets it right away though, because he's known me for so long. He jumps to my rescue.

"She wants you home on time. You've said that, and you've been trying and succeeding to some degree. Why does she want you home for dinner or whatever, though? It's not like she doesn't have all day to herself. Maybe she's hinting at help with cleaning or something like that?" he suggests.

I shake my head. "No, Katie has always been adamant that she doesn't want help with the housework. In fact, she said she wouldn't have any purpose at all if it weren't for the cleaning and laundry."

As soon as I say it aloud, I hear it. The guys do, too, because they both grimace.

"That's sad," Ben says.

"Yeah, I see that now," I mutter.

"Does she want to go back to work at a gallery?" Daniel asks. "Or anywhere?"

"I don't think so. The last time we talked about galleries specifically, she said Christine was still so young, and she thinks the galleries are kind of..." I trail off and glance at Ben. It's one thing to admit my issues in front of him. It's another to air Katie's dirty laundry. "Toxic." I finish cryptically.

"Katie got sober when she was pregnant with Mason," Daniel fills him in helpfully. When I glare at him again, he shrugs. "What? It's nothing to be embarrassed about."

"It's really not," Ben reassures me.

"I'm not embarrassed. I just don't know how much of her business she wants out there." And it's been a minute since I have had a true friend around, even though Daniel and I have talked on the phone at least weekly since he moved out here. I'm out of practice trusting people, I guess. "But what *is* embarrassing is I have no idea what Katie wants or needs, and I should."

Daniel tilts his head, studying me. "Does she know what she wants?"

I frown at him, considering. "No, I don't think so."

"Then that's not embarrassing, either." He leans back in his seat and crosses his arms, as if that's the end of that. Which I suppose it is.

"You need to be persuasive, then," Ben says more to himself than to us, but when we both snap our heads to him, his face flushes. "Not in a creepy way. But you said once she makes up her mind, she doesn't change course very easily. How long has it been?"

"Before his wedding," I indicate Daniel, who winces sympathetically.

"Oh, shit," Ben curses.

I nod, twisting my wedding band around my finger with my thumb.

"You should try taking her out on a date. I know finding a babysitter in New York was next to impossible, but your parents are watching the kids now. What if they watched them every week? Or we could. We'd be happy to." Daniel suggests.

"Maybe," I say slowly. I'm unconvinced a few dates will have Katie falling in love with me again, but at this point, I'll try anything.

"Or a night in." Ben waggles his eyebrows. "You know, sexy pajamas, gray sweatpants..."

"This is going too far," I groan.

"The ladies love gray sweatpants," Ben insists.

Yeah, on you. You're jacked, I think, but that's not something I'm willing to say aloud to a man I practically just met.

Ben's eyes light up, and for a second, I'm afraid I did actually say that out loud. He leans forward, resting his forearms on his knees. "You should ask Jenny for some book recommendations. You know, those romance ones?"

"I'm not reading those," I protest quickly. "I'm still working on Daniel's."

"You've been working on that for a year," he mutters good-naturedly.

Ben shakes his head. "Trust me, man, you don't have to. Buy them and just leave them around. She'll pick one up. Jenny devours those things, and I can't say I mind." He stops short of winking at me, but I can tell he wants to. I grimace.

Daniel smirks. "They show up in our library sometimes, which I would assume is Jenny's doing." He looks to Ben, who tries to look innocent for all of one second before he nods in confirmation. Daniel smirks. "I catch Mac reading those things and she lights up, if you know what I mean."

"Everyone on the planet knows what you mean," I mumble.

Daniel is amused as he stands and collects our forgotten paper plates to throw them in the trash. "We'll figure it out." He claps his free hand on my shoulder in reassurance as he passes me. "But I think you should start by helping her determine what it is she needs out of life. From what you said, she seems a bit..." He searches for the word. "Adrift."

I chew on the inside of my bottom lip as I think about this. "Adrift" is putting it lightly, but he's got the gist of it.

"I heard Mason and Brody hit it off." Ben changes the subject, and while I'm grateful to not be talking about my sex life and my sad wife anymore, I have to rack my brain to remember who Brody is. "My nephew," Ben supplies when he sees me struggling.

I nod. "Oh, right. Yeah, they're in the same class." He's only been in school for a week, but I should know who my son's friends are.

Daniel comes back into the living room after clearing away the food. Ben seems not quite sure what to say next, which is fair. It dawns on me that I should ask if he can meet with my team to talk about ideas for the addition, since he teaches at the high school, too. I decide against it, though. I don't want to drag work into every aspect of my life. I'm doing a bad enough job of leaving work on time, and apparently an even worse job at leaving work at the office when I am home.

We sit in awkward silence for a few minutes. I hope Katie's night is less uncomfortable than this is. Eventually, Ben suggests we watch whatever hockey game is on. Daniel grimaces, but hands him the remote, and we settle in to watch the game. My heart's not in it, though. As happy as I am to have friends here, I have a nagging feeling that I have some things to figure out on my own.

Chapter 16
Katie

Two more weeks. That's all it takes for everything to fall back into exactly the way it was in New York. Well, not exactly the way it was. At least here, I've been added to a group text with Mac and Jenny. Jenny started it just after I left her house, then promptly renamed the group *Jenny's Book Club* and texted a few screenshots of covers with half-naked men on them asking which we should read first. Mac sent back a picture of her holding one up in front of what I think is her home library, typing: *This one appeared the other day. Might as well start here.*

Since then, the conversation has devolved into some complaints about domestic life, though they can't really relate to my texts about Brandon's work-life balance, or lack thereof—Daniel is *always* home, which is an issue for Mac in its own right, and Jenny and Ben commute together. They also can't relate to the struggle of trying to get two kids ready for school or keeping them occupied during the cold winter months without too much screen time. I leave out the part about wanting to claw my ears off when the kids inevitably end up running in loud circles around the house to get their energy out. But they try to understand, and I appreciate the effort.

Brandon, however, is showing next to zero effort to change his ways. He has come home after dinner almost every night for the past two weeks. Two of those nights, he didn't get home until the kids and I were in bed.

I knew the honeymoon period wouldn't last, but I'm surprised how quickly things shift back. At my therapist's gentle insistence, I haven't demanded Brandon move back to the guest room, but I'm getting close. Each night, I have to inform Mason or Christine that he won't be home to read them bedtime stories or hear about their days at school. And every time, my resolve to leave this place at the end of our two-month agreement hardens. If their father has to disappoint them, he may as well do it in a city that feels more familiar.

Any other wife would probably wonder if there was another woman at this point. For some reason, I don't. I trust Brandon; I just don't like how he operates when it comes to our family. I hate it when our kids are sad, especially when he's the one causing it, and I'm the one who has to deliver the news. I'm sick of it.

But I'll have to wait until my next appointment with Nora to unpack that, because it's Monday again, and I have lunches to pack, shoes to find, and a toddler to wrangle into something suitable for school.

"Mama?" Christine asks from her little table in the corner, but I'm too busy being angry at Brandon and packing Mason's lunch and trying to shovel some breakfast in my own mouth to respond. "Mama. *Mommy!*" she exclaims just as Brandon swoops in and squats next to her.

"What's up, baby?" His voice is gentle, and I harden my heart against how soft he always is with our kids. I will not let the image of his giant body sitting on the floor next to Christine's toddler-sized table worm its way into my feelings. I don't have any room for anything but resentment right now.

"What's dis, Daddy?" She points to something on the table as I smear some jelly on a piece of bread and shove it against the slice where I already spread sunflower seed butter.

"That's a koala bear," Brandon says.

"What's 'ko-all-ah-bear'?" She says it slowly and all mushed together, trying to get her mouth around the unfamiliar term. I love it when she tries out new words. Her little voice sounds like someone who sucked in helium from a balloon while chewing on a wad of gum.

"It's a bear," he responds.

"It's not a bear," I say tersely as I shove the sandwich into a reusable silicone bag. I mentally pat myself on the back for doing my part to save the planet like I do every time I use one of these bags.

Brandon looks up at me. "If it's not a bear, what is it?"

"It's a marsupial." I grab a container of strawberry yogurt from the fridge and toss it in the lunch bag along with an ice pack to keep it cold.

"What's a marsupial?" Mason asks, coming over to inspect his lunch. He'd better not have an issue with it, considering I've asked him to help prepare it six times now, and he's ignored me every time.

"An animal that carries its babies in a pouch on its belly," I respond.

Brandon frowns, looking at what must be a picture of a koala next to Christine. "Why do people call them 'koala bears,' then?"

"Probably because they look like bears? But they shouldn't because they're not." I also grab a bag of baby carrots and a packet of bite-sized cookies and throw them in the lunch bag as well.

"What should they be called, then?" Brandon wants to know.

I look up to scowl at him. I do not have time for this conversation, especially with a grown man who can search for the answer on the internet. I know he's trying to be helpful by responding to Christine, but if he wanted to *actually* be helpful, he could jump in on some of the more practical details of the morning rush.

His expression isn't challenging, though. He genuinely looks curious. I blink a few times, trying to remind myself to calm down. "Just 'koalas,' I'm pretty sure."

He looks back to where Christine is pointing. "That's a koala, then." But in the time it took us to have that conversation, she's sloshed milk from her cereal all over the table and the floor. Brandon sighs deeply and pushes himself to stand. "Next time try getting some of that in your mouth, yeah?"

He walks over to the coffee pot and pours himself a mug. I track him, my mouth agape, as he leans against the counter and takes a sip.

"What?" He asks innocently. He really doesn't get it.

I can feel my face turning red. This might be the day I lose it and become one of those women on Jenny's podcast. Maybe I'll write a book about it.

I grit my teeth. "Oh, I don't know. You could grab a towel and clean that up before she steps in it and freaks the f—" I catch myself before I let out the rest of the word while the kids are in the room—"out because her socks are wet?"

"Mom. Language," Mason chides jokingly. I whirl on him, my eyes wide in warning, and he wisely slinks away to the mudroom to hopefully find his backpack and shoes.

Brandon must value his appendages because, by the time I face him again, he has a towel in his hand and is moving toward Christine. I shove the rest of Mason's lunch in his lunchbox and pour my own mug of coffee. If Brandon can do that for himself in the midst of morning chaos, then so can I.

Somehow, the coffee makes everything that happens in the next thirty minutes slightly more tolerable. Maybe he's on to something. Maybe everyone who preaches about self-care and putting on your own oxygen mask first are on to something, too. Can simply pouring yourself a cup of coffee while getting your family ready to leave for the day be considered self-care? I don't know. But what I do know is that, by some miracle, everyone gets out of the house on time with no tears shed, and by the time the house is silent, I'm on my second cup. Maybe I'll make this a new habit.

There hadn't been any time to paint over the weekend. Brandon wanted to visit some museums, so we did that. Then, he had to "get some work done." I'm not sure what kind of work he needed to bring home over the weekend when he stays so late every night, but he seemed kind of distant and distracted even while he was with us, so I didn't have the heart to argue. I wanted to ask him if he was doing okay, but he disappeared to lock himself in his basement office. I played with the kids until he finally came out for dinner, and then fell into bed, exhausted.

So, as soon as everyone is on their way, I don't waste any time getting into my studio. My fingers are practically twitching to paint something, but I stare at a blank canvas for a while, not sure where to start. My eyes keep snagging on the pictures of Brandon and the kids lined up against the wall behind the easel, and my mind keeps wandering.

He makes it so hard to focus. When my brain is tired from the merry-go-round of thoughts about him and the kids, it's difficult to be creative in any way.

I know I shouldn't complain. I have whole days to myself now. Even the laundry and housework are getting easier as the kids get older and less messy. They can take on some of their own chores, too, which I demand they do despite my mother-in-law's insistence that little kids shouldn't have to clean up after themselves. It took me *three years* to finally break Brandon of the disgusting habit of leaving bits of food and dirty clothes lying around our home, and I refuse to let either of my kids' partners—should they choose to have them—deal with that, too.

But with physically easier children comes more emotional work. Fighting about chores and schoolwork, talking about our feelings when things get tough, pent-up energy that needs to get out before bed every night. All of that is so much easier with two parents around, and I don't have that. The days I have to myself mean nothing when the nights are rife with struggle.

I know disappointment is a part of life, and kids need to learn to deal with it in a healthy way. But being sad their father isn't home in time to tuck them in, or have dinner with them, or hear about their day... That's different than being sad I said no to a new toy.

Brandon spent so much of my pregnancy with Mason persuading me that he'd be a good father. That he'd be there for us. That he *wanted* to be there for us. And, for a while, he was. But his parents became more demanding, and around the time Christine was born when they didn't give him that promotion, he had started slipping away little by little.

At first, I told myself it was temporary. That the kids were too young to remember how often he was gone. But, it kind of stuck. Even after his parents moved out here, Brandon continued to bust his ass for them. The kids just got used to him only being around some mornings and in his office on weekends. They stopped asking when he'd be home. Now, after a few weeks of him being around more often, they're asking where he is at night, and I don't know how to tell them he's chosen work over us again.

If I allowed myself to stop and think about my own emotions for longer than a second, I'd have to admit I'm hurt, too. Because he's not only choosing work over his kids. He's choosing work over me. He's breaking his promises to me. I've been down that road before. It happened with my parents, and it's happening with him. History really does repeat itself.

I sigh heavily, but it does nothing to release the tension building in my shoulders. My coffee is gone, and I haven't even bothered to reach for a pencil or paintbrush. I swivel on my stool to face the window, hoping some light will perk me up, and I catch the date jar sitting on my desk. We're set to host the dinner where we pick a date this Friday. I haven't added anything to it yet. It felt shady and unfair to add date ideas just to mess with Brandon.

But is it?

What's a little discomfort for one night? He can handle it. It seems so small compared to what I've had to deal with. He might even admit it's fun. Or maybe it'll help knock us out of this funk. Besides, there are so many other slips of paper in there, the odds are probably low that we'll pick one of mine, anyway.

I cut up some strips of paper and write a few outrageous suggestions on them. I place them in the jar and mix them up, a smirk playing at my lips.

Chapter 17
Brandon

FRIDAY MORNING, BEFORE THE sun even peeks above the horizon, Mason bursts into our room. I groan and cover my eyes with the crook of my elbow. Katie barely stirs.

"Today's the day I get to have a playdate with Brody after school!" he squeals.

I wince as Mason's voice pierces through my brain. It is way too early for this.

I roll over and grab my phone, tapping it awake. "What are you doing up at five-thirty in the morning?" I half-grumble, half-growl, trying not to open my eyes too far and fully wake myself up. There's still a chance I can get some more sleep if I can just get him to leave.

"I'm excited!" he shouts again.

I shush him. "Your mother is sleeping."

"Only the dead could sleep through this," she mutters out of the side of her mouth, not opening her eyes.

"Go back to bed, Mason. Wait for your alarm," I say.

"Okay!" he exclaims, and practically skips down the hallway back to his room. He leaves our doorway and the hallway light on, though, so I have to get out of bed to at least shut off the light. The cold air immediately hits my bare chest and jolts me further toward fully awake. I crawl back into bed as quickly as I can.

Katie hasn't moved. I'm almost certain she hasn't fallen back asleep yet, but I don't want to take any chances and wake her again. I lay on my back and fold my arm beneath my head, tilting so I can watch her for a moment. Her closed eyelids flutter ever so slightly, and her full lips are parted and relaxed. Her blonde hair falls over her jaw, and I want to brush it away. I don't, though, fearing my touch would wake her.

For the next hour or so, I move in and out of sleep. Just when I start to doze off again, something bumps me awake, and by the time I can hear Mason's alarm going off down the hall, I feel more run down than I did when he burst through our door.

Katie's breath is deep and even. I roll over slightly and press a kiss to her temple. She groans and opens one eye.

"I'm not feeling great. Do you think you can do the morning stuff today?"

"Of course," I say. "Do you want me to cancel tonight?"

She closes her eye, looking content. "No. It's... I'm not sick. I just need some extra time."

I look down to where the comforter has slipped down to her waist from when I moved, and she's clutching a hot water bottle to her lower abdomen. I didn't even notice she had that last night, though she was reading in bed by the time I got home.

Katie has always had terrible monthly cramps with her period. She said they got worse after she had Mason, too. She's seen several doctors over the course of our marriage and never received any answers aside from the advice to use a heating pad and take some over the counter pain medications. She was hopeful her IUD would help, but no such luck.

I hover my hand above the hot water bottle. It's lukewarm at best. I slide it out from under her hand. She doesn't protest, but she does curl further into herself as she presses her eyes closed. Her breathing has become more labored, and a slight line has appeared between her brows.

No one else seems to be stirring yet—there isn't even a sound besides the alarm coming from Mason's room, so I throw on a shirt and pad down to the kitchen. I run the tap and as it heats up, I distribute the old water from the bottle into the potted plants by the window. Then I refill the bottle once the water is as hot as it will go. I fill a glass with cold water and grab the bottle of pain meds, too, and make my way back upstairs.

Katie is still curled up, so I gently pry her fingers open and press the medicine into her palm. She opens one eye at me again, and I hand her the glass of water. She props herself up on her forearm and greedily shoves the medicine into her mouth before she downs the whole glass of water and flops back on the bed. I slide the hot water bottle back over her abdomen, and watch as her expression smooths out.

I walk through the bathroom and into our walk-in closet to start getting ready for the day. It doesn't take me long, but when I'm done, I'm surprised Christine isn't up and Mason's alarm is still blaring. A quick look at my watch tells me that we'd better get moving if everyone is going to make it to where they need to be on time. I walk over to the bed and pull my phone off my charger, but as I turn to leave the room, Katie grabs my wrist and tugs gently.

I lean over the bed so I can see her face. She smiles slightly.

"Thanks," she whispers.

My heart swells almost out of my chest. One word. That's all it took, and I'm a goner.

I squeeze her hand, and when she releases her grip on me, I pull the comforter up over her shoulders. She shimmies a bit to snuggle underneath it, and it's so fucking cute I can barely contain myself. If I had the time, I'd hold her tight until the aching stopped—hers and mine.

No time for that, though. I've got to get these snails moving or we're going to be late.

I leave the bedroom and close the door behind me as quietly as I can. Christine's room is closest, but Mason is the most self-sufficient, so I start with him. I burst through his door in a little bit of retaliation for earlier. Not my proudest moment, but I'll take the wins where I can. I find him in his loft bed, just a lump under a blanket.

"Hey! What are you doing?" I ask, crossing his room to shut off his alarm.

He only groans in response.

Luckily, I'm tall enough to reach into the loft bed and poke him, which elicits another groan. I count to ten, and when he hasn't moved yet, I drag the blanket off of him.

"Let's move! If you miss school, you'll also miss your playdate." Truthfully, he won't miss his playdate. Katie set it up with Ben's sister for both of our kids to go over there and play while the adults are here for a few hours, but he doesn't know that.

"Fine," he grumbles as he descends the ladder.

He's already dressed, but since he got back in bed after waking us up, his clothes are completely wrinkled.

"Mason, you're going to have to change."

That wakes him up. "What? No! I picked out this outfit special to hang out with Brody!" he whines.

"You can't go to school looking like you pulled your clothes straight out of the laundry," I insist.

He stamps his foot on the ground and folds his arms across his chest, pouting his bottom lip. He actually looks like he might cry. I check my watch again.

I do not have time for this.

"Fine, do what you want. Brush your teeth and go start packing your lunch," I sigh as I make my way to Christine's room.

She's awake, at least, but she has tried to dress herself with about as much success as you might expect from a newly-three-year-old. Her pants are on backwards and she only has one arm through her shirtsleeve. She's truly struggling, little grunts escaping as she turns in circles trying to grab the other sleeve, like a dog chasing her tail.

"Oh, baby. Here, let me help you." I try to stay calm because I'm not sure if she's going to laugh or have a meltdown.

She stops turning and looks at me, her eyes wide and brimming with tears. A meltdown, then. Great.

She lets out a wail as she tries to say something, but I can't make it out. I scoop her up and press her head gently into my shoulder. I can feel the tears moistening the fabric of my shirt. It's okay. They'll dry. But, once she's calmed down, she turns her face to rub her runny nose on my shoulder.

Gross, kid.

I don't say anything about it, though, because we're late and this will cause another meltdown. I simply put her on the ground, get her other arm through the sleeve, take her pants off so I can put them on the right way, then let her pick her socks. I know it's going to take her a good five minutes to pick out the pair she wants, but that's shorter than the ten minutes it'll take if I try to do it for her and she melts down again.

I can hear Mason in the kitchen slamming cabinet doors, which is a good sign he is working on his lunch. Maybe this morning can be salvaged.

When Christine is finally dressed, I take her to the kids' bathroom to brush her teeth. She wails again as I do it, but at this point, I don't have time to care. I carry her downstairs despite her protests that she can walk by herself—no time for that, either—and when I enter the kitchen, it looks like packages of food have exploded all over the kitchen island counter.

"Mason, what are you *doing*?" I ask, setting Christine on her feet. She immediately marches off to find something to soothe whatever hurt I caused.

"Packing my lunch and eating breakfast," he says around a mouthful of food. "But I need you to make my sandwich."

Shit. Breakfast. Okay. I grab a packet of bite-sized muffins from where Mason had tossed it on the corner of the island and tear them open. I hand them to Christine, who has returned with her favorite doll. Thankfully, she reaches in and shoves a fistful of them in her mouth before sitting right there on the floor to play.

Good enough.

Mason goes to the mudroom, presumably—hopefully—to find his backpack and shoes. I take the peanut butter out of the pantry and start smearing it on a slice of bread.

"Dad!" Mason sounds alarmed as he comes back into the room. "What are *you* doing?"

The hand holding the knife stills as I shift my eyes to him. "Making your sandwich. Like you asked." I don't mean for my words to sound clipped, but this morning is turning into a shit show real fast.

"I can't take *peanut butter*." He spits the words out like they're disgusting. "There's someone in my class who's allergic!"

I school my face to neutrality as I slowly push the two pieces of bread together and hover them over the garbage can that Mason already pulled out of its drawer under the island.

On second thought, no sense letting good food go to waste. I raise it to my mouth and take a bite. Peanut butter sandwich isn't my first choice for breakfast, but it'll do.

Mason grimaces as he watches me eat, then puts the sunflower seed butter down on the counter. I glare at him, daring him to comment. He does not. Smart kid.

"Dad?" he asks. "Am I allergic to anything?"

"No," I answer simply, picking a new knife from the drawer and making a new sandwich. Then, I look around. "Where are the plastic sandwich bags?"

"We don't use those anymore. We use the reusable ones."

"The what?" I ask. Mason tosses one to me. I pick it up and turn it over in my hand. "Huh. These are kind of cool."

"Mom says they save the planet *and* our money." There's a note of pride in his voice. While saving the planet from plastic pollution is admirable, I resist the urge to tell him we don't need to save the two dollars on a box of plastic sandwich bags. And that corporations could do a hell of a lot more to reduce pollution than we ever could.

How does Katie do this every day? I find myself wondering, which makes me pause. Katie does this every day. While I sip my coffee, not once thinking about how much she does in such a short amount of time. She makes it look so *easy*.

It's definitely not easy.

But we're late, so I'll have to come back to this revelation later. Finally, with lunches packed, kitchen tidied, breakfast eaten, shoes on, water bottles filled, and backpacks loaded, we leave the house. Ten minutes behind schedule, but not terrible, all things considered.

I drive as fast as I can without endangering anyone, and we make up a little time. We drop Christine off first, despite Mason's whining that he doesn't want to get out of the car to walk her into the building. Too bad. I'm not leaving him alone in the backseat.

By the time we make it to Mason's school, the bell to let the kids in the building is just ringing. He hops out of the car and waves, running into the front door with his backpack bouncing behind him.

Made it. I'm counting this as a win.

I reach down to the center console to take a celebratory sip of my coffee, only to find the cupholder empty. Right. I didn't have time to make coffee this morning.

There are about ten coffee shops on the way to the office, though, so it's still a win.

It's hard for me not to get lost in my work. I tried to explain it to Katie once, and she told me to set an alarm. It sounds dismissive, but it wasn't; she just wanted me home, which was fair. If it weren't for her and the kids, I'd probably sleep on the sofa in my office more nights than not. I used to do that before Katie and I got married. But that was because my office was closer to her studio apartment than my place was, and I wanted to be near her every extra second.

Today, though, I'm not working very well. I can't focus. I've been staring at the design I've been drafting for a good three hours, with no progress to show for it.

My mind continues to drift to that time when Katie's belly was swelling more and more each day. Feeling Mason's surprisingly powerful kick against my hand. Her finally agreeing to let me spend the night once after I showed up daily for months. Her admitting how embarrassed she had been about the drinking. How hard it was to throw it all away and not reach for it. How much calmer she felt about it all when I was around. Me gripping her hands, telling her how in awe of her I was. How much I loved her and the baby.

It took her so long to let me in, but once she did, it was like the rays of a thousand suns shining on me. It sounds cliché because it was. There's no other way to describe it. She had this crusty exterior that I had to chip away at, but it was so worth it to get through.

And now, that crusty exterior is back. I tried to start chipping at it again, and I was probably doing a pretty good job, but work got busy, and I haven't been able to step away. My red flag is that I'm the type of person that once I start something, I need to finish it. This does not bode well for balancing home life and large-scale projects. Like additions to high schools. Like managing an architecture firm.

I'm worried about Katie. I know she doesn't want to fall back into her old patterns, and I'm afraid to ask her how tempted she's been to do so. I'm also worried about this job. I know how important it is for me to knock this one out of the park—for my career, and for the firm. It's turning out to be a larger job than anyone had expected.

The school board wants several options to choose from. So, while the basics of the addition will remain the same—larger cafeteria, faculty lounge, and these nebulous educational spaces—they want options for layout and design. Which means my team and I have had to draw several versions of the blueprints, and also render 3-D mockups, while putting together presentations about each. It's no small task, that's for sure.

The senior architect, Jasper, and I are each drafting one design option, and the three junior architects are working on another. At least, I think they are. I'll find out at our team meeting on Monday. But, with about one month until our final presentation, the clock is ticking.

I skip lunch and set an alarm to pull me out of my reverie. I want to be sure I leave on time for dinner. I won't leave Katie alone with our friends if I can help it, and the way this day is going, I'm going to be lost in thought for the rest of it.

Sure enough, I jump about a foot when my alarm goes off at the end of the day. My mind had drifted once again, but this time, to my brother, Shane. I haven't heard from him in a while. Not since he called a few weeks ago asking for money. My brain often connects Shane and Katie, usually when I'm worried about one or both of them. Right now, it's both.

I shake it off, silencing the alarm and shutting down my useless computer. Well, I suppose the computer is only as useless as its user today. I shove the laptop in my bag, throw my coat over my shoulders, and power walk out the door with my head down. By some Friday miracle, no one stops me.

By the time I make it home through some awful Chicago traffic, there are two extra cars parked on the street, and I can make out multiple silhouettes throughout the kitchen. It seems everyone is here but me.

I rush into the house and shrug out of my coat, making sure to hang it up before joining everyone. When I enter the room, everyone but Katie lights up with greetings. My wife just turns her back to me to check on the food in the oven.

"It smells amazing," I offer.

"Chicken parmesan," she grumbles. The whole room falls silent. Daniel catches my eye from across the kitchen and smiles sympathetically. Mac winces.

"I'm sorry I'm late."

Katie turns, a small, disingenuous smile plastered on her face. "You're not. They were early."

Mac slides her gaze to Jenny, who sighs dramatically and glares at her. "Oh my god. I can be on time, you know."

Ben snorts, and she smacks him with the back of her hand. He rubs the spot as if she hurt him, which I'm sure she did not. "Last I heard, Brody and Caleb were over the moon to have friends to play with tonight," he informs me. I nod gratefully, then grab a soda out of the fridge.

"Not as excited as Mason was at five-thirty this morning." Katie raises an eyebrow.

"Mmm," Jenny hums. "You're not going to get any sympathy from this one. He's up at five every morning to work out."

"I'm sorry. I misheard that. I thought you said five in the morning." I lean forward to hear better.

Ben chuckles. "Teacher life, man." He turns to Jenny, who is smiling at him like she can't help it and is completely unaware she's doing so. "We have to leave for work at seven. Day starts early. Then, with practice after school, there's no other time for the gym if I want to hang with this one." He loops an arm around Jenny's shoulders, and she practically melts into him.

Katie clears her throat pointedly. I look at her, my brows pinched, but her face is blank.

"Dinner should be ready in about fifteen minutes." Her voice is bland.

"I spoke with your architect today, Brandon," Mac slides in to change the subject. "I think we came up with some good ideas, but we're going to follow up sometime next week."

Jenny groans. "I know you're excited, but can we not talk about work, please?" She turns to Katie, an eyebrow raised mischievously. "This might be the first time I've seen you and Brandon together since you were here for the wedding, and everything was going to shit then."

"For all of us," Katie mumbles. I cough.

"So, tell us more about you." Jenny flaps her hand back and forth. "Not about the jobs and stuff. How did you meet?"

Katie looks across the room, catching my eye. We have a silent conversation, wherein I tilt my head in deference to her. She can tell it if she wants to.

"I stole him from my friend, who had brought him to a gallery party," she says simply.

Mac makes an offended noise. "That's it? That's all you're going to tell us?"

Katie smirks at some private memory. "Let's put it this way. You've heard of slow burns?"

Mac and Jenny chuckle at each other across the table. "Yeah, we're familiar," Jenny says.

"Well, our love was more like a wildfire." Katie's eyes find mine again, glinting with a passion I haven't seen in her in a long time.

"It's a good thing wildfires are hard to put out." My voice is gruff and low. The room goes still for a moment, and I don't even care that everyone's eyes are on us.

Mac suddenly claps her hands, shaking us out of it. "Let's choose the date before dinner. It's tradition."

"The jar is in my studio. I'll grab it." Katie shoves off the counter where she had been leaning. "Daniel, stay away from the oven."

He raises his hands, palms out. "Why would I touch it?"

She glares at him, though there's an element of playfulness to it as she backs through the door of her studio. She returns a minute later and plops a clear glass jar that has folded up slips of paper in it onto the counter.

"So, how does this work?" she asks the room.

"Usually, we take turns drawing out of the jar. But you all haven't had a turn, so maybe you should do it?" Mac proposes.

Katie shrugs and meets my gaze. She takes a wooden chopstick out of a drawer and uses it to stir up the slips of paper. Then, she tilts the jar at me. "You want to do the honors?"

"Sure." I reach my thumb and forefinger into the jar, pinch a piece of paper, and pull it out. I unfold it to find Katie's unmistakable, curly handwriting.

And as soon as I register what's on the paper, I devolve into a coughing fit having choked on my own saliva.

"What does it say?" Jenny pulls the slip of paper from my hand. She reads it and starts giggling, then hands it to Mac, who barks a laugh and smacks the counter. Both women look at Katie appreciatively.

"Um, excuse us," Mac says. She grabs Katie's arm, and the three women disappear into the studio.

"What is this, the 1950s?" Daniel asks, affronted.

"What the hell did that paper say?" Ben asks.

I drag a hand over my face, laughing humorously. "Pole dancing lessons."

Ben guffaws. Daniel snickers. I stare at both of them.

Daniel leans his forearms on the counter. "Was that Katie's addition?"

"It's her handwriting." The oven timer goes off, and I take the chicken out, then move back to the counter, slinking into a seat next to Ben.

He claps me on the shoulder reassuringly. "It won't be so bad."

I pointedly look him up and down. "Says the guy who wakes up at five in the morning to work out. It's probably just another day at the gym for you."

He pulls the corners of his mouth down, conceding.

"She's messing with me, isn't she?" I ask no one in particular.

"Probably. At least you got pole dancing. I got a cooking class." Daniel muses.

My jaw drops. "Do they have a death wish?"

"Ha ha," he says with zero humor. Then, his face breaks into a wide grin. "Maybe this is exactly what you both need. You can be playful. Laugh about it together. Who knows, maybe it'll even be sexy."

"It'll definitely be sexy." Ben nods in reassurance.

I haven't had sex in over four months. *Everything* is sexy.

The women come back out from the studio and file off to stand or sit next to their partners. Mac and Jenny are wearing expressions of feigned innocence, but Katie catches my eye, and one side of her mouth tilts up in what looks like apology. I purse my lips against a smirk.

"How's next Saturday for everyone?" Jenny waves her phone. "There's a place about thirty minutes away that has availability for a group lesson at seven in the evening."

Katie looks at me questioningly, but there's a gleam in her eye that I haven't seen in a while. She's enjoying this.

I scrape my knuckles against my jawline, pretending to consider, but the truth is, I'll make a complete fool of myself pole dancing if it makes her this amused.

"I'll ask my parents to watch the kids."

Chapter 18
Katie

THE NEXT SATURDAY COMES fast. I'd say it's the mundanity of parenthood and the whirlwind that is the morning and evening routine, and that is definitely part of it. I decided to accept Brandon's absence and move past it. We're already a month into this little endeavor, and while I like the group of friends we've settled in with, I still feel like an outsider most of the time.

What is mostly contributing to the passage of time is my art. Something about letting go of a little of my anger has unblocked me, and I'm sketching scenes faster than I can keep up with them. I'll start on one scene, and before I know it, there's a painting in front of me and it's time to get the kids from school.

The only frustrating part of it is that every single sketch that forms is of Brandon and the kids. It's like the harder I try to ignore his absence, the more present he is in my mind. I've scribbled words or sentences on some of the panels, and toward the end of the week, I spend some time lining them up against the wall in what seems to be a sequential order.

Something about this is calling to me. What seemed to be unrelated paintings are starting to look like a story. A story calling out to be told.

I'm in my studio on Saturday, arranging and rearranging paintings between doing some searches on my tablet for photographers in the area. I don't know if this could be a book or not, but I'm sure the first step is to digitize the images on these canvasses. So, I search and send some emails while Brandon wrestles loudly with the kids outside the door. The louder they get, the harder it is to concentrate, and by the time the doorbell rings signaling the arrival of his parents, I'm just about on overload with the noise.

I take a deep breath, hold it, and blow it out slowly through pursed lips, reminding myself to relax my shoulders as I leave my studio, closing the door behind me.

"There's dinner in the fridge for you and the kids," Brandon is saying to his mom. "Christine goes to bed at eight. Mason can stay up a little later, but he should be asleep by nine. They'll fight it, but remember, you're the boss."

"Oh, you don't need to worry about that with me," his mom insists. She's probably right. That woman is intimidating when she wants to be.

Brandon turns to me. "I think that's it, then. You ready?"

I slide my purse over my shoulder as I muster up a friendly smile. "Thanks for watching the kids, Maria."

"I'm happy to do it," she says, taking my hand and squeezing it. "Patrick is so sad he can't be here." It's the most genuine thing she's ever done with me, and I'm sort of thrown off by it.

She turns to the kids, who have realized she's here and rush up to her. Christine squeezes her legs, and Mason wraps his long arms around her waist.

"Okay, kids. Are you ready to have some *real* fun, now that Grandma's here?"

And there it is. The implication that she's better at everything than we are.

Brandon catches my eye, grins, and shrugs. "Let's get out of here while they're distracted."

We sneak out the door and to the car. "I'm glad we escaped before Christine realized we were gone," I say as Brandon rushes to open my door for me. I shoot him an amused glance. It's been a while since he's opened a door for me.

"Yeah, let Mom deal with that tantrum, since she's the *real* fun adult." Brandon rolls his eyes good naturedly.

For the first time today, I have a moment to take him in. His rusty hair is pulled back in a single loop behind his head. He's wearing a green t-shirt that brings out the color of his eyes, and a puffy coat over it. My eyes trail down his body to his lower half. He's wearing his favorite pair of gray sweatpants.

I bite the inside of my cheek. I haven't seen these in a while. Which makes sense because he sleeps in boxers, and is home so late most days, he goes directly to bed without the need for loungewear.

But I do love them, that's for sure. He knows it, too, because I've told him. I squeeze my inner thighs together, but it does nothing to relieve the pressure between my legs. I had put the idea for pole dancing lessons in the jar in a fit of anger before we picked. I figured dancing around a pole in leggings and a sports bra would taunt him a little. Looks like two can play at that game.

Well played, Conley. Well played.

When we arrive at the studio, the others are pulling up, as well. We all walk in together, Mac and I devolving into nervous fits of giggles. Jenny looks completely unfazed. The guys stroll ahead of us, bumping into each other jokingly.

Jenny laughs darkly. "Check out their pants."

Mac and I direct our attention to the men walking in front of us and note that they're *all* wearing gray sweatpants. Matching ones. Almost like they planned it.

"What are the odds they did this on purpose?" Mac's eyes are practically bulging out of her head as she ogles Daniel's ass. He's also wearing his favorite gray cardigan, which makes him look like a bad mashup of work-from-home and workout. But I'm certainly not going to judge Mac if she's into it.

Jenny tilts her head with a light smile playing at her lips, clearly doing some ogling of her own. "Who are we to over-analyze this gift from a higher power?" she breathes.

I watch them for another second, but they don't take their eyes off their partners' backsides. "Do you think we should be objectifying them like this?" I ask. But I can't stop myself from raking my eyes over Brandon from behind, either. He's not lean like Daniel or built like Ben, but he definitely fills out these sweatpants nicely.

Jenny nudges me with her shoulder. "You're not immune," she teases.

No, I most certainly am not.

When we enter the studio, two cheerful and impossibly thin women in tiny shorts and sports bras are waiting for us. They introduce themselves as Brittani and Chelsea, then show us where we can hang our coats and leave our shoes. Ben is the first to shed his outer layers, and he quickly walks right over to one of the poles in the center of the room. He reaches above his head, grabs it, and pulls himself up, then lowers himself a few times. Then, he takes a running start and twirls around it. He lands on his feet with a whoop.

Jenny slow claps. "Show-off," she calls as she kicks off her shoes and joins him at the pole next to his. She reaches up and grabs her own pole, leaning into it seductively and resting her other hand on the waistband of her bright pink leggings. Ben licks his lips, and I look away to find Brandon looking at me, smiling widely. His gaze is heated, and I realize too late that he's not looking at my face. He's taking in my black sports bra and leggings.

"Hey. Eyes up here." I cock an eyebrow at him. He shifts his gaze to my eyes, still smiling, then turns to take his place at a pole. I take the one next to him.

"You'll all want to remove any bracelets or rings," one of the instructors announces. Everyone but Ben fiddles with their wedding or engagement rings, twisting them off their fingers and slipping them into pockets or dropping them in their shoes for safekeeping.

"Soon," Ben winks at Jenny and wiggles the fingers of his left hand. She does a giddy dance and kisses his cheek.

Daniel and Mac follow us painfully slowly to two other poles, and then we're ready to get started. Brittani turns up the feel-good music, and Chelsea leads us in some stretches. Jenny teases Ben because, even though he's jacked, he's supremely inflexible. Daniel can't take his eyes off Mac. She seems unaware of him staring at her, but her over-excellent form tells me there's not much that escapes her notice.

I don't know if it's the sweatpants or the promise of pole dancing, but I'm feeling feisty tonight. I lean over one leg, close enough to Brandon to whisper, "Chelsea is hot."

He hums and glances at her as she wiggles her butt to the beat of the music. When he looks back at me, the sharpness in his gaze suggests he's done playing. "You can look all you want, Cat," he whispers back, "but remember. You're mine."

An absolutely delicious thrill passes through me, raising the hairs on my arms and making me shiver. I wanted to rile him up a little, but he turned that right back on me. A second point goes to Brandon. From the wry smile on his face, he knows exactly what he's doing, too.

Once the stretches are done, Brittani takes over for the warm-up. "Okay, first, we're going to practice gripping the poles. No spins yet." She directs the last statement at Ben, who has the good sense to look sheepish. "Face the pole, everyone. Now reach your hands up above your head and put them on the pole. One on top of the other. Good. Now, take the knee of your right leg and press the inside of it to the pole." She and Chelsea walk back and forth checking our form. "Perfect. Now, wrap your shin around the pole to grip it."

Chelsea stops at Brandon and squats down. "No, not quite."

"You know shins are basically bone, right? They don't bend like that," he grumbles.

I laugh, and he whips his head around to look at me, his eyes shining. I smile back, then nod to Chelsea on the ground next to him. "Better pay attention," I caution.

He turns back just as she grips his ankle and wraps it the way she wants it around the pole. "Like that," she says.

He inhales sharply through his teeth, and I chuckle again. Down the line, Daniel is having similar issues. He hops on his standing leg a few times to fight falling over.

"You didn't have dance lessons in your fancy private schools?" Mac taunts. I have to say, I thought she was demure and sweet when we were here last for their wedding, but the lady has some bite, and I like it.

Jenny snorts, and Ben lifts himself up on the pole, using the momentum to spin himself around.

"No spinning yet," Brittani and Chelsea say in unison. Ben groans like a petulant teenager.

"Okay," Brittani continues over the music. "Now, you're going to practice pulling yourself up and down on the pole. Just get a feel for it." She grabs a pole and sets herself up to demonstrate. "Push off the floor with your back leg, then pull yourself up with your arms until your chest touches the pole, then back down. Do that a few times on each leg."

We do, though some of us have more success than others. Brandon tries, to his credit, but after a while, he stops and shakes his hands out, wiping them on his sweatpants. He takes the opportunity to watch me, and that gleam is back in his eyes. He's starting to look almost feral, watching me raise and lower myself on the pole.

I plant both feet firmly on the ground and put my hands on my hips, which makes his hazel eyes flame even more as they land where my hands rest. "You okay?" I ask quietly.

His eyes meet mine again. "No," he says simply.

I meant to provoke him today. That was the whole point—to make him uncomfortable like he did to me by moving us out here, leaving me in the dust every night again, and making promises he obviously can't keep. What I *meant* was for him to be embarrassed at swinging himself around a pole. I didn't mean to be watching his semi-hard dick, barely hidden by his sexy-as-hell gray sweatpants.

Realizing I need to own the result of my too-elaborate prank, I straighten my shoulders. Unfortunately, that has the effect of pushing my breasts out, a movement Brandon does not miss. His Adam's apple bobs.

His gaze lingers on me for a second more, then a new song comes on, and he snaps out of it. He turns back to his pole and situates himself, then starts raising and lowering himself in time with the music.

I'm no saint. Any warm-blooded woman watching her husband pull himself up and down against a metal pole is going to start thinking about sex. I'm not an exception to this rule. But it's been so *long*. Which, yes, is somewhat my doing, though I like to think that if he had been home before I had fallen asleep more often these past few weeks, I wouldn't have held out.

But, *fuck*. My husband is hot right now, all rippling muscles and sensual motions. I want to tear him out of here this very moment, and I only have myself to blame for the warmth building in my core.

Luckily, the desire becomes somewhat easier to ignore as we transition to doing some spins, much to Ben's delight. Watching Brandon flop around the pole is much less sexy than watching him practically make love to the thing in the warm-ups. I manage to get a few good spins by the end of class, and I know Brandon catches some of them by the way he's looking at me as we all gather our things to leave.

As we say our goodbyes, the other two couples are practically drooling over each other, so it seems they had a similar experience. I suppose I can see this as a service to our new friend group; I got all of them laid tonight, that's for sure.

Our kids aren't used to having babysitters, so we drive straight home. By some miracle, they're both in bed and Maria is dozing on the couch when we arrive. I say a half-hearted good night, then make my way quickly up to our bedroom to shower and change.

Brandon enters the room just as I'm peeling my sweaty sports bra over my head. My back is to him, but I quickly grab a shirt and hold it in front of me. Not like he hasn't seen it all before, but after having his eyes on me throughout a ninety-minute sexy dance class, I'm feeling slightly modest.

"Do you, uh, need the shower?" I ask over my shoulder.

"I'm pretty sticky." I hear a drawer open and close as he takes a new shirt out and lays it on the bed. "You can go first. If you want." His voice sounds strained.

I nod, but don't move. There is a dampness starting to build between my thighs that I'm certain is not sweat. I face him, and his eyes immediately dance to where I'm holding the shirt in front of me and back to my face. He's shirtless, standing there in only gray sweatpants, his ink on full display. I'm just about to cross the room and tear those fucking pants off of him when he speaks.

"At least four of us are getting laid tonight, if their body language was any indication," he jokes, though it's laced with bitterness.

That's enough to snap me out of whatever foolish thing I was just about to do. "Are you going to try to guilt me into fucking you?" I try to keep my voice down so as not to wake the kids, but there's no mistaking the anger in it.

He runs a hand through his hair. "No, Cat—"

"Do not call me that," I hiss. "Do not. You keep calling me that, but it doesn't mean what it used to."

He tilts his head, regarding me. "What?"

"You called me that in my apartment. When it was just you and me. When things were easy. Now..." I trail off and swallow hard, the hand clutching the shirt to my chest trembling. "Now, I don't even know. You promised it would be different here. You promised you'd spend more time with the kids, with me." My voice cracks on the last word. I have a tenuous control on my emotions right now, and I'm afraid it's not going to take much for me to break down.

"Katie." He sounds agonized, and I immediately regret asking him not to call me by my nickname. My name sounds so much colder on his lips. "Tell me what's going on here."

"I'm sorry I got pregnant, Brandon." I spit it out like I've been holding it in my mouth for too long and it has gotten sour. "I'm sorry I wanted that baby more than I had wanted anything before he came along. I'm sorry I thought I could fix my issues with my parents by becoming a parent myself. I know it was a long time ago, but you've made it pretty clear that this whole family business really cramped your style. So, I'm sorry. I ruined your life just like your mom figured I would. I'm sorry the kids and I are such a drag on your career."

He shakes his head, imperceptibly at first, then with more vigor. "No," he whispers. "Where would you ever get that idea? You and the kids mean more to me than anything. It may not have been on purpose, but I wouldn't have had it any other way. You *have* to believe that, Katie."

I blink, and a tear falls down my cheek before I can stop it. "If that's true," I whisper, unable to raise my voice any higher, "then why are you gone all the time?"

He stares at me in silence, his chest rising and falling rapidly. His fists clench and unclench at his sides, as if he's trying and failing to grasp onto the words he wants. But he's quiet for so long that I'm pretty sure the conversation is over. My gaze falls to the floor, and I feel myself practically slump in defeat.

He's never going to choose us over the job. I either need to accept it, or I need to leave. I don't like either of these shitty options.

"I'm going to shower," I mutter, then move as fast as I can to the bathroom, closing the door with a final click behind me.

Our shower is huge, with a rain showerhead and a lower, handheld one. Brandon certainly spared no expense on this house, and I feel like I deserve a little luxury right now. I turn the faucet on and let the steam start to build while I wait, letting the static sound of the water soothe my nerves. Maybe if I can wash that fight off me, I'll feel better. Maybe I'll feel less like I need a drink to take the edge off.

The dire nature of that thought hits me, and my body goes cold all over. I lean my hands against the counter, pressing my palms into the edge of it to the point of pain. I take a deep breath and hold it, pressing my eyes closed.

I hate that this is who I've become. For years, I was so blissed out on motherhood and with Brandon that I didn't feel like I needed alcohol. I never even joined a program. I mean, sure, I was nauseous about it at first, and I craved weird food and drink, but that could have easily been first trimester hormones, too. My drinking was never something I needed to function throughout my day; it was something I turned to when I was stressed or wanted to have a good time or needed to impress a client. I just leaned on it a little too much. No big deal, right?

I figured since it was relatively easy to walk away from when I was pregnant that it hadn't been as much of an issue as I had made it out to be. Any time I felt shaky about it, I was able to lean on Brandon. He was *always* there. And he always steadied me. Once I let myself believe he was there for the long haul, once I let him into our lives, it was like magic. Who needs wine when you have magic?

But now, I don't have him. He's never here, I'm lonely as hell, and the kids have only gotten louder and more emotionally needy as they've gotten older. Even the hours of my day when they're not here aren't enough to recover from the chaos they bring. I've felt shakier and more stressed. And, without any permission, these thoughts about booze have started to poke their way back in.

I curl my hands into fists and pound the counter, welcoming the jolt of pain. I'm not as strong as I thought I was. I've depended too much on him to soothe me, and now I can't do it myself. This is exactly what I was afraid of. That I had replaced the booze with him, and one day, he'd decide that this all happened too fast. That he wants out. That he has changed his mind.

And I'd be left alone, with thoughts like these, unable to resist.

The door clicks open, but I keep my eyes pressed shut. A sob escapes me, then another. Brandon quickly steps behind me, his bare chest pressing against my exposed back. He brings his hands around my torso, pressing his palms into the skin of my stomach. He opens his fingers wide, so my whole middle is covered by his warmth.

I didn't realize until exactly this moment how much I wanted him to follow me in here. How good it would feel to let him support some of this weight, even for a little while.

Suddenly, I'm desperate to feel something other than this anguish. My need for his hands on me, for him inside me, is too great to control. I press my back into his front, feeling the hard length of him against my lower back.

"Brandon," I moan. "Touch me."

"You're crying." He squeezes me tighter, leaning down to rest his chin on my shoulder.

"I'm upset," I admit, my eyes still closed.

"I'm not going to touch you like that when you're upset," he insists, though it sounds like his resolve is cracking.

"Brandon..." I trail off, wiggling my ass against his cock and eliciting a sound from him that I want to bottle up and bring back out on lonely nights without him.

"Look at me, Cat," he commands softly, his breath tickling my ear.

I keep my eyes closed.

He tsks, then licks my earlobe. "Look at me."

I open my eyes and meet his in the mirror, which is starting to fog from the steam of the shower. There is an undeniable desire in him, but also a resolve.

"I want you more than I've wanted anything in my entire life," he whispers, and my knees go weak. He tightens his grip on me to keep me upright. "But I'm not going to have the first time I make love to you in four months be a hate fuck. I love you, Katie." This time, my name on his lips sounds like a plea. It's pulsing with heat and want. "I haven't done a good job of showing that. I want to talk this out."

"I don't want to talk," I say, breathless.

He hums, then kisses the place where my neck meets my collarbone, his hands moving over my leggings, caressing the dip just above my hips, then splaying over my lower abdomen. "I'm having a hard time committing to a conversation when you're half naked and there's a perfectly good shower ready to go behind us."

I lean my head further away so he can access my neck, which he does. "We wouldn't want to waste any more water."

"Mmm-mmm," he agrees, still pressing a hot line of kisses along my neck and collarbone.

"We've wasted so much already. We should probably shower together to make up for it," I suggest.

He pulls away and spins me to face him. My breasts press up against his upper torso. He reaches a hand between us to cup one, gently twisting the nipple. My head falls back as he snakes an arm around my shoulders, pulling me closer. "We talk later," he insists. "Promise me."

I let out a deep moan, which will have to do because words are failing me at the moment.

He pinches my nipple harder, and my center aches for him. "Promise me," he says again, his voice hard and commanding. *Fuck*, that's hot.

"I promise," I manage to say, and that's all it takes for his lips to crash into mine. He backs us into the shower, pants be damned, and presses me against the wall. The cold tile combined with the hot water and Brandon's hands skating all over me overwhelms my senses, but in a good way. In a way that brings me out of my head rather than settling me further into it.

I break my hands free to shimmy myself out of my wet leggings and underwear. He does the same with his sweatpants and boxers, kicking the pile of it out of the shower with a wet plop. I giggle at the sound.

Brandon rests his forehead in the place where my neck meets my collarbone, breathing heavy. "Do it again," he says softly.

"What?" I loop my fingers around the hair tie holding his hair in place and pull. His hair cascades around his shoulders, darkening under the water.

He pulls back, his hazel eyes searching mine. "Laugh. Again."

My eyebrows pinch together. I run my fingers through his hair, and his eyelids flutter closed. "You don't laugh nearly enough, Cat. Not anymore. I want to hear it again."

"Mmm," I hum. The tip of his cock presses into my hip. I wrap my hand around it, pumping a few times. My hand glides over him easily with the added slickness of the water. "I don't think you want me laughing while I'm doing this."

He lets out a sound somewhere between a laugh and a loud moan.

I laugh again, and his eyes fly open. "Shh," I hush him. "This isn't going anywhere if you wake up a kid." I stroke him a few more times as he lowers his lips to my nipple. The coarse hair of his beard burns the sensitive skin on one side as he plays with the other with his fingers. My back arches into him.

I reach between us and cup between my legs, pressing against my swollen opening with a finger. Brandon practically growls.

"No, Cat. That's mine," he says, then sinks to his knees. He plants his palms firmly on my hips, then moves me directly into the stream of water. It splashes over his shoulders as he looks up at me. His hand skates down my right thigh, and he lifts it over his shoulder, opening me to him. He drags a finger ever so slowly through my center. I shudder and buck my hips involuntarily into him. His eyes meet mine as he slides a finger into me, then another. A low rumble escapes me, my eyes never leaving his.

He pumps his fingers a few times, then trails a line of kisses up my right inner thigh. I glide my hands up over my full hips to my breasts, cupping and kneading them to heighten the sensation.

"Yes, Katie. Fuck, I could worship you on my knees like this all day. You're a fucking goddess."

Goddess. This draws another laugh from me, though breathier this time, the image of his lips on my thigh mingling with memories of sculpture and art. His hands are molding my skin like clay. Brandon looks pleased. I'm not sure if it's because I laughed again or because of the shared memory. My hips and breasts are fuller now than they were then. I look down at where the fingers of his free hand dig into my left hip, leaving little indents behind, and I can almost see what he sees. It's sexy as hell.

My gaze shifts to where his fingers are fucking me, his face upturned and enraptured. I take in a shuddering breath as the pressure builds in my core, leaning my head back against the tile and letting the water fall over me.

I'm not looking when his lips kiss my clit, but when his tongue licks that sensitive spot, it has the same fervor and reverence his expression had a few moments ago. His beard scrapes the delicate skin on the insides of my thighs, and again, I'm overwhelmed.

"Oh," I breathe. "I think... I'm going to..." I can't finish the thought, because Brandon picks up the pace with both his finger and his tongue, and I fall completely over the edge. I cover my mouth so as not to shout too loudly.

Brandon pulls his fingers out of me, and I make a small noise of protest. He's not done with me, though. He turns me to face the glass door, then runs his fingers from my shoulders down to my hands. He grips them, bringing them up in front of me and placing my palms on the shower door. He bends me over just slightly, then uses his palms to spread me for him.

His cock enters me in one, desperate thrust. I moan at the sudden fullness, still a bundle of nerves from my orgasm. He thrusts once, then twice, then stills.

"Dammit, Katie," he curses. "I don't think I'm going to last very long."

I chuckle, then wiggle my backside closer to him, drawing him deeper inside me. He inhales sharply. I look at him over my shoulder. He's wearing a mischievous smile.

"Do not move your hands," he demands, pulling out ever so slowly, then ramming back into me. My head falls between my arms as I moan. He feels so good. He's always felt so good.

I hear a noise to my left and turn my head. Brandon has taken the handheld showerhead off its mount. He clicks it a few times to change it to the massage spray, then holds it with his left hand, bringing it around to the front of me. He angles it so the water hits just the right spots, and my hips buck into him. His other hand lands on my ass, gripping its fullness as I imagine he was clutching my hips earlier. The image of it has me close to coming again, but I try to breathe through it, to wait it out until he's ready.

His thrusts become more powerful and rhythmic. His fingers are almost painfully pressing into my skin, but it's the kind of pain that is so wonderful that I lean into it. I leave my hands on the shower door like he told me to, but I use it as leverage to push back into him, meeting his thrusts. The only sounds are the meeting of our skin and the pulse of the water still trained on me.

I risk moving one hand from the door and snaking it down my body, touching where we meet. His breathing becomes even more labored as he feels my fingers on him. I reach lower, cupping his balls in my hands, massaging them.

"Cat," he moans. "Fuck yes."

"I know what you like," I tease. I feel him go even harder inside me, and I know he's close. I use my arm between my legs for some added pressure, and I come undone again just before he thrusts erratically into me, grunting, then sighing.

He stills for a moment, then kisses my shoulder. He pulls out of me, and I shift to stand upright, but his hand on my lower back stops me.

"No, let me look."

I look over my shoulder at him again, a coy smile playing at my lips. "You didn't have enough of a view before?"

His eyes meet mine, darkening. "Never."

We hold each other's gaze for a moment longer, then he takes a washcloth off a hook and lathers it with soap. He gently cleans between my thighs, then over my back and breasts, then kneels again and works on cleaning my legs. His touch is smooth and sensual, and it has me fighting another warmth building.

"Brandon," I breathe a warning. "If you keep this up, I'm going to jump you again."

He chuckles darkly, looking up at me from where he still kneels. "I'm not twenty-four anymore, Cat. I'm going to need a few more minutes."

He glides the soapy washcloth over himself quickly. I pout my lower lip dramatically. "You got to do me. I would have done you, too." I'm still leaning over, pressing my hands into the shower door which probably should be weird at this point, but I like the way he's looking at me a little too much.

He shakes his head, droplets of water falling off the ends of his hair and down his chest. "I want to take care of you, Cat. I hardly ever get to." His expression is more earnest than I've ever seen it.

My heart squeezes. I sink to my knees in front of him, the water falling over both of us now. A tear creeps its way down my cheek, too, but I'm hoping he doesn't notice. "I'm right here. Every day. You could take care of me all you wanted if you just came home." It's a plea, and I probably should be ashamed of how desperate I've become for his attention, but I can't muster up the energy.

He gently touches my cheek, pushing a wet piece of hair behind my ear. He leans in and kisses my nose. "I know."

He pushes to standing, then pulls me up with him. He shuts the water off and steps out, grabbing a towel. He comes back to me with it, toweling me off, then wrapping me in it. All the while, he's silent, his expression unreadable.

Tiny little prickles of anxiety bubble up in me, feeling like little toothpicks poking my heart. My breathing catches. He dries himself off with another towel, then finally looks at me. He takes my chin between his thumb and forefinger, tilting my head up. He kisses me passionately, dissolving most of my anxiety as his hands scrape over my still-exposed skin.

"Why don't we move this to the bed?"

My eyes dip to his waist, then lower, then trail slowly back to his face. "You haven't had enough yet?"

He runs a hand through his wet hair, shaking it out a little. The muscles on his forearm shift delicately underneath his tattoo as he moves his palm to absent-mindedly stroke the letters on his chest.

"Not possible." He says it with such fervor that the lingering prickles of anxiety are soothed completely. "But I'm freezing. Let me find some dry sweatpants, and I'll meet you out there."

Chapter 19
Brandon

I'M A PIECE OF shit, and I know it. I've barely been able to admit to myself how much I am struggling at work, let alone tell Katie that I'm wondering if taking this promotion was a terrible idea. Mason has been so happy. I thought Katie would turn a corner when she had her studio and some new friends. I have friends here, too. Fuck, I went *pole dancing* with them, and we had a great time, which is something that never would have happened back on the East coast.

But when I saw Katie breaking down earlier, I froze. I've been so worried about this job, but I've been more worried about her, without any clear ideas for how to help. I hadn't meant for things to go as far as we took them tonight, but as soon as I touched her skin, it was like little fires erupted in my veins. When she told me to touch her, my resolve crumpled.

I can't resist her. I never could.

We should have talked first. I knew it, but my dick took over because I'm an idiot. And she's perfect.

Now, she's sitting outside the bathroom, sated but probably confused, because I can't keep my dick in check long enough to talk to her while she's not wearing any clothes.

I'm sorry I got pregnant, Brandon.

Those words hit me like a knife. I have never been sorry she got pregnant. Not once. It's fair to say I didn't know her very well, but what I knew, I liked. A lot. It's also fair to say I had no idea what being a parent would be like, but it had always been something I knew I wanted. The timing felt irrelevant. And now, after six years of marriage and two kids, I always thought it was a moot point.

It worked out. At least, I thought it did.

We've avoided this for too long, been interrupted too many times. I need to come clean about what has drawn me to the office so late these past weeks, and I need her to tell me what's going on with her. I saw the agony on her face as she pounded her fist on the bathroom counter. I heard her say she's sorry she got pregnant, taking all the blame for something we were both complicit in—something that doesn't even need an apology.

I lean on the counter, studying myself in the mirror. I'm older than the last time I really looked at myself. My expression lines are deeper; my skin has gotten rougher and more weathered. But I can't help but wonder how much I've grown as a person. Am I really all that different from that wide-eyed, impulsive, twenty-four-year-old, asking Katie to marry me every single day from the day she told me she was pregnant to a few months after Mason was born when she finally said yes?

You got spooked by Katie drinking one time, then moved your entire family halfway across the country on the empty promise that you'd be a better man for them. And you think you've changed?

I sigh and hang our wet pants over the edge of the tub to dry, feeling that ache of desire again at the memory of how they got in this state. I take a deep breath, shake my head, and rummage through my clothes in the closet to find an acceptable pair of lounge pants and a t-shirt. I pull them on quickly, then run a brush through my hair and go out into the room.

It's dark, so I wait for my eyes to adjust. Katie is just a lump under the comforter. As I approach the bed, I can only see her eyes and nose poking out above the top, her wet hair falling in wavy clumps on her pillow. Her eyes are closed, and the comforter rises and falls with her deep breaths.

I smile softly as I climb in beside her. She never could stay awake very long after we made love. As if drawn by a force outside her control, she scoots closer to me without fully waking. I shift my arm underneath her head and tuck her in close to me. She sighs deeply, her cheek pressed against my chest.

Tomorrow. We'll find time to talk tomorrow. We'll come up with a better plan.

We do not come up with a better plan the next day. We barely even have a chance to talk. I should have known better. Sundays are always a shit show, and this Sunday is no different. During breakfast, Mason remembers that he's been selected as student of the week, so he has to create a poster all about himself to share with the class on Monday. There are themed days for the remainder of the week, too, but he can't remember what they are. So, a thirty-minute-long search of his backpack ensues wherein we empty all its contents and open every book in search of the paper with the themes. We find a lot of papers, but not the one we need. Christine grabs some of the papers and runs off to color on them. We figure as long as she's coloring quietly, she's one less issue to deal with, but when we can't find the information sheet, Katie narrows her eyes in her direction. Sure enough, Christine has been coloring on the paper we needed the whole time. Mason snatches it from her, sending Christine into a panic tantrum about her masterpiece. Katie tries to ploy her with some paints from her studio, but she will not be appeased. Mason is unrelenting in his grasp on the sheet of paper, so it takes us a good thirty more minutes to calm Christine down.

Once that's settled, Katie takes Mason to the art supply store to get the materials he needs to create his poster. When they get back, they set up in the kitchen. Katie brilliantly bought an extra poster board for Christine, too. The two kids work in peace with Katie supervising until lunch time. They both refuse to eat lunch, so I drag a screaming, over-tired Christine to nap.

During her nap, Mason and Katie gather everything he's going to need for the week, lining it up in the order of the day he'll need it on his dresser. I take the time alone to pull up designs on my laptop, only to stare at them unproductively. Guilt nags at me that I should be the one helping Mason so Katie can have her time in her studio.

Before long, Christine is poking her head out of her room and calling out to let us know she's awake.

Shortly after that, it's time to make dinner—fish sticks, green beans, and macaroni and cheese. It's not even an adult meal, but it's good enough. We wrestle the children into their respective baths and showers. I read a chapter of Mason's book to him in our bed since there's no way I'm squeezing my giant body into his loft bed.

As I send Mason off to brush his teeth, I hear singing coming from Christine's room. I wander quietly out into the hallway, not wanting to interrupt. Through a crack in the door, I see Katie as she rests her back against the headboard. Christine is snuggled close, her head resting on

Katie's chest and her eyes closed. Her hands are clasped under her cheek in a purely storybook position I wasn't aware real people did.

Katie's voice drifts into the hallway as she sings a lullaby and rocks our daughter gently. I stand there, a silent voyeur in a stolen moment. Simply put, it's the most beautiful scene I've ever witnessed. My heart expands, squeezing the air out of my lungs.

Katie's gaze shifts to mine. Her voice trails off, and her eyelids flutter as she takes a deep breath. Christine doesn't stir, so she must be asleep. Katie must come to the same conclusion, because she presses a kiss to Christine's hair and scoots quietly off the bed, covering our little girl with the pink blanket and rubbing her back lightly before leaving the room and closing the door quietly behind her.

She meets me in the hallway, tilting her face up to me. I'm completely at a loss for words, so I just wrap my arms around her shoulders and pull her close. She wastes no time burrowing herself into me and folding her arms around my torso. I breathe in her rose-and-paint scent as we stand there, pressed together.

"Ew," Mason says as he comes out of the bathroom. "Are you gonna kiss?"

"Not anymore." Katie's voice is muffled into my shirt.

I give her one last squeeze before we part. "Okay, buddy," I say to Mason. "Let's get you to bed."

By the time Mason is settled and I'm descending the stairs to the living room, Katie is sprawled out on the couch, her eyes half-closed. Instead of talking to her like I know I should, I suggest we both go to bed. She sleepily agrees, dragging herself up the stairs and into bed next to me. She snuggles up just like the night before, and I drift off with the sound of a lullaby playing on a loop in my mind.

The next day is just as busy. Drop off is a disaster again. Mason forgets his poster, so we have to go back to get it, which makes me late for my morning meeting with the team. Turns out it doesn't matter, though, because the only person who is on time is the senior architect, Jasper. He's beyond annoyed when I walk in, but when he reports on his design work, there's nothing special about it. He shows no spark of passion for the project, like he'd rather be anywhere but here, presenting anything but this project to anyone but me.

Thalia comes in next, rushing as usual. "I'm so sorry. I was on the phone with your friend, Mac. The only time she could talk was before school started, and then I wanted to write up my notes before this meeting and lost track of time."

I tone down the edge that has been building. I hadn't realized she had been in the office this whole time, or I would have reminded her as I walked in. I probably rushed past her cubicle and didn't see her in my own tardiness.

I motion for her to sit. "It's okay. I was late, too." I eye Jasper, daring him to make a remark, but he doesn't.

Thalia looks around the otherwise-empty room. "Where are the others?"

Jasper snorts. "Your guess is as good as anyone else's."

Thalia frowns and folds her hands on the table in front of her. "Do you want me to wait for them before I tell you what Mac and I discussed?"

"No," I say a little too sharply. Something tells me Marianne and Orlando don't have anything noteworthy to present, anyway. "I'm interested to hear what you and Mac talked about."

Thalia lights up, her back straightening and her hands clasping tighter. "She had some great ideas for these educational spaces." She pauses to open her notebook. "She said there's nowhere in the building now for groups to convene. The library has some study spaces, but they aren't large enough for clubs or faculty to use them with any purpose. She says the teachers probably aren't interested in study spaces as much as they are large group workrooms. She got into a lot of detail about the spaces." She shakes her head. Mac must have talked her ear off. "They'd ideally be big enough for two classes of students to meet together for collaboration. So, maybe they'd house sixty to one hundred people. She suggested a movable wall so it could be two separate spaces or one combined space, depending on what it's needed for."

I nod slowly, rubbing my beard between my thumb and forefinger as I listen. "I've seen those. Like accordion walls."

Thalia snaps and points at me. "Exactly." She writes this down. "She also started brainstorming about projector screens and walls painted to function like white boards for collaboration, which is something we can incorporate in our design, but we'd want to ask the engineer about materials and costs before we finalize anything."

"Would we have one large room with the accordion wall, or would we have several rooms?"

"I think just one would work, but if we could fit two, that would be really cool." She turns to a blank page and starts a rough sketch. "What if we had the cafeteria here, then there were stairs to another floor? Maybe a loft area overlooking the cafeteria. There could be some seating outside the room, too, to allow for extra space or reading areas?"

Jasper perks up and leans forward to look at the sketch. "Are these spaces going to be in use during lunch periods?"

"Mmm." Thalia chews her lip. "I didn't think of that."

"Think of what?" I ask.

"The noise," they say in unison. Thalia fights a smile as she looks at Jasper's gruff face across the table.

"Hmm. Right. Okay, so what if we build the cafeteria out further from the building. May I?" I hold my hand out for Thalia's pencil. She hands it over and flips the notebook to a new page, sliding it to me. "If there is a walk-through space between the cafeteria and the existing building, we can have offshoots on either side. That would give us plenty of space for two huge rooms like Mac described." I make a rough sketch as I talk.

Jasper nods. "Or, you could have communal space on one side, along with an entry to the outside, and two stories on the other side. Two identical rooms, one on top of the other."

"I like that, too." I lean back in my chair. "The board wants options. Can we draft these as two of them? If they want a third, we can maybe present the loft idea after pricing out some soundproofing. I'll contact Calvin to get his engineer perspective, and we can tweak the designs from there before we render them for the presentation."

Jasper nods once. "I'll take the two-story design. Thalia can take the double-sided one."

I slide the notebook and pencil back to Thalia. "That sounds good. Let's meet again on Thursday and see where we are. The deadline on this is going to sneak up on us," I warn.

"Especially if we're down two junior architects," Thalia says, eyeing the empty chairs.

"Right. I'll... deal with that, too, somehow. In the meantime, come to me if you need help. Orlando and Marianne are off this project until further notice."

Jasper chuckles darkly, and Thalia's eyes grow wide, but they both voice their agreement before shuffling out of the conference room to get to work.

I snap my laptop shut, silently reminding myself that personnel issues are an unfortunate part of this job and wondering how mad my parents will be if I dissolve the team they set me up with before I've even really started.

By the time I've made a few phone calls, tracked down my missing junior architects, had a longer-than-necessary conference call with our engineering team, and drafted a formal email to HR about the afore-mentioned missing junior architects, it's dark outside. A quick glance at my laptop clock has me groaning and burying my head in my hands.

I'm sorry I got pregnant, Brandon.

Her words have been on repeat all day. Every time I get a second of quiet, they cut through me again. I can't avoid it anymore. We can't be interrupted again. We have to talk about this. It's not fair for her to go on feeling this way when I've never felt anything but the opposite.

My door is open, but a slight tapping comes from that general di-rection. I peek over my hands to see Thalia standing in my doorway. I straighten and try to look at least a little like I'm not in danger of a Monday evening mental breakdown.

"Thalia, what are you still doing here?"

"I could ask you the same question." She lifts one eyebrow. "May I?" She indicates the chairs positioned in front of my desk, and I nod, leaning back in my seat.

She sits, crossing one leg over another and clasping her hands on her knee. "I asked my mom to watch the baby for a few extra hours so I could work on the proposal we talked about this morning." She eyes the steam rising from the fresh cup of coffee on my desk. "How many nights have you been here burning the midnight oil this month?"

I glance at the cup, then back to her. "Too many," I admit.

She hums. "I thought you were going to make it a priority to get out of here in time to see your kids more."

"I was. I am. I..." I slump in my chair. "There's a possibility I'm out of my depth here."

Thalia tilts her head. "How so?"

I pass a hand over my mouth, considering. "I like designing. I'm good at it. I can look at a space, measure it, do the math, and create something that's both functional and looks cool. I'm not so great at the more managerial tasks."

"What makes you say that?"

"Did you see Marianne or Orlando in the office at all today?" It's a rhetorical question. Neither of them bothered to show up or notify anyone they were using a personal day. Hence the formal email to HR.

Thalia chuckles. "Can I speak frankly?"

"Of course." I lean forward and fold my arms on top of the desk.

She pauses for a moment, considering how she wants to proceed. "Do you remember doing group projects in high school? Where, inevitably, at least one person would let everyone else carry the project for them?"

I nod. "You're telling me those two haven't been pulling their weight."

"I've been gone on my maternity leave, as you know, but they've been like this since before I had the baby. I'm not surprised to see they haven't changed."

"Why have my parents kept them on?" I say, more to myself than to her.

She barks a laugh. "Your parents haven't had a great read on this place for a year, at least." Her eyes go wide, and she claps a hand over her mouth as if she didn't mean to let that out.

"You're not going to offend me," I assure her. "I had no idea."

She lowers her hand back to her lap. "Don't get me wrong. This is an amazing firm to work for. They're just…"

"Ready to retire?" I fill in. She nods, conceding.

"The cookies should have been a dead giveaway," I mutter.

"Excuse me?"

I shake my head. "Never mind. So, you're saying they don't know Marianne and Orlando aren't working as hard as everyone else?"

"Probably not. I think we all figured they were young. That they'd step up eventually. We covered for them more than we should have. No one wanted to be the one who got the kids in trouble, so to speak."

I smirk. "Except for you."

She shrugs, but there's a gleam in her eyes. "I wanted you to know their bad behavior is well-established. You looked like you were beating yourself up in here. Whatever else you do with that information is up to you."

"Ah. Well, thank you, Thalia." I mean for it to be her cue to leave, but she stays right where she is. "Was there something else?"

"You should go home."

I busy myself shuffling some papers on my desk. "I just have a few things to wrap up—"

"Is any of it necessary for tomorrow?" She cuts me off.

"Excuse me?"

"Does any of it have to be done before, say, ten tomorrow morning?" Her expression is smug, as if her question is also rhetorical.

"No."

"What is it about it that can't wait, then?"

I smooth down some hairs on the top of my head. "I don't know. Nothing, I suppose."

She slaps her hands on her thighs and makes as if to stand. "Well, I'm leaving. And, today aside, I've been taking your earlier advice to get home to my baby, which has been great. Maybe you should practice what you preach." She's teasing, but she's looking at me in that piercing way like Katie does when she's waiting for me to come to the same conclusion.

I snap my laptop shut. "Understood. Thank you, Thalia." She smiles and leaves. I check my watch. If I hurry, I can probably make it just in time for the tail end of dinner.

So, I hurry.

Chapter 20
Katie

I'M SCOOPING PEAS AND mashed potatoes on plates to a rhythmic chorus of "we hate vegetables" when the door to the garage bursts open. The kids go blissfully silent, look at each other wide-eyed, then take off running.

"Daddy!" they yell as they practically tackle him to the floor. He scoops Christine up and pulls Mason in for a tight hug.

"Mom said you wouldn't be home," Mason accuses.

"I'm sorry." Brandon starts turning to go back the way he came. "Should I go, then?"

"No!" Mason giggles. I smile quietly at the sound, and Brandon catches my eye from across the room.

"We hate vegetables!" Christine shouts as she pounds her little fists on Brandon's shoulder in time with her words. Brandon rubs his ear, wincing.

"Welcome home," I say sardonically, though my heart is beating faster at the sight of him. I might be more excited than the kids that he's home.

He chuckles. "What's for dinner?"

"Vegetables," I joke. "And meatloaf."

"It's a good thing your mom hides vegetables in the meatloaf, then, since you won't eat the ones on your plate," he says to the kids with fake enthusiasm.

Mason rolls his eyes. "She does not."

"I don't?" I ask, playing along.

"Mom. No, you don't," he insists. Then, he comes over to inspect the meatloaf in question. "Wait, do you? What's this orange thing?"

I lean closer and squint where he's pointing. There's nothing orange there. "A piece of carrot," I deadpan.

"Oh no. You're not getting me to eat vegetables by hiding them in meatloaf. No way." He folds his thin arms across his chest, stomping his foot.

"We hate vegetables!" Christine screams again. This time, Brandon puts her down to get some distance.

I sigh deeply. "Relax. I wouldn't dream of trying to trick you with hidden vegetables." Then, I smirk. "I'd much rather torture you with vegetables in plain sight."

Mason groans as if I'm the absolute worst person on the face of the planet. It feels like almost overnight, he became so dramatic. He's really been letting this new facet of his personality shine, too. It's delightful.

"Okay, buddy. Why don't you take your sister and go wash up for dinner." Brandon ruffles his hair. Mason swats him away with another noise of disgust, then takes Christine's hand, leading her out.

Brandon hangs up his coat in the closet. As he walks back to the kitchen, he unbuttons his shirtsleeves and rolls them up, his forearms and cat tattoo on full display. I run my tongue over my bottom lip as I watch him. Now that we've scratched that particular itch, I find it's all I can think about, especially when he's in the room. Especially when I can see his ink.

He must notice how unexpectedly turned on I am, because he crosses the room in two long strides and cups my cheek with his hand. He curls his fingers into my hair, loosening my messy bun and using it for purchase to angle my head. He kisses me deeply, but I'm still holding the serving spoon I was using to dish out the vegetables, so I feel both completely swept up and awkwardly grounded at the same time.

Brandon breaks the kiss, then plants a quick one on my cheek before leaning against the counter and dipping a finger in the mashed potatoes.

I swat at him with the spoon. "Get out of there."

"You know mashed potatoes are my favorite." He suggestively licks the stolen dollop off his finger, rubbing his tongue around it again and again.

My insides turn molten, but the kids are going to come back any second, so I busy myself with taking down another plate and serving a huge heap of potatoes. "I have been making them every night for a week, trying to summon you."

He chuckles at my sarcasm. "I deserved that," he says. He kisses my cheek again, taking the plate from me and serving himself some meatloaf before making his way to the table.

"Excuse me," I say pointedly. He frowns at me, confused, so I forcefully indicate the bowl of peas, raising my eyebrows to suggest he take some as a good example for the kids.

"Oh," he says, finally catching on. "No thanks. I hate vegetables."

The kids, having chosen that exact moment to re-enter the room, cheer. My nostrils flare as I stare him down. He's joking, of course, but I'm not amused. I have to play bad cop all day. The least he can do is eat some damn peas.

"Sorry." He smirks. "I was teasing. Peas are great. Peas are especially fun when you can launch them at each other across the table." He winks at Mason, who tries—unsuccessfully—to hide a laugh.

"Launch them wherever you want, as long as some land in your mouth, and you clean up whatever doesn't." I help myself to a serving of everything, then hand full plates to each of the children. It's absolutely a mistake to let Christine carry her own plate to the table, but if we don't, she'll throw a fit, so I follow her closely, my arm out to catch the plate should it fall out of her tiny hands.

They do shoot peas into each other's mouths, and enough of them make it into the kids' bellies that I'm happy with the result. Between that and the kids telling Brandon every painstaking detail about their days at school, dinner takes a lot longer than usual.

Normally, I'm counting down the minutes until dinner is over. It's always a cacophony of noise, mess, and touching. Mason poking at Christine, both of them throwing food at each other, Christine begging to sit in my lap, each of them vying for my attention at the same time, various sauces or yogurts landing on my clothes and arms. The whole thing is almost always capped off with one or the other out of their seat and running laps around the table.

But something about Brandon's presence always calms them. Or, maybe a better way to put it is that he focuses their attention. He takes their boundless energy and channels it into something productive. Tonight is no different. They're not polite, well-behaved children, but they're funny and engaged. They eat enough food with some nutrition in it that I won't mind if they raid the pantry for snacks in an hour. Which they will do.

The whole scene tears me in two. One part of me is warmed to my very center at the way the three of them interact. One part is angry. The kids love him and me in very different ways. I'm the one who always has to do the day-to-day drudgery. I'm the one who has to make them sit to eat when they're wild or do homework and count screen time minutes when they'd rather zone out in front of the television. Brandon gets to witness the more settled moments. They don't get riled up around him as much because they don't have as many chances. It's novel when he's here, whereas I'm the norm. It makes me feel so completely outside the relationship they have with Brandon that it almost physically hurts. And, not for the first time, I have the fleeting thought that a glass of wine would take this edge off.

I do what Nora tells me to do when I feel like an outsider looking in. I widen my perspective, like I would with a painting. I step back and see myself in the scene, because I am there, whether I feel like it or not. It helps take the edge off enough that I make it through the rest of dinner feeling less twitchy.

When we're finally done eating, Mason grabs the broom and sweeps up the peas without being asked. Brandon takes over baths and bedtime. I load the dishwasher, wipe off the surfaces, then fall onto the couch.

By the time Brandon has both kids in bed, I'm already half asleep, my arm hanging limply off the side of the couch and my eyes focused on an invisible spot on the ceiling. Brandon sits on the coffee table and rests his elbows on his thighs, steepling his fingers in front of his lips.

I roll my head to look at him. "It's a huge couch. You don't have to sit there."

"I know." He studies me, his hazel eyes intent. His expression darkens, and a little thrill passes through me. I shiver, quickly sitting up so our knees touch. I press my palms into the couch cushion.

I'm not sure how to interpret his body language, which is new for us. Usually, he's so open I can read him like a book. But right now, I'm not sure if he's going to have his way with me right here on the couch or tell me he's moving out.

Little pinpricks of anxiety rush through my chest, and my eyes widen. "Is everything okay?"

He takes a deep, shaky breath and runs a hand over his rusty hair. "Yeah." He blows out through pursed lips, his breath tickling my bangs. He grabs my hands and squeezes them. "That's a lie. It's not okay." He lets go of my hands and pinches his temples, squeezing his eyes shut.

He's silent for a long moment, and my right leg starts bouncing up and down completely without my permission. He eyes it, and I force it to stop.

"I'm sorry, Katie." His gaze finds mine, his eyes shining as if he's going to cry. He grasps my hands again, and it feels desperate. "I made promises to you, and I broke them. It didn't even take me very long. I'd love to tell you it's not my fault, but I can't. I should have seen this coming. This job is..." He trails off, his eyes going skyward. He laughs humorlessly. "It fucking sucks."

His shoulders sag as if the sheer weight of carrying those words has fallen off them as soon as they are out of his mouth.

I should comfort him, but instead, I let out an involuntary sob. It's loud and unexpectedly wet. In a heartbeat, he's off the table and next to me on the couch, pulling me close.

"Shit, Brandon." I smack his shoulder. "I thought you were leaving me or something."

He holds me at arm's length, a deep crease between his eyebrows. "What?" he barks. He pulls me close again, squeezing me harder. "Fuck. I'm not very good at this. I was trying to open up to you."

I laugh harshly. "Oh my god. You're terrible at this. You stared at me like what you were about to say was the hardest thing, and I thought—"

He cups my cheeks between his palms, wiping a stray tear with his thumb. He leans forward so our faces are less than an inch apart, our eyes locked on each other. "Why would I ever leave you? What would make you think that?"

I raise an eyebrow, sniffling. "You really don't get it, do you? You're never here. And even when you are, you're distant. Like your mind is somewhere else."

He pulls back, dropping his hands. "Right. Well, I can see how you would come to that conclusion. I haven't been very good to you or the kids, Cat." He fiddles with a loose thread on the couch cushion. "This job is not what I expected. Or what I was promised."

I lay my hand over his. "Tell me about it, then."

He spends the next hour filling me in on everything that has been going on. He starts with his useless junior architects that he's pretty sure he's going to have to fire. After that, he describes his unimaginative senior architect who seems so much like a crotchety old man that I'm surprised when he tells me Jasper is probably only in his early forties. He's frustrated with his parents for being almost completely hands-off. Even though he wants to take over the firm, he feels stalled because they're technically still there. He seems to find a lot of promise in one of his junior architects, but she's a new mom and he doesn't want to overload her.

When he talks about her, I'm unexpectedly jealous. I know she must be busting her ass with a new baby and a job, and I should feel fortunate that I never had to do that. But I can't help but wonder if I'd feel differently if I had some kind of purpose outside of motherhood these past seven years. My mind goes to the panels starting to line up in my studio, but now's not the time to talk about that. Not when Brandon is in crisis.

I blink rapidly and rejoin what Brandon is saying about having to do all the personnel stuff on top of more design work than he expected to make up for the lost productivity of his team. He doesn't seem to notice I checked out for my own little pity party, which is good. This isn't about me.

With each sentence, he relaxes. Some of the color comes back to his face, and a little of the wide-eyed optimism I fell in love with comes back, too.

Eventually, he trails off into silence. I take his hands and rub my thumbs over his knuckles.

"I'm so sorry, Brandon. I had no idea how hard this was for you. I really thought it was just the same old work stuff." A little bubble starts to rise in my chest, like maybe if I can tell him everything that's been weighing on me, I'll feel better, too. But I shove it down. He needs to have this moment for himself, and he needs my support.

He shakes his head vehemently. "No, Cat. I'm the one who needs to apologize. I need to set better boundaries like I promised I would. At the very least, I'm not going to miss more time with you and the kids." He takes a shuddering breath and presses my fingers between his own. "If you want to go back to New York, I'd go with you. Right now." His face is eager, and it's so boyish that for a second, I'm taken back to the night I told him I was pregnant with Mason. He was outwardly thrilled and ready to jump in, feet first. But just like now, I knew he wasn't sure. That he was posturing for my benefit.

A corner of my mouth pulls up as I slowly shake my head. "Brandon Conley, you are not a quitter."

His eyes dip to my lips, then shine before making their way up to mine again. "How do you figure?"

I laugh, my smirk turning into a full grin. The sound is clunky from the stress of the conversation and almost foreign to my ears, though Brandon's brows loosen all the same. "You asked me to marry you every single day for almost an entire year," I say as if it should be obvious.

He leans in, brushing his nose back and forth against mine. A rumble starts deep in my throat, and he inhales, breathing me in. "When I see something I want, I don't give up easily." His voice is husky, and I'm grateful we're sitting because it makes my knees go weak.

"Yes," I breathe. I clear my throat, pulling away from him just a bit. "Right. Focus for a second." My voice is steadier, in control. "Do you want this job?"

He narrows his eyes, but his gaze never leaves mine. "I do," he admits. "But not if it's going to come between us like the last one did. Not again. You're too important to me."

"Then we need to figure out how to make the job work with the family," I say firmly.

It feels like a lot of things have been solved for him, or at least they should be, but he's still looking at me a little strangely.

"I'm confident we can figure it—"

"Why did you apologize for getting pregnant the other night?" he blurts out.

I reel back, my shoulders tensing. "What?"

"You told me the other night you were sorry you got pregnant. That it cramped my style or something. Why did you say that?"

"Why are you asking about this now?" I'm still reeling from the topic switch.

"It's been on my mind all day." He frowns when I don't respond. "Why did you say that, Katie? Please."

"I was upset," I say simply.

Apparently, that's not good enough for him. He shakes his head without speaking. I run a hand through my hair in frustration. He's really all about unburdening himself tonight, I guess. Well, I wanted my turn. Now I have it.

Resigned, I drop my hand to my thigh with a smack. "You never got to choose us. The choice was made for you. It wasn't my fault, per se, but it happened. And you're a great guy, so of course you were going to do the right thing by us." I sigh, turning my gaze to the ceiling. "But I had a couple years on you. You were fresh out of school. Unprepared for this." I shrug, returning my eyes to him. "You didn't know anything about me, Brandon."

"I knew enough," he insists, his voice barely a whisper.

"You didn't." I lean forward to punctuate the words. "You didn't know anything about my family. You knew I drank a lot, but you didn't know I—" The words catch in my throat. "All of a sudden, I was knocked up, and you hadn't had the chance to run."

"You were..." he pauses, swallowing audibly. "You are everything, Katie. I wouldn't have run."

I jump to my feet in a fit of frustration. "You've *been* running. What else could you possibly call this?" I throw my arms wide, encompassing the house, the kids, the sheer size of the loneliness I've been trying to shove into a too-small box. "I understand where you're coming from. I do. But you can't just open up a little and expect that to fix everything.

You promise again and again that you'll be here. I believe you every time. Even now, you have me hoping things will be different." I don't mean to sound patronizing, but he winces. "What am I supposed to think?"

I want to tell him more. I want to tell him about all the times I've felt overstimulated. When I've just needed five minutes of quiet. When I've thought a drink might take the edge off—something that's been happening more and more lately.

But I don't because pain crosses his face, clear as day. I might as well have struck him with my open hand across his cheek. It feels equal parts devastating to know I caused it and exhilarating to have finally gotten it out.

He stands slowly. Normally, he towers over me, but he's so deflated that he seems about three inches shorter than usual. He looks at a spot over my shoulder. "I'll take the guest room tonight," he whispers. He steps past me toward the basement stairs.

I whirl around as he passes. "No. Please." My voice cracks. If I had known this was going to be the result, I would have continued to keep it all bottled up. I finally thought we were getting somewhere, and he's running. Again. "I want to figure this out." I mean to sound confident and assertive, but it comes out more as a plea. A prayer. Desperate.

He stops but doesn't face me. "I'm going to try, Cat. I just... I need some space." He continues his way to the stairs, descending them silently.

I watch until he's well out of sight, hoping he'll change his mind, but he doesn't. I get ready for bed and fall into a restless sleep, alone.

Chapter 21

Brandon

I ASK KATIE A hard question.

She answers honestly.

And what do I do? I leave. I do exactly what she says I've been doing. I run away.

I need time to think, and there's rarely any thinking when I'm pressed up against her under the covers. The problem is, the only thing I can think about is how much I've fucked this up and how much I'd rather be showing her how much she means to me, but I said what I said, and now I have to live with the consequences.

I try calling Daniel, but it goes to voicemail. He's probably having a nice evening with his wife, and I fight the jealousy that comes with the realization.

Katie is right. What is she supposed to think of my absence, especially when I haven't been able to communicate how difficult this job has been? How was she supposed to read the late nights in New York? I thought it was obvious I was working hard for my family, but she was working hard *with* the family. The family I convinced her I wanted.

I sit on the edge of the bed with my head in my hands for what feels like forever. Eventually, I get up and go to our room. I listen at the door for any sounds, but it's silent. I crack the door open and peek inside, only to see a dark room, the outline of her hips visible in the light filtering in from the hall. As much as I want to wake her up, pull her close, and shower her with promises that this time it's going to be different, I know that wouldn't be helpful.

She wants to believe me. I could tell in her voice. No matter how many times I've shown her evidence to the contrary, she sees the potential. She always has. It's time I live up to it.

I close the door quietly behind me as I make my way back to the guest room. I grab a notebook from my office and settle into bed, though I don't sleep. I stay awake long into the night, hashing out a schedule for my work that will allow me to be home in time for dinner for the rest of the week. The project might suffer. Then again, if I put it in the right hands, it might not. I flip to a new page, writing up some notes on what we've done so far and what Jasper and Thalia can take over from here.

Once it's done, I feel good enough about it to get a few hours of sleep, but I'm jolted awake by Mason bursting through the guest room door.

"Mom sent me in here. She told me it's your turn to 'do the morning shit.'"

"Don't say that word," I grumble into my pillow.

Mason shrugs. "That's what Mom said. Is she mad at you?"

Yes. I sit up slowly, grabbing a t-shirt off the floor next to the bed and sliding it over my head. "What makes you ask that?"

"You're sleeping in here," he says. We had done a pretty good job of hiding the separate sleeping arrangements from the kids the last time, but I knew that couldn't last forever.

"Nah," I lie. "I was snoring, and she kicked me out. No big deal. Come on, let's get ready for school."

I lead the kids in the usual morning routine. While they're getting dressed, I slip into our bedroom to brush my teeth and grab some clothes, but Katie hides under the covers and doesn't say anything to me. I know I asked for space, but it stings all the same.

As the kids are eating breakfast, I text Thalia to let her know to meet me at the high school instead of the office. I text Jasper to tell him that I plan to be on site for a few hours, and I won't be in the office at all today. Then, I pack the kids up and head out.

When I get to the high school, Thalia is beyond grateful she didn't have to go into the office today. We walk the site where the addition will be. I take a look at the outside of the building and make some notes about options for entry points, connecting the new and the old. All in all, it's uneventful but useful, and I send Thalia home early to her baby.

"You know what I'm going to do?" she asks on her way to her car. "I'm going to let my parents keep hanging out with the baby, and I'm going to take a nap." She smiles dreamily, as if just the thought of it makes her so happy, she could burst.

I chuckle. "I remember those days. Take the naps where you can get them."

She nods, and I notice a stain on her shirt as she gets into the car. I remember those days, too, when I had to change my shirt three times before I was able to get out of the house. I smile fondly at the memory as I watch Thalia peel out of the parking lot on her way home.

I check my watch. It's just about lunch time. I could call my new teacher friends and see if they're available during their lunch periods, but there's only one person I want to see right now, and she's at home.

I get into my car and quickly google Thai restaurants. The pickings are slim, but I eventually find one that looks good enough. I order Katie's favorite and bring it home, hoping to surprise her.

When I get inside, the house is completely silent. Katie's car is in the garage, though, so I know she's here. I put the food on the island and catch movement in her studio from the corner of my eye.

I don't say anything as I walk to the open door. Once I get closer, I see her back is to me and she's wearing her huge over-ear headphones. I lean against the doorframe to watch her. She's perched on the stool in front of her easel, a small table set up next to it with various paints and cups of water set haphazardly on top of it.

I can't see what she's painting because her body is blocking the canvas, so I move further into the room. She has only painted the clothes and one set of hands, but the rest of the sketch is clear. It's the kids and me, playing a board game. Christine is on my lap, leaning forward to touch a game piece, and Mason is clearly frustrated she's messing up the game. She's captured it perfectly.

Suddenly, Katie turns my direction. I'm closer to her than I thought I was because she swipes purple paint over my shirt and onto my bicep.

She must not have known I was there, because she yelps and jumps back, pulling the headphones off her ears and streaking her own cheek with purple in the process.

"Brandon!" She presses a hand to her heart as if she could calm it. "You scared me."

"Sorry," I say sheepishly. "I got home early and came in to see if you wanted lunch. You must not have heard me with your headphones on." It's a half-truth, but I don't think she needs to know that I have been creeping behind her to see her painting for the past few minutes.

She narrows her eyes as if she doesn't believe me, but I shrug and point to her work in progress. "You're painting me and the kids?" I can't help the note of hope in my voice. Surely, if she's painting us together, she can't be totally angry with me for the way I behaved last night.

Katie scratches her head with the hand holding the paintbrush. A few drops of paint land in her hair. "Uh..." she falters. "Yeah. That's kind of all I paint."

That's when I finally look around the whole room and notice the stacks of paintings in various stages of completion leaning against the wall and hanging on the hooks I installed when we moved in. Every single one of them features the kids and me in some way. Making pizza, ice skating, making a snowman. And there's the one she started in New York of us at the pumpkin patch. Some are scenes that really happened, and others are made up from other references, but they are all clearly the kids and me having fun together.

My jaw drops as I take them all in. They're stunning.

"I started with the pumpkin one," Katie is saying. She moves her hand, wielding the paintbrush as a pointer. "And then I got inspired, I guess? I don't know." She sounds unsure, but I wish she had more confidence about these pictures. They're perfect, and there's so much love in them. It makes my heart hurt.

"Why aren't you in them?" I ask quietly.

She chews her bottom lip, considering. "Well, that's a good question. I didn't realize I was gone at first, but when I did, I thought maybe I should talk to my therapist about it. We're working on it."

I nod slowly, still looking at each painting in turn.

"But I kept going with them, and I think there's a story here? Maybe something about a hero dad, or a dad who makes some mistakes, but is always there for his kids? I thought it might make a good children's book." Her voice is shaking a little, which rips my attention from the paintings to land solely on her.

"You want to write a children's book?" My eyebrows pinch together.

Katie blushes. It's so beautiful, I can hardly stand it. I could sweep her up in my arms right now, but I can see she's struggling to get something out in the open, so I wait patiently for her to speak.

She runs a hand through her hair, looking at it as it comes away with purple paint on it. "Maybe? I started contacting some professional photographers to take pictures of the paintings so they can be digitized, but I don't know. It's kind of expensive."

"I don't care about the money," I say, my voice still quiet.

Katie snorts a laugh. "I know. It just feels wasteful."

"What's wasteful about it? It's something you love. It's something you want to do."

She shrugs as if it's truly no big deal, then steps closer to her table to put the paintbrush down and start cleaning up. I take her hand and she turns to face me. "Cat." I'm completely in awe of her, and I don't quite know how to express it. "It's brilliant."

Her face lights up ever so slightly, her eyebrows raising and her eyes widening. "Do you think so?" She wears the exact same expression our kids make when we tell them we're proud of them—excitement mixed with hope.

I step closer to her, intoxicated by her budding happiness. I want to put it in a box and keep it with me to pull out and look at on bad days.

I cup her cheek with my hand, threading my fingers through her hair. "I do."

Her eyelids flutter closed. "I'm sorry—"

"No," I stop her. "I shouldn't have run off last night. And I shouldn't have made you spend all those nights alone with the kids while I was at work." Her eyes open softly, her face tipped up to mine. My hand is tangled in her hair, mixing with the paint splattered there. I want desperately to kiss her, but we've gotten side-tracked too many times, so I force myself to continue. "I never felt like I deserved you and the kids. I assumed I was too lucky to have landed this perfect family, basically by accident. My parents practically handed me a job, and now they've handed me another one. I wanted a promotion, yes, but I wanted you to be proud of me. I wanted you to feel like you made the right decision marrying some idiot right out of grad school with nothing to show for himself but some money his parents gave him, a strung-out brother, and a broody writer friend."

Katie starts to shake her head, but I don't let her get a word in. "You make everything in my life better. You always have. From the night I met you until this very moment, you've continually made our lives magical. I wanted to be worthy of that magic."

"All I wanted was for you to be with me." She pauses, dragging her bottom lip through her teeth. "I was okay until I wasn't, you know? And it happened so fast. I didn't even know I was turning to old habits until I did, and I didn't know how to ask for your help. You were stressed. I didn't want to be a burden."

I pull her into me, her head on my chest, paint smearing on the other side of my shirt. "I love you, Cat. You could never be a burden. 'In sickness and in health,' remember?"

She shrugs and buries herself deeper into me. I wrap my other arm around her shoulders and press a kiss to a paint-free area of her hair.

"I'm going to be better. You don't have to believe me, but I'm going to show you," I insist.

Katie turns her face upward and snakes her hands up my back. I shudder, fisting her hair without thinking, and kissing her deeply. It's urgent, and we're all tongues and teeth and swollen lips as we crash into each other with fervor. I part my lips from hers just long enough to pull her shirt over her head and groan when I see her lacy, blue bra barely covering her perfect breasts. I kiss my way down to them, pulling each strap off her shoulders on the way. She pulls my shirt over my head, then goes to work on the fly of my jeans, shimmying herself out of her leggings at the same time. It's a feat that shouldn't be possible, except we're the parents of small children who have learned a thing or two about how to undress quickly.

I unhook her bra and let it join the pile of clothes on the floor. She smooths her hand over my chest, lingering over my tattoo. Some of the remaining paint leaves its mark. Katie eyes it, purring. Her eyes gleam at the mark she's left and, I have to admit, it's hot as hell to know she's claimed me.

"I'm yours," I say, my voice rough. "And you're mine." Her eyes darken as I dip my fingers in some purple paint, drawing a line over her jaw and down her neck. I circle her nipple, and she looks down at the trail of it, laughing breathily.

I kiss her jaw on the other side, then lean to whisper in her ear. "You were beautiful painting like that. So peaceful. So happy." I punctuate each sentence with another kiss. She sighs, her hand finding my cock and pumping a few times. But it feels impatient, and I can't wait either. I pull her to the floor with me. I lay on my back, and position her above me, my hands gripping those hips that haunt my dreams nightly.

Katie rests her hands on my chest as she leans forward, her round breasts dangling above me. As she lowers herself onto me, I cup one of her breasts, the paint smearing. She feels so fucking good. She's so warm and tight, and she takes all of me inside her almost immediately. It's better than two people who were made for each other. It's two people who have mapped each other's bodies over the years, knowing exactly where the treasure is, and the best route to get there.

I press a finger to her clit, and she moans. Her thighs flex as she raises and lowers herself rhythmically on my cock. I watch myself as I thrust in time with her, letting her control the depth. She takes all of me every time.

"Look at you." I tighten my grip on her hip, pressing my fingers into her flesh. She leans back so she can sit up, letting me get the view she knows I like. "You're fucking perfect." She skates her hands over her curves, up on top of her breasts, and into her hair. She lifts it off her shoulders so I can see her neck.

I can't stand not kissing the long column of her throat, so I hold her hips down to keep myself inside her as I sit up. I press my hands to her back, bringing her closer to me, and she obliges, circling her hips and driving me wild. The friction between us lands right where she needs it, and she picks up speed. Breathy moans escape her, and I know she's close.

"Yes, Cat. That's it," I gently encourage her. "Fuck, you feel so good." It's just enough to send her over the edge. She clenches around me, her thighs slick with sweat and paint and arousal. With a few more thrusts, I'm following her, burying my cock in her warm body and my face in the crook of her neck.

After we wring every last ounce of pleasure from each other, I lay back on the floor. Katie curls up next to me, her head on my shoulder and her hand on my chest. She delicately traces the letters there. I kiss her forehead. I know we're going to have to move soon. The floor is cold, and we're both covered in paint. But I want to soak up this moment for a minute.

A low rumble works its way up her throat as I absentmindedly draw circles on her upper arm.

"You were right," I say quietly. "I didn't know you very well when we got married."

She turns her head so her chin is resting on my chest and her eyes meet mine. "Careful. Hearing I'm right is a major turn on."

I chuckle, moving my light circles to her upper back. "The thing is," I say slowly, "that I love you more with every piece I learn about you."

She studies me for a long moment before turning her head and nestling into my shoulder again. She doesn't say anything, but I feel her smile against my skin. And her smile is all I need.

Chapter 22

Katie

EVERYONE IS AT SCHOOL or work and the house is quiet when I click the red *Join Call* button on my tablet. While I wait, I run through all the things that have happened since the last time I spoke with my therapist. It's probably too much to cover in the short time we have together, and I can't decide where to start or what's important. My mind feels like a snow globe after a child shook it up, all the thoughts glittering in their freefall through my brain. They're all pretty, and they all look important, but they're a mess.

Before long, Nora's face fills the screen. She smiles warmly, the dark skin around her eyes crinkling. "Good morning, Katie. How are you doing today?"

"Fine, I think?" I don't mean to ask it as a question, but it comes out that way, anyway. I grab a paperclip that's laying on the desk and start twisting and untwisting it between my fingers.

"You think? What's going on?"

I take a deep breath, eyes trained on the paperclip in my hands. "Everything feels like it's going really well," I say with more certainty than I feel.

"But?" Nothing gets by Nora. I should have known better.

I force myself to look at the screen where Nora waits patiently for me to answer. She's wearing a loose-knit ochre sweater that compliments her warm skin and giant, dangling gold earrings. I wonder how she wears those all day without ripping them out of her earlobes.

She probably isn't in a constant state of overstimulation like I am, that's how.

I sigh, stretching my neck to the right, then the left. "On the outside, things seem great. Brandon and I had a few talks about the important stuff. Mostly why he's been staying at work so late and how I've been feeling about it." I pick at a thread on the sleeve of my sweatshirt. "He kind of bared his soul to me, but I wasn't able to give him much. I still feel like a mess."

"What feels messy to you?" She asks it without judgment, and I try to apply the same lens to my own thoughts. I try to look at them for a moment as if I'm not anxious or disgusted by them.

"I believe him when he says he's going to come home on time. I believe he wants to be a bigger part of the kids' lives and mine. I always believe him, though, so..." I shrug.

Nora chuckles. "There must have been something different about it this time to make you say it."

"There was. He seemed so upset with himself. Like all he wants is to be better for us. But as he was saying it, I kind of realized..." This is the part that's going to be hard to admit. I swallow, then push through. "I realized I wasn't really asking him to come home for the kids. I mean, that's part of it, of course, but I was asking for me. Somewhere along the line, I lost everything. I have no family to speak of. All my friends were either work or drinking buddies; some of them both. Trying to paint with two small kids ended up being arts and crafts time for everyone rather than something I did for myself, so I just... stopped." I finally look back to the screen.

"You didn't have your coping mechanism anymore, either," she suggests.

"Yeah. Everything changed so fast. And I was happy. I really was. But with the kids in school and Brandon still working late nights, I guess I was left looking at myself and wondering who the hell I was anymore."

Nora hums as she nods slowly. "And did you like what you saw?"

"Not all of it." It comes tumbling out without thinking, and I'm a little surprised.

"What is it you do like?"

I scrunch up my nose, and Nora laughs.

"I know it's hard to talk positively about yourself, but try," she insists.

"Okay... I guess I like that I'm a good mom. I'm a good wife, too. I'm passionate about my art again, which feels like I'm moving in the right direction. I think I'm fun to be around, though Brandon says I'm a grouch. Grouches can be fun, too, though, so..." I trail off, smirking.

Nora's shoulders shake as she tries, unsuccessfully, to hold back her laughter. "What is it you don't like, then?"

"I've been thinking about drinking way too much lately." After the other night with Brandon, I must be ready to tell someone, because the admission comes easily. But I cringe, waiting for her admonition or judgment or disappointment.

It doesn't come. She shifts in her seat, her expression remaining completely neutral. "Have you had alcohol since we last spoke?" It's a loaded question, but it sounds so simple coming from her. There's no value behind it, just did I, or didn't I?

It makes it easier to answer. "No."

Nora nods, but it's not a nod of approval. She's considering her next words. "Katie"—she leans forward, resting her elbows on her desk—"you've been thinking about drinking, but you haven't had a drink. I'm proud of you."

I straighten, shaking my head slightly. "What? Why?"

"So far, up until recently, staying sober has been relatively easy for you, yes?" she asks. I nod my agreement, and she continues. "That makes sense. You had other things to focus your attention on. But when you were left to yourself again, those old thoughts started creeping back in. That also makes sense. That's to be expected. But you didn't give in to them like you would have in the past. That's fantastic."

I frown. "I'm not following."

"They're just thoughts, Katie. You are not your thoughts. How many times have you thought something terrible and not acted on it?"

"Like punching Brandon in the face?" I joke.

Nora chuckles. I'm glad I somehow found a therapist who appreciates my dark humor. "Exactly. Do you feel bad about those thoughts?"

"Not usually," I deadpan.

"In all seriousness, you probably don't feel bad about those thoughts because you didn't act on them. You'd feel terrible if you did actually punch him in the face, but you didn't. So, what makes the thoughts about drinking any different?"

I consider this for a moment. "I guess they're not. But that doesn't explain why you're proud of me about this."

"I'm proud of you because it's easy to stay on course while you're distracted and happy. It's much harder when you're not. But you're doing it anyway. You will have to work at this for the rest of your life, and sometimes it'll be hard like this. But you're doing what you set out to do, even though it's difficult, and that's something to be proud of. It shows immense growth."

Tears prick at the corners of my eyes. I quickly wipe them away.

"What's going on?" Nora asks. "What are you thinking?"

"That felt really good to hear," I admit. More tears threaten to fall, but I talk through them. "I've been over here beating myself up about wishing I could have a drink when things get stressful, but you're right. I haven't had a drink, even though things have been *very* stressful, and maybe I should celebrate that."

"You should *definitely* celebrate that." Nora's smile is wide.

And, for the first time in a while, I can feel my smile is, too.

Nora and I talk for a little longer about ways to let those disruptive thoughts go. By the time we end the call, I'm feeling lighter than I have in a long time. It's almost as if I can start to forgive myself for some of this. Or, maybe, like there was never anything to forgive in the first place.

But with this new lightness also comes a new exhaustion. I guess baring your soul to your husband and then your therapist can make you pretty tired. I glance around the studio, but I'm mentally drained. I don't think I'll be able to paint today, or at least not until I get more coffee. But when I go out to the kitchen to make more, I find we're out of coffee beans.

I tip my head back and groan, cursing past me for not putting coffee on the grocery list. To be fair, though, we've been going through it a lot faster between Mason's five-thirty wakeup calls and a few late nights.

Since the kids are at school and Brandon is at work, I have nothing but time to treat myself. I pull out my phone and search for nearby coffee shops. The first search result looks like a bookstore with a coffee bar inside, which sounds perfect, actually. As much as I have resisted Jenny's smutty book recommendations, I am starting to get curious about them. And now that Brandon and I have reignited that particular flame, maybe reading one won't make me feel like an outsider looking in.

It only takes a few minutes to get there. When I pull up, it's clear I'm in the middle of downtown Leade Park. I certainly wouldn't call this a small town, but it's quaint, with a train running through the middle of it on its way to Chicago. The buildings look like they've been updated several times since they were built at the turn of a past century.

All Booked Up, which is a sickly-sweet name for a bookstore, is a storefront sandwiched between an indoor plant shop and a furniture shop that looks like it has long passed its heyday. When I pull the door to the shop open, there's a ding of a bell—because of course there is. The inside is just as quaint as the outside, with oak bookshelves lining the walls and creating faux-aisles through the front of the store. The faint sound of a milk steamer comes from the back of the store, and I'm overwhelmed by the inky, faintly almond smell of books and coffee. It's not the same kind of overwhelm as kids screaming and making dinner, though. It's more akin to a soft blanket covering my brain, soothing over some of the raw edges from my recent conversations.

A faint smile plays at my lips as I stand just inside the door, taking in the space. Maybe I'll paint this later. I'd like to try to capture the comfort of the moment just after you walk in the doors of a space that feels like home.

The store is relatively empty, which makes sense for a weekday afternoon. A blonde woman sits at the counter to my left. She had been reading but puts her bookmark in the book to mark her page and looks up at me.

"Hello!" she says cheerfully. "Anything I can help you find?"

"Romance?" I ask.

She smiles conspiratorially and ticks her eyebrow up a bit. "Rom-com or something steamier?"

I laugh, then give her the title Jenny mentioned in her text messages. The woman hums, still smiling, as she leads the way toward the back of the store. She points out the book I'm looking for, then winks and leaves me to browse. The cover pictures only a half-naked man whose pants are slung lower on his hips than anyone would wear them as he wraps his arm behind his head to flex his chest muscles. I figure I may as well lean into this new-to-me genre, so I pull two other books with similar covers off the shelf before I make my way back to order coffee.

The café area is empty save for one table absolutely covered in papers and notebooks. A man sits there with his back to me. He's wearing a well-loved gray cardigan, and one of his hands is shoved in his dark, wavy hair while the fingers of the other tap out an erratic rhythm on top of the table.

I laugh silently and put on my best, high-pitched fangirl voice. "Oh my god. Is that the famous Daniel Evans?"

He stiffens and his fingers go still on the top of the table. I shouldn't mess with him, but it's too easy. He hates when people recognize him in public.

Daniel turns around slowly, and when he sees me, his shoulders sag in relief.

"Dammit, Katie." He narrows his eyes at me.

My shoulders shake as I try to control my laughter. "Sorry."

"No, you're not."

"You're right. I'm not." I walk toward his table. "Writing the next Great American Novel to torture high school students all across the country?"

Someone snorts from behind the counter. I whip my head toward the sound, unaware there was someone back there. It's a younger version of the blonde woman who welcomed me into the store. She covers her mouth quickly. "Oh, sorry."

Daniel smiles good-naturedly. "Aimee, meet Katie. She's a friend from New York. Katie, this is Aimee. She was a student in Mac's class when I shadowed her a few years ago. Her mom owns this place."

"Ah, so you're well acquainted with Daniel's torturous prose, then," I tease.

She laughs brightly. "We all read the book Mr. Evans wrote about us, so, yeah, I guess."

I turn to Daniel and silently mouth, "Mr. Evans?" Daniel shrugs, though I can tell the name makes him proud.

He nods toward the books I'm holding. "What torturous prose are you after today?"

I feel color rising to my cheeks. Daniel must see it, too, because his smile turns wicked. I flash the cover at him, then quickly turn it back toward my body.

He gives a hearty chuckle. "Oh, I read one of those once."

My eyes bug out of my head. "You did not," I say in disbelief.

He nods, smiling. "I did it to impress a girl."

"Did it work?" I ask, though I think I already know the answer.

Sure enough, he replies, "It did." He ticks an eyebrow upward and motions toward an empty chair, indicating I should sit. "Jenny got to you, too?"

I sink into it, putting the books face-down on the only remaining space on top of the table. I'm not sure how weird it is to have one of Daniel's former students—if you could even call her that—knowing I'm reading smut. "You could say that."

Aimee giggles. "Miss Green always had interesting taste in books."

I arch my eyebrow at her. "She told you about the books she reads?"

"Oh, no. Never." She shakes her head vehemently. "But I worked here all through high school. Mom was always the one to ring her up, but I figured it out eventually." Her face lights up as if something just occurred to her. "Is it true her and Coach are finally a thing?" Her wide, blue eyes bounce quickly back and forth between Daniel and me.

"Finally?" I ask, just as Daniel says, "Yes."

"Should you be talking about teachers' personal lives and reading habits with former students?" I ask him.

"Probably not." He dips his chin to give Aimee a pointed look.

"I'm an adult now. It's fine," she insists. We both continue to stare at her in silence. When she realizes she's not getting any more gossip out of us, she sighs, resigned. "Would you like anything to drink, Katie?"

"Just black coffee, please."

"Oh good. That's way easier than Mr. Evans' order," she says as she pours me coffee in a mug and brings it over. "On the house," she says as I reach for my wallet. Having no more customers, she bounces past me to the front of the shop. I get up to put a five-dollar bill in the tip jar to compensate, then sit back down, cupping the warm mug with my hands and resting my feet on the bottom rung of the chair. I'm effectively curling into the warmth of the shop and the coffee. It feels good after the emotionally draining days I've had.

Daniel drops the pen he's been holding, then leans back in his chair. "How are the Conleys?"

"Good." I respond automatically, but Daniel has known me for a long time. He crosses his arms and waits, his gray-blue eyes soft.

"Really. We're good," I insist.

"Pole dancing was as effective as couples therapy, then?" he teases.

My face flames at the memory of what happened after we got home that night. Daniel smirks. His damn writer brain doesn't miss anything.

I trace my finger along the spine of one of my books. "It ended up being good for us, I think."

He's still smiling to himself, but he nods. "Glad to hear it."

We sit in awkward silence for a minute. I sip my coffee for something to do, turning my attention to the mismatched tables in the café, noting how they somehow all look like they belong here, even though not one of them is the same as another.

Daniel leans forward in his chair, his forearms resting against the table. "Brandon is like a brother to me. You know that. But that makes you my de facto sister-in-law, Katie. I care about you, too."

I've always liked Daniel. He was a little lost when I met him, but he has always been genuine, and now is no exception. He doesn't need anything from me, and he's not after any information. He's not even looking out for Brandon right now. He simply wants me to be okay.

My gaze falls slowly to my hands, which are clasped on the table in front of me. I'm surprised when my inhale is a little shaky. "How did you know you wanted to stay here?" My voice is quiet and unsure, but somehow, I know he'll have the answer I'm looking for.

"Mac was here," he says simply. "It was the easiest decision I've ever made."

"She could have come back with you," I suggest, though I know she probably wouldn't have.

Daniel shakes his head, confirming my suspicion. "This is her home. She has roots here." He pushes back away from the table and runs a hand through his hair. A lock of it falls over his forehead. "I don't really think I've ever had roots anywhere." He pauses, then smiles softly. "Until now."

He does have roots here. It's a quiet realization, but I see it clearly. Even if that small conversation with Aimee a few minutes ago didn't prove it, his demeanor would. He seems settled, relaxed. Where there used to be doubt and chaos brewing, now there's contentment. Happiness. Belonging.

I chew on the corner of my lip. "Didn't you miss New York?"

"A little, at first." He lets out a breath through pursed lips, looking skyward. "But I think you and I both know there wasn't anything left there for me. Not really."

I nod, falling silent. I grip my coffee mug again, taking another slow sip. Daniel tilts his head, watching me. I carefully set the mug down on the table and press my palms flat against it, letting the cold tabletop ground me.

"Do you miss New York?" he asks.

"I thought I did." I give him a sad smile. "But I think maybe what I really missed was who I was when we were there."

"What do you mean?"

"I was fun, you know? And then I was head-over-heels in love and a new mom at the same time. Now..." I trail off and shrug.

"You're different. And it's not the same city you loved anymore."

"Yeah."

Daniel leans forward further and covers my hand with his. "We're all rooting for you, Katie."

I had my suspicions about how much Brandon had told Daniel about his decision to move us all out here, but at this moment, I'm sure Daniel knows everything. But instead of embarrassment, what I feel is relief. He knows, and I don't have to hide it. I swallow hard and roll my lips between my teeth. I bite down hard to distract myself from the tears that are threatening to fall. When I feel composed enough, I let out a slow breath. "Brandon has been struggling with his job. He says he'd go back with me if I want."

"Do you?"

He hasn't moved his hand from mine, his expression open and concerned. It's a brotherly moment, or I would assume it is. I don't have siblings, so I don't exactly know what that would feel like, but this feels close.

It's another realization that settles on me, this one softer than the others over the past few days. Brandon and the kids are my family, but Daniel has always been, too. And maybe his new crew could be something like family, as well. I think of Ben and his sisters, and his nephews who have made my children feel so welcomed. Jenny's warm humor and Mac's ability to make me feel like I've known her my whole life. Even Brandon's parents, who are trying to be a bigger part of our lives.

Maybe this is how you build a home. It's not you and your tiny family against the big, bad world and all its temptations. It's you and your family and the people who want to hold you up, for no other reason than that they love you and want you to be happy.

And all those people are here for us. In Leade Park. We never had that in New York, and we were never going to.

I look at Daniel, his question hanging in the air between us. I frown. "Do you think Brandon wants to go back?"

"I think Brandon wants to be where you are. It'll probably be the easiest decision he'll ever make." He smirks at his own reference to the earlier part of the conversation. I roll my eyes. He's insufferable.

I shake my head slowly. "Then, I think I want to stay."

A smile stretches across his face as he squeezes my hand. "Well, then. Welcome home."

Chapter 23
Brandon

KATIE IS UNCHARACTERISTICALLY QUIET all through dinner—a dinner I made sure I was home for—and into the kids' bedtime. When I ask her what's going on, she says she's not feeling great. I half-believe her; she looks a little paler than usual and seems to be dragging, but I have a feeling that's not the whole truth.

When the kids are finally in bed, I find her in our room, changing into her pajamas. She barely spares me a glance when I enter the room, which has me running through all the things that could have happened today. Finding nothing, I switch to wondering if I did something wrong.

"I can hear you thinking," she says as she folds her shirt and sets it in the drawer.

"You don't seem like yourself tonight."

She shuts the drawer and turns toward me, leaning back against the dresser and crossing her arms. "I think I'm getting sick," she insists again.

I narrow my eyes, perching myself on the edge of the bed. "And?"

Her nostrils flare slightly as she presses her lips into a straight line. She's clearly at war with herself about whether or not she wants to tell me what's on her mind. My heartbeat ticks up slightly as I start to worry about what she could be afraid to tell me.

But before my brain can go too far down that road, she lets out a frustrated puff of air. "I want to stay in Leade Park."

I blink several times, surprised. "I'm sorry, what?"

"Don't make me say it again." She frowns.

I chuckle, a sly smile spreading as I push off the bed and make my way to her. I put my hands on the dresser, enclosing her. Her full lips part slightly as she tips her head up to look at me. My gaze meets hers, and I lean in close. I drop my voice a register. "Was it that difficult to admit I was right?"

The desire that was clear in her eyes lights up in flames. She smacks my chest. "Way to ruin a moment."

I kiss her neck softly. She curls toward me, letting out a gasp.

"What are you talking about?" I ask before planting another kiss a little lower on her neck. "Hearing I'm right is a major turn on."

She huffs, but there's no commitment to the sarcasm. "I never said you were right."

I kiss her jawline. "It was implied."

She rests a hand on my chest, pressing me away. Our eyes meet again, hers serious even as they're laced with wanting. "You said you'd go back to New York. Do you want to stay here?"

This woman. This beautiful, wonderful woman. She's so grouchy and guarded so much of the time, but she has such a soft and caring soul. Not for the first time, I'm overwhelmed with how lucky I am to have met her. I lean in to press my lips to her forehead, then lean mine where my lips just were. "I want to be wherever you are."

She barks a harsh laugh at that. I pull away, lowering my eyebrows in question. She draws in a deep breath through her nose. "I ran into Daniel today. He said you'd say that."

"You asked Daniel for advice?" I don't mean to sound incredulous, but Katie is so rarely willing to ask advice from others. She's usually the one to dish it out.

"He was being nice." She shrugs, as if it's no big deal. I guess it's not, really, except that she was with a friend today, unprompted, and she asked that friend for advice. Something has shifted in her. I can see it now that she's not struggling through admitting her realization. The air around her lately had been charged and tense, but now it's more relaxed. It's as if she only needed to make a decision, and that settled her.

I kiss her again. "It's a good thing you want to stay," I say against her lips. "Because I dumped the apartment a week after you moved out here."

Her eyes fly open, her mouth agape. "You cocky bastard. You were that sure I'd come around?"

I laugh heartily, tipping my head back and pulling her into a tight hug. She leans her head against my chest, and I hold her there, stroking her hair. "I'm kidding. But I did put it on the market, and there has been some interest."

She wraps her arms around my waist and melts into me. I might be a cocky bastard, but I'm a lucky one, too.

"Are you going to be okay with this job?" Her voice is muffled by my shirt.

"Yeah. I have a plan."

She pulls back to look at me, a skeptical look on her face. "What plan?"

"It's a half-plan. Step one is to get my parents out of there."

"What's step two?"

I scrunch up my face, closing one eye in the process. I look at her with the other. "That's why it's a half-plan."

She chuckles, and her laugh feels easier now than it did even a few days ago. I soak it in, allowing it to reassure me. We hold each other like this for a while longer, until we finally climb into bed, falling asleep easily.

The next morning, my parents are in my office. Mom sits across from me, her black suit perfectly pressed, a string of pearls around her neck. Dad stands behind her, slightly more casual in a pale blue button-down shirt and navy tie. They're so stoic, they could be stand-ins for the couple in that famous painting of the farmer and his wife.

I pinch the bridge of my nose, closing my eyes to collect myself. This is not going according to my half-plan. "Look," I say as I drop my hand back to the desk. "You brought me out here to take over. I understand why you felt it necessary to transition me into this new role, but there are staff issues that have come to my attention. Jamie has informed me that, until I'm officially in charge, there's not much I can do about it."

"Who is Jamie, again?" Mom asks.

"From HR, dear." Dad lays a hand on her shoulder.

I give both of them a pointed, if not exasperated, look. "You're so hands-off, you don't even know who heads HR. And that's fine," I add quickly. "It's not a judgment. It's a statement of fact. You're both ready to retire. You should. Let me take this on."

"Honey." Mom's voice is patronizing. She's not going to let go. It's a good thing I didn't spend any time planning past step one, then. "Why don't you tell us what's going on with the staff, and we'll take care of it?"

"Tattling to Mom and Dad isn't a great look for someone who is supposedly going to be the new boss."

Dad squeezes Mom's shoulder again. She looks up at him, and he smiles down at her. "We've been talking about it for a year, Maria. The firm is ready for the transition. This won't even come as a surprise."

Mom swallows hard. "I don't know if *I'm* ready for the transition." She faces me again, her hands clenched so hard in her lap that her knuckles are turning white. "I don't know what I'll do without this place."

It's a rare, vulnerable moment for her, and I don't want to discount that. At the same time, if she doesn't go now, she'll end up half-running this place well into her nineties. "You have each other," I say gently. "You'll figure it out."

Mom groans, but it's good-natured. "That's what I'm worried about." She smiles up at my dad, whose eyes go darker for a second. I shudder and look away. I am so grateful that my parents still love each other, but I don't need to see it play out right in front of me.

I clear my throat to remind them I'm sitting right here, before turning my attention back to them. Luckily, they've returned to their platonic state. Mom looks resigned. Dad looks happy. That tells me all I need to know. "So, it's decided?"

Dad nods once. "We'll send a memo at the end of next week."

Turns out after step one, step two is easy. I write up some new plans for how things are going to work around here. Jasper is going to take over as lead architect on the Leade Park High School project. Thalia will assume the role of senior architect, while I shift fully to my leadership role. Frankly, I'm glad to step away from the project, even though it's unfinished. It'll still be my responsibility to review and approve final plans, but I won't have any more involvement in the design process. To say Jasper is happy would be an understatement. He's so grateful, he's even willing to agree not to give Thalia any more shit about her work hours.

And speaking of work hours, I draft a memo that will go out after my parents' stating that I'm excited for this new role, and I know I'll do a good job. I also write that I will be leaving the office at five every day, and any non-emergency communication will be returned the next business day. I hope that this will begin to create a new culture here, where people have time to spend with their families and don't burn themselves out.

My final act of the day is to send an email to Jamie in HR, making her aware that I'll be filing a formal complaint against Orlando and Marianne. They won't be fired, but it'll only take one more strike. Hopefully, this will be the reminder they need to get themselves back on track, but we'll see.

It's still early when I finish, but everything else I need to do can wait. It's Friday, anyway, so it feels like a good time to get out of here. Katie should be picking up the kids from school right about now, and above all, I want to be with them. I want to cook dinner and tell Katie everything that happened today. I want to play with the kids and make her roll her eyes. I want to give her time to work on her paintings—or, her book, I suppose—if that's what she wants.

I snap my laptop shut and shove it in my bag. I glance across the way. My parents' office light is off, which makes me chuckle to myself. I waste no time putting on my coat and walking out, wanting to be sure I beat rush hour traffic.

By the time I pull in the driveway, I have a whole romantic speech ready to sweep Katie off her feet, and I am determined to deliver it, even if I'm interrupted twelve times by tiny humans in the process.

When I come into the house, I can hear the television from the living room. I frown; it isn't like Katie to let the kids watch TV right after school. Then again, I guess I haven't been home for the after-school routine in so long, I don't know what they do now.

I hang up my coat and walk further in the house to see Mason and Christine sitting on the floor, their eyes glued to some cartoon on the screen. Katie is belly-down on the couch, her arm hanging off the edge and her eyes barely open.

"Um, hi everyone?" I say cautiously. No one moves. I try again, louder. "Hey! I'm home!"

Mason is the first to peel his eyes away from the TV. "Dad!" He jumps up and runs over to hug me.

Christine is slower, but she follows. "Dad! Dad! Mama's sick!"

I glance at Katie, who is rubbing her eyes with the palm of her hand and trying to get up. "I see that."

Katie groans and flops back on the couch. I walk around to kneel on the floor so we're closer to eye-level.

"Can't move. Everything hurts."

The kids start chasing each other around the living room, squealing at each other. Katie winces. I run a hand over her forehead to find her much warmer than usual. "How long have you felt like this?"

"Told you yesterday I felt sick," she mumbles.

"Why didn't you call me?" I'm trying to hide my concern, but I don't think I'm doing a very good job of it.

"Dunno." She closes her eyes. "Please make the kids stop screaming."

"Right." This springs me into action. I jump to my feet and corral the kids. "Everyone, upstairs."

"Dad," Mason whines, but I shush him quickly.

"Nope. Upstairs." I march up behind them as I pull my phone out of my pocket to call Daniel.

He answers on the second ring. "Hey, what's up?"

"Oh thank god. I have a huge favor to ask. Katie is sick. Can you and Mac hang out with the kids for a while? Order dinner or something? I don't care. They're loud and she needs to rest."

"Who's that?" Mason asks.

I move the phone away from my mouth. "Uncle Daniel."

His face immediately brightens. He practically vibrates with excitement. "Can we sleep over at his house? Please Dad? Please?"

Christine, probably unsure what we're even talking about, jumps right in. "Pweese Dad?"

"No, buddy."

"We can take the kids tonight. I'll come get them now, and we can do breakfast here tomorrow morning. It's not a problem," Daniel is saying.

I push the phone back to my ear. "I can't ask you to do that."

"I work from home and make my own hours. Mac has weekends off. This is why you have friends nearby. It's no big deal," he insists.

"Are you sure? I'd call my parents, but it'd take them forever to get here—"

"I'm sure. You can return the favor someday, maybe. Hopefully." There's something in his voice there that I'm going to have to ask him about later, but I have two kids hanging on me and a sick wife downstairs, so it'll have to wait.

"Okay. Yeah. That'd be awesome. Thank you."

"No problem. You got cold and flu medicine for her?"

I wrack my brain, but I don't know. "Can you pick some up just in case? The non-drowsy kind." She's said before that she can't have anything that makes her loopy because it feels too close to being drunk, and she doesn't want to risk it.

"Sure thing. See you in a few." He hangs up.

I take a deep breath and look at the kids. "Pack a bag. You're spending the night with Uncle Daniel."

Mason whoops, and Katie moans from downstairs. I glare at Mason, and he covers his mouth with his hand as he slinks away to his bedroom. I scoop up Christine and take her to her room to pack.

By the time we have everything ready, Daniel is knocking at the door. Mac is jogging around to the driver's seat of his car. She waves at me. "Tell Katie I hope she feels better soon," she calls.

"We can keep the kids with us all weekend if you need. Or, you know, if you want." Daniel winks as he hands me the bag of cold medicine.

"Careful with that offer," I warn as I usher the kids to my car and get them buckled in. I give them each a kiss and tell them to be good before I trade keys with Daniel.

"Are you two ready to eat chocolate and stay up all night watching rated-R movies?" he asks as he climbs in the car. The last thing I hear before the car door shuts behind him are cheers of "best uncle ever!" from the back seat.

I watch and wave as they pull away, fighting a little pang of sadness that I haven't heard from their biological uncle, Shane, in a while. I send up a quick prayer to the universe that he's doing okay, but I don't have time for more than that. Katie's sick, and I need to take care of her.

I find her curled in the fetal position on the couch. I fill a glass of water and take it to her, along with the medicine. "Hey, Cat." I push some hair out of her face. "Can you take this for me?"

"Mmm-mmm." She shakes her head.

"I know, baby. This will make you feel better."

"Can't."

"It's just a pain reliever and a decongestant. It's okay, I promise."

She winks one eye open, then the other. "Promise?"

"Yeah, I do."

She takes the pills from me and pops them in her mouth, chasing them with the water. She grimaces as they go down. "Did your parents come get the kids?"

I shake my head. "They're spending the night at Daniel's."

She scowls at me. "I don't have the energy to tell you all the reasons that's a terrible idea."

"You're sick. They're loud. I want to take care of you and not them." I shrug. "They'll probably come back alive." I climb up the couch to sit next to her. I loop my arm around her shoulders, tucking her in next to me.

Her frown deepens. "You think you're funny. You're not."

"So grouchy," I mutter into her hair.

She sighs, then groans as she folds herself further into me. "I feel like shit, and I hate everything," she says into my shirt. "You try not being grouchy when you feel like this."

"You're only proving my point," I tease. I'm trying to keep her mind off how terrible she feels. It seems to be working; some of her normal edge is back already.

She's silent for a moment, then she wraps her arm around my torso, her over-warm body almost sprawled over mine. "I wasn't always grouchy." Her eyelids are fighting to stay open, and her words are a little slurred with almost-sleep. "I know you think I am, but I'm not really. I look grouchy next to you. You get to come home and be fun. I have to do all the rules." She goes quiet for a minute as her body relaxes. Then, she stirs awake again. "Everything got so loud and sad and hard. So lonely." I can feel her slipping into sleep again. "I wasn't born grouchy. I was made grouchy."

My heart shatters right there. I'm not sure she even knows what she's saying, but that makes it all the more truthful. "Fuck, Cat." I press her head into my chest. She uses the opportunity to nestle closer. "I'm so sorry. You're right, and I'm sorry."

"Careful," she warns a little playfully, her eyes drifting closed. "Hearing I'm right is a major turn on." She smirks.

I chuckle, though her teasing does little to soothe my heart. If I hadn't already made a promise to myself to be better for my family from now on, I would do it now. This strengthens my resolve to send that memo and keep strict watch over my hours. She shouldn't have to feel like this. I'm going to make sure she never does, ever again.

I kiss the top of her head, breathing in her rose-and-paint scent that's now mixed with sticky sweat. "Come on, Cat. Let's get you to bed."

Chapter 24
Katie

BRANDON IS A DAMN hero. Even though he sends the kids to Daniel's, which would personally be my last choice, he has the forethought to get them out of the house. For two nights, he's at my beck and call. He makes sure to give me cold medicine I can take, and it works like a dream. He dozes off and on with me for two days, but he's at the ready no matter the hour. I'm vaguely aware of him checking in with Daniel to make sure the kids are alive, but I don't have the energy to talk to them on the phone, so I take him at his word that it's going well. He doesn't even complain when I insist on sleeping curled up against his side, even though I know I'm a human space heater on a good day, so I must be a furnace with this fever.

He doesn't leave my side. He's glued to me, like he needs to know how I'm doing every second. The worry is a little overboard, but it's sweet.

At one point on Saturday evening, he turns on a movie in the bedroom. I don't remember what movie it is, but he sits with his back against the headboard and his arm around me. He's still wearing the soft yellow t-shirt he put on when we went to bed the night before, and he's slipped on some sweatpants. I look up at him, studying him for a moment. His beard is untrimmed, and his rusty hair falls in loose waves to his shoulders. He hasn't taken a moment to shower in over twenty-four hours, but he's easily the most handsome man I've ever seen.

He looks down at me and notices my staring. "Do you need something, baby?" he asks gently.

"No."

"What's up?"

"Nothing. I just love you."

The corners of his mouth turn up. He presses a kiss to my forehead, then nods sagely. "Yep, you definitely still have a fever."

I give him a little shove. "I'm not saying that because I have a fever."

"I know." He squeezes me tighter, and before I know it, I'm dozing off again.

Luckily, my fever breaks sometime in the early hours of Sunday morning, and I fall into a deep sleep after that. When I wake up in the morning, I check the clock to find it later than I expect it to be. I must have needed that sleep. Either that, or it's much easier to sleep when the kids aren't bursting in your room at the crack of dawn. Maybe both.

Brandon is nowhere to be seen, which feels odd after him being attached to my side for two nights. I listen for a second, but I don't hear him in the bathroom. He must have gotten up and left me to sleep. I smile softly at the thought. I don't remember much about last night aside from how awful I felt, but I know he went above and beyond taking care of me, and I feel giddy at the thought.

My stomach rumbles, which is probably a good sign. I wrack my brain trying to remember what I've eaten the past day or so. I remember Brandon bringing me food, but I don't remember eating much of it. But then, I catch a whiff of myself and cringe. Shower first, then food.

I shower quickly, and by the time I'm dressed, Brandon still hasn't come back in the room. He must have realized my fever broke and decided to take a few minutes to himself. I can't blame him. Caregiving is exhausting.

I pull on some leggings, a sweatshirt, and my favorite fluffy socks and make my way downstairs. Brandon is sitting at the island, his back to me, sipping some coffee.

"There you are." I grab a banana off the counter and peel it. I take a bite and speak around the mouthful. "Should we get the kids? I bet Daniel and Mac are going, well, bananas." I laugh at my own joke.

"How are you feeling?" He doesn't turn around to face me, which is weird, but I shake it off.

"Much better, thanks to you. No more fever, and that shower felt like heaven."

"Good. Because I have something to ask you."

"That sounds ominous," I joke again, but it falls flat. My heart starts picking up speed. "Is everything okay? Is it something with the kids?" My voice is starting to sound panicky.

At that, he does turn around. His expression is serious, almost pained. "The kids are fine."

My relief only lasts for a second. "Okay," I say slowly. "What's going on?"

"Have you been drinking, Katie?"

I stare at him in silence, trying to get my mouth to work. I blink rapidly, trying to absorb what he's saying, but I can't. "I'm sorry, what?" I finally ask.

His expression changes, but there's still a hard edge to it that I can't quite read. Is it worry? Anger? "You can tell me, Katie. You're not in trouble or anything—"

"In trouble?" I fire back. "You're not my parent, Brandon. What the hell is going on?"

He puts his hands up, palms out. "That was the wrong thing to say. I just mean I'm not mad. I want to help. It makes sense, why you'd want me home more often, why you struggled so much with the kids both being in school—"

"I can't believe this," I cut him off again. Everything Nora and I spoke about the other day flies out the window. All the pride she instilled in me, all the faith she helped me find in myself means nothing if he doesn't trust me. "Where this is coming from, Brandon?" I sound a little desperate, but I don't try to hide it. He's pulled the rug out from under me.

He stands and takes a step toward me, and that's when I see it. A half-drunk bottle of whiskey on the island next to his coffee cup. I inhale sharply. "Where did you get that?" I whisper.

"The place was a mess with medicine and food everywhere." His eyes don't leave me. "You were finally sleeping soundly, so I came down here to clean up. I found a box under the sink and figured it was some stuff you hadn't gotten to unpack yet or hadn't wanted to until you decided we were going to stay."

"That box says 'Katie's Stuff.'" I'm seething and trying, unsuccessfully, to control it.

"I was trying to help by putting it away."

"You had no right!" I explode. "I don't go through your shit in your office. Can't I have one private—*clearly labeled*—box?"

"Have you been drinking, Katie?"

I throw my hands wide and smack them loudly against my thighs on the way down. "I can't believe you even have to ask. Would you believe me if I said no?"

He stares at me for a moment before he says quietly, "That's not an answer."

"Neither was that." I narrow my eyes and tilt my head, the pain in my heart almost overtaking the anger I felt just a minute ago. "Actually, I suppose it was. You wouldn't believe me. Because if you would, you'd know the answer already. If you really looked at how hard I've tried to keep it together, you wouldn't even have to ask."

He doesn't respond. His face is carefully neutral, and I can see he isn't going to say anything. I bark a humorless laugh and turn on my heel, grabbing my keys and boots as I pass them.

"Katie," he protests.

"I need some space," I parrot his words from not too long ago. I don't turn around to look at him. I just throw open the door to the garage, get in my car, and back out of the driveway.

I don't know where I'm going. I only know I need to get out of there, so I drive around aimlessly for a few minutes until driving in my socks starts to get too annoying. I pull over in a coffee shop parking lot and put my boots on, then go through the drive-thru to order some coffee and a muffin. I sit in my car and eat. It takes the edge off my hunger but doesn't do much for my frustration.

By the time I'm done, I still don't have a plan. Brandon hasn't even tried to call or text, which figures. It's possible he's giving me the space I asked for, but I'm not going to give him the benefit of the doubt. He's usually one to avoid issues and hope they blow over.

Well, two can play at that game. I can get the kids and hang out with Mac for a while or bring them home and use them as a buffer. They owe me for all those diapers I changed, anyway.

I don't bother calling Mac or Daniel. They have to guess we're coming soon, and I don't want to know if Brandon is there or not. Part of me wants to completely avoid him for as long as I can, and part of me wants him to come looking for me. But zero part of me wants to know if he's there already, because then I'd lose my nerve.

I drive the short distance to their house. Brandon's car is in the driveway, which makes my heart skip nervously a few times, until I remember he and Daniel switched cars to avoid the car seat shuffle. There's another car parked on the street, but it isn't Daniel's, so that must mean Brandon isn't here. Which is fine, I tell myself. Totally fine.

Muffled shouts come from the other side of the door. I bet Daniel and Mac are losing their minds with my wild children. I ring the doorbell quickly, both because it's cold and I forgot my coat, and because it's probably time to get the kids home and let the newlyweds get back to their peace.

Daniel answers the door with a huge smile, which falls immediately upon seeing me. "Aww, man." He's clearly annoyed I'm there.

"Sorry to disappoint you," I snap.

He furrows his brow briefly, then relaxes. "Oh, no. We were playing with the roller coaster in the living room—"

"The what?" There's no way I heard that right.

Daniel laughs with no small amount of trepidation. "The roller coaster. Do you want to come see it?"

I raise an eyebrow. "I don't know. Do I? Is it going to give me a heart attack to know what you've been up to all weekend?"

He chuckles, moving out of the way and motioning me inside. "No," he says as I pass him. "It's small. It's a little baby thing I picked up at the store that we set up. I promise, it's totally safe."

Mason whoops from the living room, and a man's booming laughter follows. Daniel rubs a hand over the back of his neck, looking sheepish. "Well, we might not be using it according to the directions."

"Who's 'we?'"

"Ben and Jenny are here, too. And Ben's sister, Ashley. She heard about the roller coaster and brought her kids. Her daughter, Amelia, is in the library reading." He motions toward the front room he had repurposed into a library for Mac. The door is closed. *Lucky girl*, I think. "The boys and Christine are playing in the living room. Seriously, come see." He takes a few steps and motions for me to follow.

I stand where I am, my feet planted into the welcome mat. "I think maybe I should just take my kids home." I don't know if it's all the noise or the unexpected crowd of people or the fight Brandon and I are in the middle of, but I suddenly want nothing more than to get out of this house. Facing Brandon at home feels easier than facing all these people with this weight pressing on me.

Mac comes into the front room. She walks right up to Daniel's side, fitting into him like a missing puzzle piece. She puts her arm around his back, and he puts his over her shoulder. It's instinctual, like they've done this a million times. I'm so fucking happy for them I could burst, but that happiness is tainted with envy. I know they've had their share of problems like everyone else, but their love is so relatively new. It hasn't had the chance to be watered down by life yet.

"Hey, Katie," Mac says brightly. "How are you feeling?"

"A lot better. Thanks for taking the kids. It was a huge help."

She eyes me with a dose of skepticism, but says, "We loved having them. We were just about to eat lunch and watch a movie in the basement, too, if you want to stay? Daniel set up a media center down there." She flashes a tight smile, and I can tell from the look on her face that she thinks his setup is ridiculous. Knowing Daniel, it probably is.

"No, we should get going. I don't want to impose on you any more than we already have." I use the voice I learned to use with Brandon's rich friends when trying to get out of something I didn't want to do. It's polite and firm, but sickly sweet, leaving no room for argument or hard feelings.

But I forget Daniel is one of those rich friends and has seen this song and dance a thousand times over the course of our friendship. "Katie, are you okay?" he asks. Mac glances at him, but I'd bet she hasn't missed it, either.

"I'm still feeling a little off," I lie.

"Okay." Daniel is clearly unconvinced. "I'll help the kids get their stuff ready."

He leaves, but Mac stays. She crosses the distance between us and puts her hand on my upper arm. "If you want me to leave it be, I will, but I don't think you're still feeling sick." She pauses for a moment, her green eyes searching mine. "We're friends, Katie. You can talk to me if you want."

Jenny's head pops around the corner. "Oh hey, Katie. Evans said you were here." She comes fully into the front room, eyes bouncing back and forth between us. "Are you two having a moment? Did I miss it?"

Mac's hand is still resting on my upper arm. She looks at me, eyebrows raised and seeming to say, *We can let this go if you want.*

But I don't want to let it go. In all my conversations with Nora about meeting people, in all my complaints to Brandon about being lonely, this is what I was looking for. Friends. Specifically, friends who get it. Friends who care about me for no other reason than they want what's best for me, and don't mind if I vent a little on the side. Friends I can return that favor for, too. I glance at Jenny, remembering some advice I gave her when she was in a similar situation only a few months ago and realize I already have exactly what I want. It's been staring at me in the face this whole time.

It shouldn't be a revelation, but it is. This is how friendships form. You seek the other people out for the fun stuff, then inch toward the hard stuff, and before you know it, you have people who will happily watch your kids for a whole weekend. People whose house you can show up to unannounced and vent about your husband's lack of faith in your sobriety. And you don't notice it until you need them and they're just... there.

"Actually," I start, then swallow hard. It's the admitting you need someone that's the hard part. "Can we... talk?"

Jenny nods once, the curve of her lips suggesting she's pleased I asked. Mac smiles warmly and squeezes my arm. "Daniel," she calls. "Why doesn't everyone take lunch downstairs for the movie? We'll be down in a bit."

Chapter 25
Brandon

I DON'T KNOW HOW long I stare at the half-empty bottle of whiskey. I should have followed Katie out, but I didn't. And now I have no idea where she could be or if she'll ever want to talk to me again.

I know I had no right to demand an answer. I found that bottle and freaked out. If she's been drinking again, it's because of me. She's been completely transparent about everything except for this. And if she's overwhelmed and wants me home because it's too hard to stay away from alcohol when she's alone, then it's all my fault. I shouldn't have been so naïve as to think her relapse at the fundraiser was a one-and-done thing.

I'm drowning in all the things I should and should not have done when my phone dings. My heart skips hoping it's Katie, and it falls when I flip it over and see Daniel's name on the screen.

Your wife is here. She used her fake party voice on me, so I thought you should know.

Thank goodness for Daniel Evans. I have never been more grateful for his ability to read a room. *Is she bringing the kids home?* I type back.

Instead of a return message, my phone rings with a call from him. I answer immediately. Before I can even say anything, I'm greeted with a cacophony of noise. It sounds like there's at least two other kids there besides mine, and another adult male is trying to corral them all in the background.

"Were my kids not enough for you?" I ask, raising my voice so he can hear me.

There's some movement on the other end of the line, then things get quieter. "I may have bought your kids a kiddie roller coaster, and Mac may have told Jenny, who may have told Ben, who may have come over with his niece and nephews and their mom. And I may have suggested we test out the new home theater in the basement with a movie during lunch. I don't know, man. It's a whole thing."

I pinch the bridge of my nose. "What movie?"

"Who cares what movie?"

"The father who will be up with a three-year-old with nightmares, that's who."

"Oh, don't worry. It's PG-13," Daniel reassures me.

"She's ten years too young for that, Daniel."

"I'm kidding. It's a cartoon. Are you avoiding the fact that Katie is here, or did I read that wrong?"

"You read it right. I'm trying to decide what to do," I rest my forehead in the palm of my hand and close my eyes.

"Want to talk about it?" Daniel asks.

"Not until I talk to her." I pause. "Should I come?"

"She's upstairs with Mac, Jenny, and Ashley right now, so I couldn't say for sure." There's another shout in the background, followed by tiny giggles. "But, in my limited experience with women, when they walk off, they usually want you to follow them."

I nod slowly, then remember he can't see me. "Right. Yeah. I'll be over in a minute."

"Let yourself in. This is chaos," he says just before the call is cut off.

"Amateur." I chuckle to myself as I get ready to leave.

The house is still standing by the time I get there. Sure enough, Katie's car is out front along with several others. I let myself in as instructed. There is some faraway laughter coming from the basement, but the bulk of the chatter is coming from the kitchen. It immediately hushes when I open the door.

Mac's red hair is visible in the open doorway between the foyer and the kitchen. She leans back in a chair to see who it is, but she doesn't seem surprised to see me. Daniel must have let her know I was coming.

She shifts forward again, out of my line of sight. I stay put, not quite sure what I'm supposed to do.

"Brandon is here," Mac says, her voice flat. "Do you want to see him?"

Katie laughs, the sound tinkling like bells. It comes so easily. I'm almost jealous I didn't make it happen, but also glad someone did. "Yeah, it's fine."

"Am I allowed in, then?" I call.

"We'll be in the basement if you need us," Mac says, not addressing me. There's the sound of chairs scraping, and a parade of women file out to cross the room to the door leading downstairs. Jenny glares at me as she passes. A woman who looks strikingly like Ben winces sympathetically—that must be Ashley. It occurs to me I've never met the mother of Mason's new best friend, and I make a mental note to introduce myself under better circumstances. Mac trails behind. She opens the door to my right and pops her head in.

"Amelia, come on down and watch the rest of the movie with us, okay?"

I hadn't even realized anyone was in the library, but a pre-teen girl walks out, holding a huge book to her chest. Mac motions for her to go, then turns to me. "Have a little faith in her, Brandon. That's all she wants," she whispers before following the women into the basement.

I take a deep breath and let it out slowly as I walk into the kitchen. Katie is sitting at their table, cupping her hands around a mug. She's sitting cross-legged on one of the chairs, her sleeves pulled down over her knuckles and her arms resting on the table. A halo of soft, winter light surrounds her from the patio door at her back. Her cheeks are rosy, and a hint of laughter plays on her lips.

She's fucking beautiful. She's relaxed and happy in a way I don't think I've ever seen. She looks like she belongs here, like she's comfortable and in her element after spending some time with friends.

I swallow audibly. "I've never been scrutinized by a crew of angry women before."

Katie hums. "That's because I've never had a crew of women friends before."

I'm silent, letting that set in. She's right, and I'm overcome with gratitude for the women that just filed out of this room. I know I can't always be everything for her. I'm glad they can help fill the gaps.

"There's coffee if you want it," she says, motioning toward the counter.

I shake my head, pulling out a chair and sitting down. I want more than anything to take her hands in mine, but I don't know where we are yet, so I rest them on the table.

"I'm sorry, Katie. I shouldn't—"

She raises her hand to stop me. "No, I need to say a few things."

"You don't have to explain anything."

"I want to." She twists her mug back and forth on the table, staring at it. She sighs, then shifts her gaze to me, her blue eyes intense. "I need you to believe me when I say I haven't had a drink since that night at the fundraiser. I'm proud of that because it's been hard. Harder than I wanted to admit to you. I wanted you to think I had it all together, and I didn't want to bother you when I knew you were so stressed with your job."

I take a breath as if to speak, but she shakes her head.

"No, let me finish," she insists. I fall silent and nod for her to continue. "I never felt like you got the chance to choose me. That, even if you loved us, it was forced on you in a way. I know what you're going to say about that, but don't." She cuts me off before I can even protest. She moves the mug to the side and clasps her hands together in front of her. She doesn't move her eyes from them as she speaks. "It doesn't matter what you say, because it's what I fear. And maybe that fear is irrational, I don't know. But it's always been there in the back of my mind.

"And it didn't help that our so-called friends in New York didn't want me, either. I was always the odd one out. I didn't work or come from money. I didn't drink. But when we moved here, I didn't feel that way anymore. You and I seemed to be doing really well. Mac and Jenny folded me into their friendship because they genuinely wanted to. Mason and Christine have friends, too.

"It was stressful. Of course it was. It took work to get here, and I wanted to drink sometimes." She raises her eyes to me, and there's an earnestness there that takes my breath away. "But I didn't. I thought about it, I won't lie about that. But I never acted on it. I didn't want anyone to know because it felt like I was failing. I was so ashamed. When I talked to Nora, though, she told me that wanting to drink and not doing it was something to be proud of. It made sense. I had those thoughts and didn't act on them. I was proud then, and I wanted you to be proud of me, too."

"And, instead, I questioned you. Katie, I'm so sorry." I grab her hands, and she lets me, the warmth of her palms seeping into mine.

"I was angry, obviously, but I know why you did it. You weren't accusing me. You hadn't lost your faith in me. You were worried because you love me. I should have seen that and just answered your question."

"I should have trusted you," I insist, still holding her hands.

"Well, yeah. You should have." She chuckles. The sound fills me up. "But what are you supposed to think when you find a half-empty bottle of whiskey hidden in a box with my name on it?" She smiles sardonically, her eyes gleaming.

"You don't have to explain it. I believe you."

"I want to. It's just kind of embarrassing." She bounces her knee a few times, then goes still again. "That bottle is just about eight years old. Remember when I took that shot when I found out I was pregnant? That was my coping mechanism for stressful situations, and that's when I realized I had a problem."

I nod, practically hanging on to her words. Suddenly, the realization dawns. "That's the same bottle?"

"The same bottle." She smiles sheepishly.

I lower my eyebrows and narrow my eyes in confusion. "Why is that embarrassing?"

She laughs self-consciously. "Because it's weird. Why would I keep that? It makes no sense. I should have gotten rid of all the alcohol and removed the temptation. But there was something about having the temptation there and not acting on it that felt..." she trails off, looking for the word. "Empowering, I guess."

I rub my thumb over her knuckles, catching on her wedding band with each pass. "That's not weird. It's your process. It works for you."

She nods silently, still not meeting my gaze.

"Is it my turn now?" I ask.

She smirks. "Sure."

"Okay." I squeeze her fingers. "I did choose you, Katie. You seem to forget that my family had a lot of money, and we could have paid you whatever you wanted to keep Mason a secret or have an abortion and never bother me with it again."

"You say that like someone put all of those options on the table for you." She arches a blonde eyebrow.

I laugh. "Not important right now. The point is, I didn't want that to happen. I wanted you. I wanted Mason. I wanted Christine, too, but that was a little different." She meets my gaze and smiles at that. It changes her entire face. The whole room lights up, and for a moment, I almost forget what I'm saying because she's so stunning. "I chose you then, and I choose you now, and I'd choose the same damn thing even if I had it all to do over again. I love this life we've built, and I wouldn't trade it for the world. But I need you to do something for me."

"What's that?"

"Have a little faith in me, too. I might make some mistakes, but it never changes the way I feel about you. You're everything. And you're mine. I'm never letting you go."

Her smile falters slightly. "Even if I drank that whiskey?"

"Even then." I squeeze her fingers again. She flips the palm of her left hand so our fingers interlace on the top of the table. I continue, needing her to hear the rest. "Loving someone isn't just about loving the easy stuff. It's about loving the hard stuff, too. I love all of you, Cat." I untangle my right hand so I can trace her jaw, tilting her chin up so she's open to me. The rumble I've grown to know so well rises in her throat.

A wicked grin grows on my face. "I especially love that noise."

She laughs a breathy laugh as I lean in and kiss her deeply, my hand trailing to grip the back of her head. Her laugh turns into a soft moan as I sweep my tongue into her open mouth and taste her.

A noise comes from my left. We slowly turn our heads in the direction of the sound. Daniel is standing there at the top of the stairs to the basement.

"Looks like you two made up." He wears a smug look as he folds his arms and leans against the wall.

"Did you need something, Daniel?" I ask gruffly.

"Well, if you're done making out in *my kitchen*, we were wondering if you wanted to join us for the end of this movie." He ticks his head toward the basement door in invitation.

I look at Katie questioningly. "We could leave the kids here and go back home to properly make up." I wink. Daniel coughs indelicately.

She shakes her head. "The gang's all here. Let's enjoy it." She leans in and nips my earlobe. "We can properly make up later," she whispers.

I keep her hand in mine as I stand, pulling her up with me. As soon as we get to the open door, we can hear the kids' joyful yelling and a few adults punctuating the sounds with warnings or laughter.

Daniel descends first, but Katie and I take an extra moment at the top of the stairs before joining everyone. It's absolute chaos, but I wouldn't have it any other way. As she gazes up at me, I know she feels the same. I give her hand an extra squeeze as we walk down the stairs. Together.

Epilogue
Katie

SIX MONTHS LATER

I'm running a few minutes late between meetings, which usually tends to set me on edge. But, this time, my first meeting of the day was with a sober community I visited at the urging of both Brandon and Nora. They both insisted it would be good for me to have a group of people with shared experiences, and I think they were right. It felt good to hear from people who had the same thoughts and temptations as I do, which brought an unexpected sense of ease to my morning. Now, I'm on my way down the hall of Leade Park High School, clutching my purse and sporting a bright orange visitor's badge.

"Hello, everyone. I'm Mr. Mac," Daniel says to a chorus of laughter as soon as I walk in the classroom door. Mac rolls her eyes from her perch on a stool at the outskirts of her classroom. "Okay, okay. I'm Mr. Evans. This is Mrs. Conley." He indicates me, and I wave. "Ms. Mac asked us here to kick off your first unit in this brand-new creative writing class. Isn't it exciting that this class got started because your brilliant teacher saw you were all interested and pitched it to your school administrators?"

"You flatter me," Mac says flatly, though she's fighting the blush rising in her cheeks. The students laugh again.

I didn't know what to expect when Mac asked me to join Daniel for a question-and-answer session with her class but watching them together in front of the students is something special. They play off each other beautifully, almost like they both belong in front of the twenty-eight students staring at us, waiting for us to say something profound.

"Anyway," Daniel continues, "I'm a writer. You may have heard of me. I've written a few books that have been pretty popular." More laughter. "And Mrs. Conley is working on her very first children's book that she's writing and illustrating."

Two of the girls in the back of the room perk up. One wiggles in her seat so she can sit up straighter, suddenly interested in what we have to say.

"Katie, do you want to talk a little about that to kick us off?" Mac asks, clearly trying to tone down Daniel's enthusiasm by letting me start.

"Sure," I say slowly. I look out at the classroom and remind myself that I belong here just as much as anyone else, even if my book isn't published yet. "I'm an artist. I've always loved painting, and a few months ago, I started drawing a bunch of panels that all kind of went together. It told the story of two kids who loved their dad, but their dad sometimes made some tough choices they didn't like. The book is about how they work through that as a family." I glance at Mac, who nods encouragingly. "I'm not sure how I'll publish it yet, but I'm looking into self-publishing."

"Which is a great way to get your work out there, and just as valid as traditional publishing," Mac adds. "This is an excellent opportunity for you all to ask questions. You have two very different writers here. Daniel writes very dense, difficult novels—"

"Wow. Thanks," he says sarcastically.

Mac simpers. *I love them*, I think as I chuckle to myself. And, not for the first time, I'm so glad they brought me into their little group here in Leade Park.

"He works with a publishing house and an agent and editor, the whole nine yards. Katie is working on a children's book, which as you can imagine, is much lighter but no less difficult. She's thinking about publishing it herself, which I assume she's done a lot of research on." She raises her eyebrows in question.

I nod. "A ton of research." I widen my eyes dramatically, and the students laugh. It feels good to make them laugh. Better than I had thought it would.

"Okay." Mac claps her hands. "Who would like to ask the first question?"

What follows is a lively, full-hour class where the students ask us all kinds of questions. They ask us about everything, from the difficulty of illustrating versus writing, to how to query agents, to whether or not I need an editor for a self-published children's book. They are so curious about the process of writing and publishing that we don't get a break until the bell rings. Even then, a few students come up to us on their way out to thank us or ask something they were too shy to say in front of class.

When the last student has filed out of the room, Mac beams at us.

"That was amazing. They were so engaged!"

Daniel crosses the room and side-hugs her as he plants a kiss on her temple. "Happy to help. Right, Katie?"

"That was great," I say. "I'd do that again any time."

Mac claps her hands and bounces a little in excitement. "And now, off to the ground-breaking ceremony for the new addition!" She giggles. Mac might be the only person more excited about this addition than Brandon's employees. After much deliberation, the school board selected the design of one of his junior architects, Thalia. He said that was a pivotal moment for her career. I love a good single-mom comeback story.

"I'll meet you both down there." I throw my purse over my shoulder, "Brandon is bringing the kids, and I want to do the trade-off early so he can get ready."

"See you down there," Mac calls as I leave the room.

The ceremony is going to be held outside, and it should be short, but it worked out well to do this session with Mac's students on the same day. The administration wanted to start it right after school for the best chance to catch the most people for a photo op.

Sure enough, the area is packed with teachers, community members, and families. There's a small stage with a microphone set up. Thalia and Jasper are already up there with Brandon. He jumps down from the stage and comes over when he sees me at the edge of the crowd.

He doesn't even say hello before pressing a long kiss to my lips. It's relatively innocent, but I can feel the promise of something more. I smile up at him as he pulls away.

"Where are the kids?" I ask.

He points to the other side of the area where people are gathering. His parents wave. The kids stand next to them with Jenny and Ben behind.

I wave back as I say to Brandon, "Good luck up there. I'll see you when it's over."

He kisses my cheek and rejoins his team. There's a bounce in his step that wasn't there six months ago. He's proud of this project, and he loves his new role. And he's been home in time to make dinner every night, without fail, since he took over.

I wave at Brandon's parents, pick up Christine who is demanding I do so, and give Jenny a one-armed hug. Ben smirks, then opens his arms wide. I roll my eyes and let him fold me into an embrace.

"Not a hugger," he murmurs sarcastically. I chuckle.

"Thank you for coming, everyone." Brandon speaks into the microphone. Mac and Daniel sidle up to our little group just as he starts speaking. "We are going to keep this short and sweet. We are very excited to begin work on the addition to Leade Park High School. We believe this new space will be exactly what the district needs to provide more space and educational opportunities for the students.

"The design is public, and we have brochures for anyone who would like one. It is the brainchild of our very own Thalia Gutierrez, and we could not be happier with how it turned out." He indicates Thalia, who waves quickly, then puts her hand back down just as fast. Brandon wasn't kidding when he said he'd do the talking because she was nervous in front of crowds.

"We're going to let Thalia cut the ribbon today since it was her design that was selected, and then we will be available for photos and questions. Thalia?" An older woman, whom I assume must be the superintendent, walks up to the red ribbon draped in front of the stage with a huge pair of scissors. Thalia joins her on the ground, and they both grip the scissors and cut slowly so the photographers can all get their shot. Everyone claps, then the majority of the crowd dissipates.

Our little crew sticks around, though. We make our way toward the stage as the crowd thins. The kids run around in circles. Brandon and his dad chase them. Eventually, Brandon catches Christine and lifts her up to sit on his shoulders. Mason ends up riding piggy-back on Brandon's dad. It's an adorable scene, and I file it away for later when I'm in my studio.

"Excuse me," someone says to my left, breaking me out of my reverie.

I turn toward the voice to see a young man holding a camera. "Yes?"

"Are you a teacher here?" he asks.

"No, but they are." I indicate Mac, Jenny, and Ben. "And my husband is the head of the architecture firm, if you're looking for a photo."

He looks relieved. "Yes, that would be amazing. My boss wanted a shot of some of the teachers, but with people from the firm, it would be perfect."

"I got you." I wink, then raise my voice. "Teachers! Architects! Line up for a photo!"

I haven't lost my authority, it seems, because they immediately fall into line. Daniel and I hang back with the kids as the only two who don't have anything to do with this project. But for once, I don't feel like I'm on the outside of anything. I feel like I'm right here in the middle of it. Where I'm supposed to be.

Daniel elbows me gently. "I'm glad you chose to stay," he says as if he read my mind.

"Me too," I say honestly.

He nods, looking back at the group as they rearrange according to the photographer's directions. "I'm glad you chose Brandon, too, all those years ago." The words are soft and sincere.

I hum, unconvinced. "He chose me."

Daniel shrugs. "You chose each other."

Brandon surprises me with a bear hug from the side. I squeal until he puts me down. He leaves his arm around me and kisses the top of my head. "Ready to head home?" he asks.

I look around at our family—both blood and otherwise—and am overcome with gratitude. I'm grateful they found us and took us in. I'm grateful they've been there for us and our kids. But, most of all, I'm grateful for Brandon as he smiles down at me, his eyes full of love.

"Sure. Let's go home."

Yeah, I chose him. It was the best choice I've ever made.

A Note About Setting

Leade Park is not a real place, and Leade Park High School is not a real school. It is a combination of all the Midwestern places I've encountered and all of the schools in which I've worked. I tried to keep it as realistic as possible while also keeping it completely separate from any real place. Any likeness to a real town or school is purely coincidental, and is most likely a result of my deep love of—specifically—the quirkiness of each school in which I've worked and—more generally—all things Midwestern.

Acknowledgments

THERE'S A SAYING IN teaching: "The first year, you know nothing. The second year, you think you know everything. The third year, you start learning." Substitute "year" with "book," and I think this is spot on. Thankfully, I have had so many people helping and cheering me on along the way.

I have to thank my husband first. He's the best of Daniel, Ben, and Brandon all rolled into one. When I say these books wouldn't exist without him, I mean it. Like Katie and Brandon, we have two kids who are a little older now. Like Katie, I'm trying to get back to my art. Unlike Brandon, my husband is always ready to take over when my to-do list seems insurmountable. You're my favorite, and I love you.

Huge thanks to my early readers for your timely and important feedback: Jillian, Alexis, Stefanie, Caitlin, Jessica, Sandy, and Elizabeth. I was nervous about this one because it's so different from the other two, but knowing you all related to these characters in a million different ways has kept me going. Thank you for the late night feedback sessions, walking me through moments of imposter syndrome, and cheering me on the whole way.

Special thanks to Alexis for the use of your name. Your contribution to literature shall not go unnoticed!

I couldn't do all of the beautiful promotions I do or offer all that cool swag without the amazingly talented Lorissa Padilla. Your illustrations of my characters are stunning, and I absolutely cannot thank you enough for bringing them to life in a new way. Thank you so much for sharing your talents.

And a heartfelt thanks to Sandy and Jessica for providing insight into those living with and loving people who experience substance use issues. Your thoughtful feedback was invaluable.

Jillian Liota of Blue Moon Creative Studio knocked it out of the park with this cover again. Thanks for making my dream of a purple cover come true!

I am one of the lucky ones who has found an editor who might actually love Leade Park as much as—if not more than—I do. She's not only my editor, but my audiobook narrator and my friend. Thank you to Megan Carver for your expertise, insight, and for answering my 10,000 voice memos. And, most of all, thank you for loving my babies and taking such good care of them. But you still can't have my em dashes.

Thank you to my family and friends who didn't bat an eye when I said I was going to write books. Your support means the world to me. I certainly wouldn't have done this without you. Thanks, especially, to my mom, dad, and brother who have unconditionally loved and believed in me my whole life. I love you all.

Finally, thank you to everyone who has read these books. I still have to pinch myself every time I see a review or message from a fan. (I have fans! This is wild.) You make me want to keep going because of your love for my words. Thank you from the bottom of my heart.

Also By Allie Samberts

Leade Park:

The Write Place

The Write Time

The Write Choice

A new standalone, coming Summer 2024!

Stay up to date on new releases and grab some bonus content! Subscribe

to Allie's newsletter at https://alliesamberts.substack.com

About the Author

Allie Samberts is a romance writer, book lover, and high school English teacher. She was voted funniest teacher of the year for 2023 by her students, which is probably her highest honor to date. She is also a runner, and enjoys knitting and sewing. She lives in the Chicago suburbs with her husband, two kids, and a very loud beagle. You can follow her on Instagram @alliesambertswrites, read her blog at alliesamberts.substack.com, and get other updates at www.alliesamberts.com.

Made in United States
Orlando, FL
02 December 2024

54795365R00195